DICK
FRANCIS

"*Forfeit* is not only an enthralling mystery, it is a moving story about very real people. It puts Francis right up there at the top among the best mystery writers in the world today."

—Stanley Ellin

"One of the most highly acclaimed novelists of the decade."

—*The Bookshelf*

"Dick Francis continues to be the hottest author going to the post. He improves with every offering."

—*Columbus Enquirer*

FORFEIT
was originally published by Harper & Row, Publishers, Inc.

Books by Dick Francis

Blood Sport *
Dead Cert
Enquiry
Flying Finish
Forfeit *
For Kicks
Nerve
Odds Against
Slayride *

* Published by POCKET BOOKS

*Are there paperbound books you want
but cannot find in your retail stores?*

FORFEIT

Dick Francis

PUBLISHED BY POCKET BOOKS NEW YORK

FORFEIT

Harper & Row edition published 1969

POCKET BOOK edition published June, 1975

Standard Book Number: 671-78884-1.
Library of Congress Catalog Card Number: 69-15289.
This POCKET BOOK edition is published by arrangement
with Harper & Row, Publishers, Inc. Copyright, ©, 1969,
by Dick Francis. All rights reserved. This book, or portions
thereof, may not be reproduced by any means without permission of the original publisher: Harper & Row, Publishers,
Inc., 10 East 53rd Street, New York, N.Y. 10022.
Front cover photograph by Carl Kravats.

Printed in the U.S.A.

FORFEIT

ONE

The letter from *Tally* came on the day Bert Checkov died. It didn't look like trouble; just an invitation from a glossy to write an article on the Lamplighter Gold Cup. I flicked it across the desk to the sports editor and went on opening the mail which always accumulated for me by Friday. Luke-John Morton grunted and stretched out a languid hand, blinking vacantly while he listened to someone with a lot to say on the telephone.

"Yeah . . . yeah. Blow the roof off," he said.

Blowing the roof off was the number-one policy of the *Sunday Blaze,* bless its cold heart. Why didn't I write for the *Sunday Times,* my wife's mother said, instead of a rag like the *Sunday Blaze?* They hadn't needed me, that was why. She considered this irrelevant, and when she couldn't actively keep it quiet, continued to apologize to every acquaintance for my employment. That the *Blaze* paid twenty-eight per cent more than the *Times,* and that her daughter was expensive, she ignored.

I slit open a cheap brown envelope and found some nut had written to say that only a vicious, unscrupulous bum like myself would see any good in the man I had defended last Sunday. The letter was written on lavatory paper and spite oozed from it like marsh gas. Derry Clark read it over my shoulder and laughed.

"Told you you'd stir them up."

"Anything for an unquiet life," I agreed.

Derry wrote calm uncontroversial articles each week assessing form and firmly left the rebel stuff to me. My back, as he constantly pointed out, was broader than his.

Eight more of my correspondents proved to be thinking along the same general lines. All anonymous, naturally.

7

Their problems, I reflected, dumping their work in the wastebasket, were even worse than mine.

"How's your wife?" Derry said.

"Fine, thanks."

He nodded, not looking at me. He'd never got over being embarrassed about Elizabeth. It took some people that way.

Luke-John's conversation guttered to a close. "Sure . . . sure. Phone it through by six at the latest." He put down the receiver and focused on my letter from *Tally,* his eyes skidding over it with professional speed.

"A study in depth . . . how these tarty magazines love that phrase. Do you want to do it?"

"If the fee's good."

"I thought you were busy ghosting Buster Figg's autobiography."

"I'm hung up on Chapter Six. He's sloped off to the Bahamas and left me no material."

"How far through his horrid little life have you got?" His interest was genuine.

"The end of his apprenticeship and his first win in a classic."

"Will it sell?"

"I don't know." I sighed. "All he's interested in is money, and all he remembers about some races is the starting price. He bled in thousands. And he insists I put his biggest bets in. He says they can't take away his license now he's retired."

Luke-John sniffed, rubbing a heavily freckled hand across the prominent tendons of his scrawny neck, massaging his walnut-sized larynx, dropping the heavy eyelid hoods while he considered the letter from *Tally*. My contract with the *Blaze* was restrictive: books were all right, but I couldn't write articles for any other paper or magazine without Luke-John's permission, which I mostly didn't get.

Derry pushed me out of his chair and sat in it himself. As I spent only Fridays in the office, I didn't rate a desk and usurped my younger colleague's whenever he wasn't looking. Derry's desk held a comprehensive reference library of form books in the top three drawers and a half bottle of vodka, two hundred purple hearts, and a pornographic film catalogue in the bottom one. These were window dressing only. They represented the wicked fellow Derry would like to be, not the lawful, temperate semidetached man he was.

I perched on the side of his desk and looked out over the Friday morning clatter, a quarter acre of typewriters and telephones going at half speed as the week went on toward Sunday. Tuesdays, the office was dead; Saturdays, it buzzed like flies squirted with D.D.T. Fridays, I felt part of it. Saturdays, I went to the races. Sundays and Mondays—officially off. Tuesdays to Thursdays, think up some galvanizing subject to write about, and write it. Fridays, take it in for Luke-John, and then for the editor to read and veto.

Result—a thousand words a week, an abusive mailbag, and a hefty check which didn't cover my expenses.

Luke-John said, "Are you or Derry doing the Lamplighter?"

Without giving me a second Derry jumped in: "I am."

"That all right with you, Ty?" Luke-John asked dubiously.

"Oh, sure," I said. "It's a complicated handicap. Right up his street."

Luke-John pursed his thin lips and said with unusual generosity, *"Tally* says they want background stuff, not tips. . . . I don't see why you shouldn't do it, if you want to."

He scribbled a large "O.K." at the bottom of the page and signed his name. "But of course," he added, "if you dig up any dirt, keep it for *us*."

Generous be damned, I thought wryly. Luke-John's soul belonged to the *Blaze* and his simple touchstone in all decisions was "Could it possibly, directly or indirectly, benefit the paper?" Every member of the sports section had at some time or other been ruthlessly sacrificed on his altar. For canceled holidays, smashed appointments, lost opportunities, he cared not one jot.

"Sure," I said mildly. "And thanks."

"How's your wife?" he asked.

"Fine, thanks."

He asked every week without fail. He had his politenesses, when it didn't cost the *Blaze*. Maybe he really cared. Maybe he only cared because when she wasn't "fine" it affected my work.

I pinched Derry's telephone and dialed the number.

"*Tally* magazine, can I help you?" A girl's voice very smooth, West Ken, and bored.

"I'd like to talk to Arnold Shankerton."

"Who's calling?"

"James Tyrone."

"One moment, please." Some clicks and a pause. "You're through."

An equally smooth, highly sophisticated tenor voice proclaimed itself to be Arnold Shankerton. Features. I thanked him for his letter and said I would like to accept his commission. He said that would be very nice, in moderately pleased tones, and I gently added, "If the price is right, naturally."

"Naturally," he conceded. "How much do you want?"

Think of a number and double it. "Two hundred guineas, plus expenses."

Luke-John's eyebrows rose and Derry said, "You'll be lucky."

"Our profit margin is small," Shankerton pointed out a little plaintively. "One hundred is our absolute limit."

"I pay too much tax."

His sigh came heavily down the wire. "A hundred and fifty, then. And for that it'll have to be good."

"I'll do my best."

"Your best," he said, "would scorch the paper. We want the style and the insight but not the scandal. Right?"

"Right," I agreed without offense. "How many words?"

"It's the main feature. Say three thousand five hundred, roughly speaking."

"How about pictures?"

"You can have one of our photographers when you're ready. And within reason, of course."

"Of course," I said politely. "When do you want it by?"

"We go to press on that edition—let's see—on November twenty-first. So we'd like your stuff on the morning of the seventeenth, at the very latest. But the earlier the better."

I looked at Derry's calendar. Ten days to the seventeenth.

"All right."

"And when you've thought out how you'd like to present it, send us an outline."

"Will do," I said; but I wouldn't. Outlines were asking for trouble in the shape of editorial alterations. Shankerton could, and would, chop at the finished article to his heart's content, but I was against him getting his scissors into the embryo.

Luke-John skimmed the letter back and Derry picked it up and read it.

"In depth," he said sardonically. "You're used to the deep end. You'll feel quite at home."

"Yeah," I agreed absent-mindedly. Just what *was* depth, a hundred and fifty guineas' worth of it?

I made a snap decision that depth in this case would be the background people, not the stars.

The stars hogged the headlines week by week. The background people had no news value. For once, I would switch them over.

Snap decisions had got me into trouble once or twice in the past. All the same, I made this one. It proved to be the most trouble-filled of the lot.

Derry, Luke-John, and I knocked off soon after one and walked down the street in fine drizzle to elbow our way into the bar of the Devereux, in Devereux Court opposite the Law Courts.

Bert Checkov was there, trying to light his stinking old pipe and burning his fingers on the matches. The shapeless tweed which swathed his bulk was as usual scattered with ash and as usual his toecaps were scuffed and gray. There was more glaze in the washy blue eyes than one-thirty normally found there: an hour too much, at a rough guess. He'd started early.

Luke-John spoke to him and he stared vaguely back. Derry bought us a half pint each and politely asked Bert to have one, though he'd never liked him.

"Double Scotch," Bert mumbled, and Derry thought of his mortgages and scowled.

"How's things?" I asked, knowing that this, too, was a mistake. The Checkov grumbles were inexhaustible.

For once, however, the stream was dammed. The watery eyes focused on me with an effort and another match sizzled on his skin. He appeared not to notice.

"Gi' you a piesh o' advishe," he said, but the words stopped there. The advice stayed in his head.

"What is it?"

"Piesh o' advishe." He nodded solemnly.

Luke-John raised his eyes to the ceiling in an exasperation that wasn't genuine. For old-time journalists like Bert he had an unlimited regard which no amount of drink could quench.

"Give him the advice, then," Luke-John suggested. "He can always do with it."

The Checkov gaze lurched from me to my boss. The Checkov mouth belched uninhibitedly. Derry's pale face twisted squeamishly, and Checkov saw him. As a gay lunch, hardly a gas. Just any Friday, I thought: but I was wrong. Bert Checkov was less than an hour from death.

Luke-John, Derry, and I sat on stools around the bar counter and ate cold meat and pickled onions, and Bert Checkov stood swaying behind us, breathing pipe smoke and whiskey fumes down our necks. Instead of the usual steady rambling flow of grousing to which we were accustomed, we received only a series of grunts, the audible punctuation of the inner Checkov thoughts.

Something on his mind. I wasn't interested enough to find out what. I had enough on my own.

Luke-John gave him a look of compassion and another

whiskey, and the alcohol washed into the pale blue eyes like a tide, resulting in pinpoint pupils and a look of blank stupidity.

"I'll walk him back to his office," I said abruptly. "He'll fall under a bus if he goes on his own."

"Serve him right," Derry said under his breath, but carefully so that Luke-John shouldn't hear.

We finished lunch with cheese and another half pint. Checkov lurched sideways and spilt my glass over Derry's knee and the pub carpet. The carpet soaked it up good-temperedly, which was more than could be said for Derry. Luke-John shrugged resignedly, half laughing, and I finished what was left of my beer with one swallow, and steered Bert Checkov through the crowd and into the street.

"Not closing time yet," he said distinctly.

"For you it is, old chum."

He rolled against the wall, waving the pipe vaguely in his chubby fist. "Never leave a pub before closing. Never leave a story while it's hot. Never leave a woman on her doorstep. Paragraphs and skirts should be short and pheasants and breasts should be high."

"Sure," I said, sighing. Some advice.

I took his arm and he came easily enough out onto the Fleet Street pavement. His tottering progress up toward the City end produced several stares but no actual collisions. Linked together, we crossed during a lull in the traffic and continued eastward under the knowing frontages of the *Telegraph* and the black glass *Express*. Fleet Street had seen the lot: no news value in an elderly racing correspondent being helped back from lunch with a skinful.

"A bit of advice," he said suddenly, stopping in his tracks, "a bit of advice."

"Yes?" I said patiently.

He squinted in my general direction.

"We've come past the *Blaze*."

"Yeah."

He tried to turn me around to retrace our steps.

"I've business down at Ludgate Circus. I'm going your way today," I said.

"Zat so?" He nodded vaguely and we shambled on. Ten more paces. He stopped again.

"Piece of advice."

He was looking straight ahead. I'm certain that he saw nothing at all. No bustling street. Nothing but what was going on inside his head.

I was tired of waiting for the advice which showed no signs of materializing. It had begun to drizzle again. I took his arm to try and get him moving along the last fifty yards to his paper's florid front door. He wouldn't move.

"Famous last words," he said.

"Whose?"

"Mine. Naturally. Famous last words. Bit of advice."

"Oh, sure." I sighed. "We're getting wet."

"I'm not drunk."

"No."

"I could write my column anytime. This minute."

"Sure."

He lurched off suddenly, and we made it to his door. Three steps and he'd be home and dry.

He stood in the entrance and rocked unsteadily. The pale blue eyes made a great effort toward sobering up, but the odds were against it.

"If anyone asks you," he said finally, "don't do it."

"Don't do what?"

An anxious expression flitted across his pallid fleshy face. There were big pores all over his nose, and his beard was growing out of stiff black millimetres. He pushed one hand into his jacket pocket, and the anxiety turned to relief as he drew it out again with a half bottle of Scotch attached.

" 'Fraid I'd forgotten it," he mumbled.

"See you, then, Bert."

"Don't forget," he said. "That advice."

"Right." I began to turn away.

"Ty?"

I was tired of him. "What?"

"You wouldn't let it happen to you, I know that . . . but sometimes it's the strong ones get the worst clobbering . . . in the ring, I mean. . . . They never know when they've taken enough. . . ."

He suddenly leaned forward and grasped my coat. Whiskey fumes seeped up my nose and I could feel his hot breath across the damp air.

"You're always broke, with that wife of yours. Luke-John told me. Always bloody stony. So don't do it. . . . Don't sell your sodding soul. . . ."

"Try not to," I said wearily, but he wasn't listening.

He said, with the desperate intensity of the very drunk, "They buy you first and blackmail after."

"Who?"

"Don't know . . . don't sell . . . don't sell your column."

"No." I sighed.

"I *mean* it." He put his face even closer. "Never sell your column."

"Bert . . . Have you?"

He closed up. He pried himself off me and went back to rocking. He winked, a vast caricature of a wink.

"Bit of advice," he said, nodding. He swiveled on rubbery ankles and weaved an unsteady path across the lobby to the lifts. Inside he turned around and I saw him standing there under the light clutching the half bottle and still saying over and over, "Bit of advice, bit of advice."

The doors slid heavily across in front of him. Shrugging, puzzled a little, I started on my way back to the *Blaze*. Fifty yards along, I stopped off to see if the people who were servicing my typewriter had finished it. They hadn't. Call back Monday, they said.

When I stepped out into the street again, a woman was screaming.

Heads turned. The high-pitched agonized noise pierced the roar of wheels and rose clean above the car horns. With everyone else, I looked to see the cause.

Fifty yards up the pavement a knot of people was rapidly forming, and I reflected that in this particular place droves of regular staff reporters would be on the spot in seconds. Nevertheless I went back. Back to the front door of Bert's paper, and a few steps farther on.

Bert was lying on the pavement. Clearly dead. The shining fragments of his half bottle of whiskey scattered the paving slabs around him, and the sharp smell of the spilt spirit mixed uneasily with that of the pervading diesel oil.

"He fell! He fell!" The screaming woman was on the edge of hysterics and couldn't stop shouting. "He fell. I saw him. From up there. He fell!"

Luke-John said "Christ" several times and looked badly shocked. Derry shook out a whole pot of paper clips onto his desk and absent-mindedly put them back one by one.

"You're sure he was dead?" he said.

"His office was seven floors up."

"Yeah." He shook his head disbelievingly. "Poor old boy." *Nil nisi bonum.* A sharp change of attitude.

Luke-John looked out of the *Blaze* window and down along the street. The smashed remains of Bert Checkov had been decently removed. The pavement had been washed. People tramped unknowingly across the patch where he had died.

"He was drunk," Luke-John said. "Worse than usual."

He and Derry made a desultory start on the afternoon work. I had no need to stay as the editor had O.K.'d my copy, but I hung around anyway for an hour or two, not ready to go.

They had said in Bert's office that he came back stoned from lunch and simply fell out of the window. Two girl secretaries saw him. He was taking a drink out of the bottle of whiskey, and he suddenly staggered against the window, which swung open, and he toppled out. The bottom of the window was at hip height. No trouble at all for someone as drunk as Bert.

I remembered the desperation behind the bit of advice he had given me.

And I wondered.

TWO

Three things immediately struck you about the girl who opened the stockbroker-Tudor door at Virginia Water. First, her poise. Second, her fashion sense. Third, her color. She had honey-toast skin, large dark eyes, and a glossy shoulder-length bounce of black hair. A slightly broad nose and a mouth to match enhanced a landscape in which Negro and Caucasian genes had conspired together to do a grand job.

"Good afternoon," I said. "I'm James Tyrone. I telephoned. . . ."

"Come in." She nodded. "Harry and Sarah should be back at any minute."

"They are still playing golf?"

"Mmm." She turned, smiling slightly, and gestured me into the house. "Still finishing lunch, I expect."

It was three-thirty-five. Why not?

She led me through the hall (well-polished parquet, careful flowers, studded leather umbrella stand) into a chintz and chrysanthemum sitting room. Every window in the house was a clutter of diamond-shaped leaded lights which might have had some point when glass could only be made in six-inch squares and had to be joined together to get anywhere. The modern imitation obscured the light, and the view and was bound to infuriate window cleaners. Harry and Sarah had opted also for uncovered dark oak beams with machine-made chisel marks. The single picture on the plain cream walls made a wild contrast: a modern impressionistic abstract of some cosmic explosion, with the oils stuck on in lumps.

"Sit down." She waved a graceful hand at a thickly cushioned sofa. "Like a drink?"

"No, thank you."

17

"Don't journalists drink all day?"

"If you drink and write, the writing isn't so hot."

"Ah, yes," she said. "Dylan Thomas said he had to be stone cold for any good to come of it."

"Different class." I smiled.

"Same principle."

"Absolutely."

She gave me a long inspection, her head tilted an inch to one side and her green dress lying in motionless folds down her slender body. Terrific legs in the latest in stockings ended in shiny green shoes with gold buckles, and the only other accessory on display was a broad-strapped gold watch on her left wrist.

"You'll know me again," she said.

I nodded. Her body moved subtly inside the green dress.

She said slowly, with more than simple meaning, "And I'll know you."

Her voice, face, and manner were quite calm. The brief flash of intense sexual awareness could have been my imagination. Certainly her next remark held no undertone and no invitation.

"Do you *like* horses?"

"Yes, I do," I said.

"Six months ago I would have said the one place I would never go would be to a race meeting."

"But you go now?"

"Since Harry won Egocentric in that raffle, life has changed in this little neck of the woods."

"That," I said, "is exactly what I want to write about."

I was on *Tally* business. Background to the Lamplighter. My choice of untypical racehorse owners, Harry and Sarah Hunterson, came back at that point from their Sunday golf-course lunch, sweeping in with them a breeze compounded of healthy links air, expensive cigar smoke, and half-digested gin.

Harry was big, sixtyish, used to authority, heavily charming, nd unshakably Tory. I guessed that he read the *Telegraph* and drove a three-litre Jaguar. With automatic transmission, of course. He gave me a hearty handshake and said he was glad to see his niece had been looking after me.

"Yes, thank you."

Sarah said, "Gail, dear, you didn't give Mr. Tyrone a drink."

"He didn't want one."

The two women were coolly nice to each other in civilized voices. Sarah must have been about thirty years older, but she had worked hard at keeping nature at bay. Everything about her looked careful, from the soft gold rinse via the russet-colored dress to the chunky brown golfing shoes. Her well-controlled shape owed much to the drinking-man's diet, and only a deep sag under the chin gave the game away. Neither golf nor gin had dug wrinkles anywhere except around her eyes. Her mouth still had fullness and shape. The wrappings were good enough to hold out hopes of a spark-striking mind, but these proved unrealistic. Sarah was all-of-a-piece, with attitudes and opinions as tidy and well-ordered and as imitative as her house.

Harry was easy to interview in the aftermath of the nineteenth hole.

"I bought this raffle ticket at the golf-club dance, you see. Some chap was there selling them, a friend of a friend, you know, and I gave him a quid. Well, you know how it is at a dance. For charity, he said. I thought a quid was a bit steep for a raffle ticket, even if it was for a horse. Though I didn't want a horse, mind you. Last thing I wanted. And then damn me if I didn't go and win it. Bit of a problem, eh? To suddenly find yourself saddled with a racehorse?" He laughed, expecting a reward for his little joke.

I duly obliged. Sarah and Gail were both wearing the expressions which meant they had heard him say "saddled with a racehorse" so often that they had to grit their teeth now at each repetition.

"Would you mind," I said, "telling me something of your background and history?"

"Life story, eh?" He laughed loudly, looking from

Sarah to Gail to collect their approval. His head was heavily handsome, though a shade too fleshy around the neck. The bald sunburned crown and the well-disciplined mustache suited him. Thread veins made circular patches of color on his cheeks. "Life story," he repeated. "Where shall I start?"

"Start from birth," I said, "and go on from there."

Only the very famous who have done it too often, or the extremely introverted, or the sheer bloody-minded, can resist such an invitation. Harry's eyes lit up, and he launched forth with enthusiasm.

Harry had been born in a Surrey suburb in a detached house a size or two smaller than the one he now owned. He had been to a day school and then a minor public school, and was turned down by the Army because as soon as he left school he had pleurisy. He went to work in the City, in the head office of a finance company, and had risen from junior clerk to director, on the way using occasional snippets of information to make himself modest capital gains via the stock market. Nothing shady, nothing rash; but enough so that there should be no drop in his standard of living when he retired.

He married at twenty-four and five years later a lorry rammed his car and killed his wife, his three-year-old daughter, and his widowed mother. For fifteen years, much in demand at dinner parties, Harry "looked around." Then he met Sarah in some Conservative Party committee rooms where they were doing voluntary work addressing pamphlets for a by-election, and they had married three months later. Below the confident fruitiness of successful Harry's voice there was an echo of the motivation of this second marriage. Harry had begun to feel lonely.

As lives went, Harry's had been uneventful. No *Blaze* material in what he had told me, and precious little for *Tally*. Resignedly I asked him if he intended to keep Egocentric indefinitely.

"Yes, yes, I think so," he said. "He has made quite a remarkable difference to us."

"In what way?"

"It puts them several notches up in lifemanship," Gail said coolly. "Gives them something to boast about in pubs."

We all looked at her. Such was her poise that I found it impossible to tell whether she meant to be catty or teasing, and, from his uncertain expression, so did her uncle. There was no ducking it, however, that she had hit to the heart of things, and Sarah smoothly punished her for it.

"Gail, dear, would you go and make tea for all of us?"

Gail's every muscle said she would hate to. But she stood up ostentatiously slowly, and went.

"A dear girl," Sarah said. "Perhaps sometimes a little trying." Insincerity took all warmth out of her smile, and she found it necessary to go on, to make an explanation that I guessed she rushed into with every stranger at the first opportunity.

"Harry's sister married a barrister. . . . Such a clever man, you know . . . but, well . . . *African.*"

"Yes," I said.

"Of course we're *very* fond of Gail, and as her parents have gone back to his country since it became independent, and as she was born in England and wanted to stay here, well, we—well, she lives here with us."

"Yes," I said again. "That must be very nice for her."

Sad, I thought, that they felt any need to explain. Gail didn't need it.

"She teaches at an art school in Victoria," Harry added. "Fashion drawing."

"Fashion *design,*" Sarah corrected him. "She's really quite good at it. Her pupils win prizes, and things like that." There was relief in her voice now that I understood, and she was prepared to be generous. To do her justice, considering the far-back embedded prejudices she clearly suffered from, she had made a successful effort. But a pity the effort showed.

"And you," I said. "How about your life? And what do you think of Egocentric?"

She said apologetically that her story wasn't as interesting as Harry's. Her first husband, an optician, had died a year before she met Harry, and all she had done, apart from short excursions into voluntary work, was keep house for the two of them. She was glad Harry had won the horse, she liked going to the races as an owner, she thought it exciting to bet, but ten shillings was her usual, and she and Gail had found it quite fun inventing Harry's racing colors.

"What are they?"

"White with scarlet and turquoise question marks, turquoise sleeves, red cap."

"They sound fine." I smiled. "I'll look out for them."

Harry said his trainer was planning to fit in one more race for Egocentric before the Lamplighter, and maybe I would see him then. Maybe I would, I said, and Gail brought in the tea.

Harry and Sarah rapidly downed three cups each, simultaneously consulted their watches, and said it was time to be getting along to the Murrows' for drinks.

"I don't think I'll come," Gail said. "Tell them thanks, but I have got some work to do. But I'll come and fetch you, if you like, if you think it might be better not to drive home. Give me a ring when you're ready."

The Murrow drinks on top of the golf-club gin were a breathalizer hazard in anyone's book. Harry and Sarah nodded and said they would appreciate it.

"Before you go," I said, "could you let me see any newspaper cuttings you have? And any photographs?"

"Certainly, certainly," Harry agreed. "Gail will show them to you, won't you, honey? Must dash now, old chap. The Murrows, you know. . . . President of the golf club. Nice to have met you. Hope you've got all the gen you need. . . . Don't hesitate to call if you want to know anything else."

"Thank you," I said, but he was gone before I finished. They went upstairs and down, and shut the front door, and drove away. The house settled into quiet behind them.

"They're not exactly alcoholic," Gail said. "They just go eagerly from drink to drink."

Gail's turn to explain. But in her voice, only objectivity: no faintest hint of apology, as there had been in Sarah's.

"They enjoy life," I said.

Gail's eyebrows rose. "Do you know," she said, "I suppose they do. I've never really thought about it."

Self-centered, I thought. Cool. Unaffectionate. Everything I disliked in a woman. Everything I needed one to be. Much too tempting.

"Do you want to see those photographs?" she asked.

"Yes, please."

She fetched an expensive leather folder and we went through them one by one. Nothing in the few clippings that I hadn't learnt already. None of the photographs were arresting enough for *Tally*. I said I'd come back one day soon, with a photographer. Gail put the folder away and I stood up to go.

"It'll be two hours yet before they ring up from the Murrows'. Stay and have that drink now?"

I looked at my watch. There was a train every thirty minutes. I supposed I could miss the next. There was Elizabeth. And there was Gail. And it was only an hour.

"Yes," I said. "I will."

She gave me beer and brought one for herself. I sat down again on the sofa and she folded herself gracefully into a large velvet cushion on the floor.

"You're married, of course?"

"Yes," I said.

"The interesting-looking ones always are."

"Then why aren't you?"

Her teeth flashed liquid white in an appreciative smile. "Ah . . . marriage can wait."

"How long?" I asked.

"I suppose . . . until I find a man I can't bear to part with."

"You've parted with quite a few?"

"Quite a few." She nodded and sipped her beer, and

looked at me over the rim. "And you? Are you faithful to your wife?"

I felt myself blink. I said carefully, "Most of the time."

"But not always?"

"Not always."

After a long considering pause she said one short word.

"Good."

"And is that," I asked, "a philosophic comment, or a proposition?"

She laughed. "I just like to know where I stand."

"Clear-eyed and wide-awake?"

"I hate muddle," she said.

"And emotional muddle especially?"

"You're so right."

She had never loved, I thought. Sex, often. Love, never. Not what I liked, but what I wanted. I battened down the insidious whisper and asked her, like a good little journalist, about her job.

"It serves." She shrugged. "You get maybe one authentic talent in every hundred students. Mostly their ambition is five times more noticeable than their ideas."

"Do you design clothes yourself?"

"Not for the rag trade. Some for myself, and for Sarah, and for the school. I prefer to teach. I like being able to turn vaguely artistic ignorance into competent workmanship."

"And to see your influence all along Oxford Street?"

She nodded, her eyes gleaming with amusement. "Five of the biggest dress manufacturers now have old students of mine on their design staff. One of them is so individual that I can spot his work every time in the shop windows."

"You like power," I said.

"Who doesn't?"

"Heady stuff."

"All power corrupts?" She was sarcastic.

"Each to his own corruption," I said mildly. "What's yours, then?"

She laughed. "Money, I guess. There's a chronic shortage of the folding stuff in all forms of teaching."

"So you make do with power."

"If you can't have everything"—she nodded—"you make do with *something*."

I looked down into my beer, unable to stop the contraction I could feel in my face. Her words so completely summed up my perennial position. After eleven years I was less resigned by it than ever.

"What are you thinking about?" she asked.

"Taking you to bed."

She gasped. I looked up from the flat brown liquid ready for any degree of feminine outrage. I could have mistaken her.

It seemed I hadn't. She was laughing. Pleased.

"That's pretty blunt."

"Mmm."

I put down the beer and stood up, smiling. "Time to go," I said. "I've a train to catch."

"After that? You can't go after that."

"Especially after that."

For answer she stood up beside me, took hold of my hand, and put my fingers into the gold ring at the top of the zipper down the front of her dress.

"Now go home," she said.

"We've only known each other three hours," I protested.

"You were aware of me after three minutes."

I shook my head. "Three seconds."

Her teeth gleamed. "I like strangers."

I pulled the ring downward and it was clearly what she wanted.

Harry and Sarah had a large white fluffy rug in front of their fireplace. I imagined it was not the first time Gail had lain on it. She was brisk, graceful, unembarrassed. She stripped off her stockings and shoes, shook off her dress, and stepped out of the diminutive green bra and panties underneath it. Her tawny skin looked warm in the gathering dusk, and her shape took the breath away.

She gave me a marvelous time. A generous lover as well as practiced. She knew when to touch lightly, and when to be vigorous. She had strong internal muscles, and she knew how to use them. I took her with passionate gratitude, a fair substitute for love.

When we had finished, I lay beside her on the rug and felt the released tension weighing down my limbs in a sort of heavy languorous weakness. The world was a million light-years away and I was in no hurry for it to come closer.

"Wow," she said, half breathless, half laughing. "Boy, you sure needed that."

"Mmm."

"Doesn't your wife let you. . . ?"

Elizabeth, I thought. Oh God, Elizabeth. I must sometimes. Just sometimes.

The old weary tide of guilt washed back. The world closed in.

I sat up and stared blindly across the darkening room. It apparently struck Gail that she had been less than tactful, because she got up with a sigh and put her clothes on again, and didn't say another word.

For better or worse, I thought bitterly. For richer, for poorer. In sickness and in health keep thee only unto her as long as you both shall live. I will, I said.

An easy vow, the day I made it. I hadn't kept it. Gail was the fourth girl in eleven years. The first for nearly three.

"You'll miss your train," she observed prosaically, "if you sit there much longer."

I looked at my watch, which was all I had on. Fifteen minutes.

She sighed, "I'll drive you along to the station."

We made it with time to spare. I stepped out of the car and politely thanked her for the lift.

"Will I see you again?" she said. Asking for information. Showing no anxiety. Looking out at me through the open window of the station wagon outside Virginia Water station, she was giving a close imitation of any suburban wife doing the train run. A long cool way from the rough and tumble on the rug. Switch on, switch off. The sort of woman I needed.

"I don't know," I said indecisively. The signal at the end of the platform went green.

"Goodbye," she said calmly.

"Do Harry and Sarah," I asked carefully, "always play golf on Sundays?"

She laughed, the yellow station lighting flashing on teeth an eyes.

"Without fail."

"Maybe. . . ."

"Maybe you'll ring, and maybe you won't." She nodded. "Fair enough. And maybe I'll be in, and maybe I won't." She gave me a lengthy look which was half smile and half amused detachment. She wouldn't weep if I didn't return. She would accommodate me if I did. "But don't leave it too long, if you're coming back."

She wound up the window and drove off without a wave, without a backward glance.

The green electric worm of a train slid quietly into the station to take me home. Forty minutes to Waterloo. Underground to King's Cross. Three-quarters of a mile to walk. Time to enjoy the new ease in my body. Time to condemn it. Too much of my life was a battlefield in which conscience and desire fought constantly for the upper hand; and whichever of them won, it left me the loser.

Elizabeth's mother said with predictable irritation, "You're late."

"I'm sorry."

I watched the jerks of her crossly pulling on her gloves. Coat and hat had already been in place when I walked in.

"You have so little consideration. It'll be nearly eleven when I get back."

I didn't answer.

"You're selfish. All men are selfish."

There was no point in agreeing with her, and no point in arguing. A disastrous and short-lived marriage had left hopeless wounds in her mind which she had done her best to pass on to her only child. Elizabeth, when I first met her, had been pathologically scared of men.

"We've had our supper," my mother-in-law said. "I've stacked the dishes for Mrs. Woodward."

Nothing could be more certainly relied upon to upset Mrs. Woodward than a pile of congealed plates first thing on Monday morning.

"Fine," I said, smiling falsely.

"Goodbye, Elizabeth," she called.

"Goodbye, Mother."

I opened the door for her and got no thanks.

"Next Sunday, then," she said.

"That'll be nice."

She smiled acidly, knowing I didn't mean it. But since she worked as a receptionist-hostess in a health farm all week, Sunday was her day for seeing Elizabeth. Most weeks I wished she would leave us alone, but that Sunday it had set me free to go to Virginia Water. From the following Sunday, and what I might do with it, I wrenched my thoughts away.

When she had gone, I walked across to Elizabeth and kissed her on the forehead.

"Hi."

"Hi yourself," she said. "Did you have a good afternoon?"

Straight jab.

"Mmm."

"Good. . . . Mother's left the dishes again."

I said, "Don't worry, I'll do them."

"What would I do without you!"

We both knew the answer to that. Without me, she would have to spend the rest of her life in a hospital ward, a prisoner with no possibility of escape. She couldn't breathe without the electrically driven pump which hummed at the foot of her high bed. She couldn't cut up her own food or take herself to the bathroom. Elizabeth, my wife, was ninety per cent paralyzed from poliomyelitis.

THREE

We lived over a row of lockup garages in a mews behind Gray's Inn Road. A development company had recently knocked down the old buildings opposite, letting in temporary acres of evening sunshine, and was now at the girder stage of a block of flats. If these made our place too dark and shut in when they were done, I would have to find us somewhere else. Not a welcome prospect. We had moved twice before and it was always difficult.

Since race trains mostly ran from London, and to cut my traveling time down to a minimum, we lived ten minutes' walk from the *Blaze*. It had proved much better, in London, to live in a backwater than in a main street; in the small mews community the neighbors all knew about Elizabeth and looked up to her window and waved when they passed, and a lot of them came upstairs for a chat and to bring our shopping.

The district nurse came every morning to do Elizabeth's alcohol rubs to prevent bedsores, and I did them in the evenings. Mrs. Woodward, a semitrained but unqualified nurse, came Mondays through Saturdays from nine-thirty to six, and was helpful about staying longer if necessary. One of our main troubles was that Elizabeth could not be left alone in the flat even for five minutes in case there was an electricity failure. If the main current stopped, we could switch her breathing pump over to a battery, and we could also operate it by hand, but someone had to be there to do it quickly.

Mrs. Woodward was kind, middle-aged, reliable, and quiet, and Elizabeth liked her. She was also very expensive, and since the Welfare State turns a blind eye on incapacitated wives, I could claim not even so much as a tax allowance for Mrs. Woodward's essential services.

We had to have her, and she kept us poor; and that was that.

In one of the garages below the flat stood the old Bedford van which was the only sort of transport of any use to us. I had had it adapted years ago with a stretcher-type bed so that it would take Elizabeth, pump, batteries, and all, and although it meant too much upheaval to go out in it every week, it did sometimes give her a change of scenery and some country air. We had tried two holidays by the sea in a caravan, but she had felt uncomfortable and insecure, and both times it had rained, so we didn't bother any more. Day trips were enough, she said. And although she enjoyed them, they exhausted her.

Her respirator was the modern cuirass type: a Spiroshell, not the old totally enclosing iron lung. The Spiroshell itself slightly resembled the breastplate of a suit of armor. It fitted over the entire front of her chest, was edged with a thick roll of latex, and was fastened by straps around her body. Breathing was really a matter of suction. The pump, which was connected to the Spiroshell by a thick flexible hose, alternately made a partial vacuum inside the shell and then drove air back in again. The vacuum period pulled Elizabeth's chest wall outward, allowing air to flow downward into her lungs. The air-in period collapsed her chest and pushed the used breath out again.

Far more comfortable, and easier for everyone caring for her than a box respirator, the Spiroshell had only one drawback. Try as we might, and however many scarves and cardigans we might stuff in around the edges between the latex roll and her nightdress, it was eternally drafty. As long as the air in the flat was warm, it did not worry her. Summer was all right. But cold air continually blowing onto her chest—not surprisingly—distressed her. Cold also reduced to nil the small movements she had retained in her left hand and wrist, and on which she depended for everything. Our heating bills were astronomical.

In the nine and a half years since I had extricated her

from hospital, we had acquired almost every gadget invented. Wires and pulleys trailed all around the flat. She could read books, draw the curtains, turn on and off the lights, the radio, and television, use the telephone, and type letters. An electric box of tricks called Possum did most of these tasks. Others worked on a system of levers set off by the feather-light pressure of her left forefinger. Our latest triumph was an electric pulley which raised and rotated her left elbow and forearm, enabling her to eat some things on her own, without always having to be fed. And with a clipped-on electric toothbrush she could now brush her own teeth.

I slept on a divan across the room from her with a bell beside my ear for when she needed me in the night. There were bells, too, in the kitchen and the bathroom, and the tiny room I used for writing in, which with the large sitting room made up the whole of the flat.

We had been married three years, and we were both twenty-four, when Elizabeth caught polio. We were living in Singapore, where I had a junior job in the Reuters office, and we flew home for what was intended to be a month's leave.

Elizabeth felt ill on the flight. The light hurt her eyes, and she had a headache like a rod up the back of her neck, and a stabbing pain in her chest. She walked off the aircraft at Heathrow and collapsed halfway across the tarmac, and that was the last time she ever stood on her feet.

Our affection for each other had survived everything that followed. Poverty, temper, tears, desperate frustrations. We had emerged after several years into our present comparative calms of a settled home, a good job, a reasonably well-ordered existence. We were firm close friends.

But not lovers.

We had tried, in the beginning. She could still feel of course, since polio attacks only the motor nerves, and leaves the sensory nerves intact. But she couldn't breathe for more than three or four minutes if we took the Spiroshell right off, and she couldn't bear any weight or pressure on any part of her wasted body. When I said after two or three hopeless attempts that we would leave it for a while, she had smiled at me with what I saw to be enormous relief, and we had rarely even mentioned the subject since. Her early upbringing seemed to have easily reconciled her to a sexless existence. Her three years of thawing into a satisfying marriage might never have happened.

On the day after my trip to Virginia Water I set off as soon as Mrs. Woodward came and drove the van northeast out of London and into deepest Essex. My quarry this time was a farmer who had bred gold dust in his field in the shape of Tiddely Pom, antepost favorite for the Lamplighter Gold Cup.

Weeds luxuriantly edged the potholed road which led from a pair of rotting gateless gateposts into Victor Roncey's farmyard. The house itself, an undistinguished arrangement of mud-colored bricks, stood in a drift of sodden unswept leaves and stared blankly from symmetrical grubby windows. Colorless paint peeled quietly from the woodwork and no smoke rose from the chimneys.

I knocked on the back door, which stood half open, and called through a small lobby into the house, but there was no reply. A clock ticked with a loud cheap mechanism. A smell of Wellington boots richly acquainted with cow pat vigorously assaulted the nose. Someone had dumped a parcel of meat on the edge of the kitchen table from which a thread of watery blood, that had soaked through the newspaper wrapping, was making a small pink pool on the floor.

Turning away from the house, I wandered across the untidy yard and peered into a couple of outbuildings. One contained a tractor covered with about six years' mud. In another, a heap of dusty-looking coke rubbed shoulders with a jumbled stack of old broken crates and sawed-up branches of trees. A larger shed housed dirt and cobwebs and nothing else.

While I hovered in the center of the yard wondering

how far it was polite to investigate, a large youth in a
striped knitted cap with a scarlet pompon came around
a corner at the far end. He also wore a vast sloppy pale
blue sweater, and filthy jeans tucked into heavyweight
gum boots. Fair-haired, with a round weather-beaten
face, he looked cheerful and uncomplicated.

"Hullo," he said. "You want something?" His voice
was light and pleasant, with a touch of local accent.

"I'm looking for Mr. Roncey."

"He's round the roads with the horses. Better call
back later."

"How long will he be?"

"An hour, maybe." He shrugged.

"I'll wait, then, if you don't mind," I said, gesturing
toward my van.

"Suit yourself."

He took six steps toward the house and then stopped,
turned around, and came back.

"Hey, you wouldn't be that chap who phoned?"

"Which chap?"

"James Tyrone?"

"That's right."

"Well, for crying out loud why didn't you say so?
I thought you were a traveler. . . . Come on into the
house. Do you want some breakfast?"

"Breakfast?"

He grinned. "Yeah. I know it's nearly eleven. I get
up before six. Feel peckish again by now."

He led the way into the house through the back door,
did nothing about the dripping meat, and added to the
Wellington smell by clumping across the floor to the
furthest door, which he opened.

"Ma?" he shouted. "Ma."

"She's around somewhere," he said, shrugging and
coming back. "Never mind. Want some eggs?"

I said no, but when he reached out a half-acre frying
pan and filled it with bacon I changed my mind.

"Make the coffee," he said, pointing.

I found mugs, powdered coffee, sugar, milk, kettle,

and spoons all standing together on a bench alongside the sink.

"My Ma," he explained, grinning, "is a great one for the time-and-motion bit."

He fried six eggs expertly and gave us three each, with a chunk of new white bread on the side.

We sat at the kitchen table, and I'd rarely tasted anything so good. He ate solidly and drank coffee, then pushed his plate away and lit a cigarette.

"I'm Peter," he said. "It isn't usually so quiet around here, but the kids are at school and Pat's out with Pa."

"Pat?"

"My brother. The jockey of the family. Point-to-points, mostly, though. I don't suppose you would know of him?"

"I'm afraid not."

"I read your column," he said. "Most weeks."

"That's nice."

He considered me, smoking, while I finished the eggs. "You don't talk much, for a journalist."

"I listen," I said.

He grinned. "That's a point."

"Tell me about Tiddely Pom, then."

"Hell, no. You'll have to get Pa or Pat for that. They're crazy on the horses. I just run the farm." He watched my face carefully, I guessed for surprise, since in spite of being almost my height he was still very young.

"You're sixteen?" I suggested.

"Yeah." He sniffed, disgusted. "Waste of effort, though, really."

"Why?"

"Why? Because of the bloody motorway, that's why. They've nearly finished that bloody three-lane monster and it passes just over there, the other side of our ten-acre field." He gestured toward the window with his cigarette. "Pa's going raving mad wondering if Tiddely Pom'll have a nervous breakdown when those heavy lorries start thundering past. He's been trying to sell this place for two years, but no one will have it, and you can't blame them, can you?" Gloom settled on him temporarily. "Then, see, you never know when they'll pinch more of our land, they've had fifty acres already, and it doesn't give you much heart to keep the place right, does it?"

"I guess not," I said.

"They've talked about knocking our house down," he went on. "Something about it being in the perfect position for a service station with restaurants and a vast car park and another slip road to Bishop's Stortford. The only person who's pleased about the road is my brother Tony, and he wants to be a rally driver. He's eleven. He's a nut."

There was a scrunch and clatter of hoofs outside, coming nearer. Peter and I got to our feet and went out into the yard, and watched three horses plod up the bumpy gravel drive and rein to a halt in front of us. The rider of the leading horse slid off, handed his reins to the second, and came toward us. A trim wiry man in his forties, with thick brown hair and a mustard-colored mustache.

"Mr. Tyrone?"

I nodded. He gave me a brisk hard handshake in harmony with his manner and voice, and then stood back to allow me a clear view of the horses.

"That's Tiddely Pom, that bay." He pointed to the third horse, ridden by young man very like Peter, though perhaps a size smaller. "And Pat, my son."

"A fine-looking horse," I said insincerely. Most owners expected praise, but Tiddely Pom showed as much high quality to the naked eye as an uncut diamond. A common head, slightly U-necked on a weak shoulder, and herring-gutted into the bargain. He looked just as uncouth at home as he did on a racecourse.

"Huh," snorted Roncey. "He's not. He's a doer, not a looker. Don't try and butter me up. I don't take to it."

"Fair enough," I said mildly. "Then he's got a common head and neck, a poor shoulder, and doesn't fill the eye behind the saddle, either."

"That's better. So you do know what you're talking about. Walk him round the yard, Pat."

Pat obliged. Tiddely Pom stumbled around with the floppy gait that once in a while denotes a champion. This horse, bred from a thoroughbred hunter mare by a premium stallion, was a spectacular jumper endowed with a speed to be found nowhere in his pedigree. When an ace of this sort turned up unexpectedly, it took the owner almost as long as the public to realize it. The whole racing industry was unconsciously geared against belief that twenty-two-carats stars could come from tiny owner-trained stables. It had taken Tiddely Pom three seasons to become known, while from a big fashionable public stable he would have been newsworthy in his first race.

"When I bred him, I was hoping for a point-to-point horse for the boys," Roncey said. "So we ran him all one season in point-to-points and, apart from one time Pat fell off, he didn't get beat. Then last year we thought we would have a go in hunter chases as well, and he went and won the Foxhunters at Cheltenham."

"I remember that," I said.

"Yes. So last year we tried him in open handicaps, smallish ones—"

"And he won four out of six," I concluded for him.

"It's your job to know, I suppose. Pat!" he shouted. "Put him back in his box." He turned to me again. "Like to see the others?"

I nodded, and we followed Pat and the other two horses across the yard and around the corner from which Peter had originally appeared.

Behind a ramshackle barn stood a neat row of six well-kept wooden horse boxes, with shingle roofs and newly painted black doors. However run-down the rest of the farm might be, the stable department was in tiptop shape. No difficulty in seeing where the farmer's heart lay: with his treasure.

"Well, now," Roncey said, "we've only the one other racehorse, really, and that's Klondyke, that I was riding just now. He ran in hunter chases in the spring. Didn't do much good, to be honest." He walked along to the second box from the far end, led the horse in, and tied it up. When he took the saddle off, I saw that Klondyke was a better shape than Tiddely Pom, which was saying little enough, but the health in his coat was conspicuous.

"He looks well," I commented.

"Eats his head off," said Roncey dispassionately, "and he can stand a lot of work, so we give it to him."

"One-paced," observed Pat regretfully over my shoulder. "Can't quicken. Pity. We won just the two point-to-points with him. No more."

There was the faintest glimmer of satisfaction in the laconic voice, and I glanced at him sideways. He saw me looking and wiped the expression off his face but not before I had seen for certain that he had mixed feelings about the horses' successes. While they progessed to National Hunt racing proper, he didn't. Older amateur riders had been engaged, and then professionals. The father-son relationship had needles in it.

"What do you have in the other boxes?" I asked Roncey as he shut Klondyke's door.

"My old gray hunter at the end, and two hunter mares here, both in foal. This one, Piglet, she's the dam of Tiddely Pom, of course; she's in foal to the same sire again."

Unlikely, I thought, that lightning would strike twice.

"You'll sell the foal," I suggested.

He sniffed. "She's in the farm accounts."

I grinned to myself. Farmers could train their horses and lose the cost on the general farm accounts, but if they sold one it then came under the heading of income and was taxed accordingly. If Roncey sold either Tiddely Pom or his full brother, nearly half would go to the Revenue.

"Turn the mares out, Joe," he said to the third rider, a patient-looking old man with skin like bark, and we watched while he set them loose in the nearest field. Peter was standing beside the gate with Pat: bigger, more assured, with far fewer knots in his personality.

"Fine sons," I said to Roncey.

His mouth tightened. He had no pride in them. He

made no reply at all to my fishing comment, but instead said, "We'll go into the house and you can ask me anything you want to know. For a magazine, you said?"

I nodded.

"Pat!" he shouted. "You give these three mares a good strapping and feed them and let Joe get on with the hedging. Peter, you've got work to do. Go and do it."

Both his boys gave him the blank acquiescing look which covers seething rebellion. There was a perceptible pause before they moved off with their calm accepting faces. Lids on a lot of steam. Maybe one day Roncey would be scalded.

He led the way briskly back across the yard and into the kitchen. The meat still lay there dripping. Roncey by-passed it and gestured me to follow him through the far door into a small dark hall.

"Madge?" he shouted. "Madge?"

Father had as little success as son. He shrugged in the same way and led me into a living room as well worn and untidy as the rest of the place. Drifts of clutter, letters, newspapers, clothing, toys, and indiscriminate bits of junk lay on every flat surface, including the chairs and the floor. There was a vase of dead and desiccated chrysanthemums on a window sill, and some brazen cobwebs networked the ceiling. Cold ash from the day before filled the grate. A tossup, I thought, whether one called the room lived-in or squalid.

"Sit down if you can find somewhere," Roncey said. "Madge lets the boys run wild in the house. Not firm enough. I won't have it outside, of course."

"How many do you have?"

"Boys? Five."

"And a daughter?" I asked.

"No," he said abruptly. "Five boys."

The thought didn't please him. "Which magazine?"

"*Tally,*" I said. "They want background stories to the Lamplighter, and I thought I would give the big stables a miss and shine a bit of the spotlight on someone else for a change."

"Yes, well," he said defensively, "I've been written up before, you know."

"Of course," I said soothingly.

"About the Lamplighter, too. I'll show you." He jumped up and went over to a kneehole desk, pulled out one of the side drawers bodily, and brought it across to where I sat at one end of the sofa. He put the drawer in the center, swept a crumpled jersey, two beaten-up dinky cars, and a gutted brown paper parcel onto the floor, and seated himself in the space.

The drawer contained a heap of clippings and photographs all thrust in together. No careful sticking into expensive leather folders, like the Huntersons.

My mind leapt to Gail. I saw Roncey talking to me but I was thinking about her body. Her roundnesses. Her fragrant pigmented skin. Roncey was waiting for an answer and I hadn't heard what he'd asked.

"I'm sorry," I said.

"I asked if you know Bert Checkov." He was holding a lengthy clipping with a picture alongside and a bold headline, "BACK TIDDELY POM NOW."

"Yes . . . and no," I said uncertainly.

"How do you mean?" he said brusquely. "I should have thought you would have known him, being in the same business."

"I did know him. But he died. Last Friday."

I took the clipping and read it while Roncey went through the motions of being shocked, with the indifference uppermost in his voice spoiling the effect.

Bert Checkov had gone to town with Tiddely Pom's chances in the Lamplighter. The way he saw it, the handicapper had been suffering from semiblindness and mental blocks to put Tiddely Pom into the weights at ten stone seven, and all punters who didn't jump on the band wagon instantly needed to be wet-nursed. He thought the antepost market would open with generous odds, but urged everyone to hurry up with their shirts, before the bookmakers woke up to the bonanza. Bert's pungent phraseology had given Roncey's horse more boost than a four-stage rocket.

"I didn't know he'd written this," I admitted. "I missed it."

"He rang me up only last Thursday and this was in the paper on Friday. That must have been the day you said he died. In point of fact I didn't expect it would appear. When he telephoned, he was, to my mind, quite drunk."

"It's possible," I conceded.

"I wasn't best pleased about it, either."

"The article?"

"I hadn't got my own money on, do you see? And there he went spoiling the price. When I rang up my bookmaker on Friday, he wouldn't give me more than a hundred to eight and today they've even made him favorite at eight to one, and there's still nearly three weeks to the race. Fair enough he's a good horse, but he's not Arkle. In point of fact I don't understand it."

"You don't understand why Checkov tipped him?"

He hesitated. "Not to that extent, then, let's say."

"But you do hope to win?"

"Hope," he said. "Naturally, I hope to win. But it's the biggest race we've ever tried. . . . I don't *expect* to win, do you see?"

"You've as good a chance as any," I said "Checkov had his column to fill. The public won't read halfhearted stuff; you have to go all out for the positive statement."

He gave me a small tight smile laced with a sneer for the soft option. A man with no patience or sympathy for anyone else's problems, not even his sons'?

The sitting-room door opened and a large woman in a sunflower yellow dress came in. She had thick hair down on her legs but no stockings, and a pair of puffed ankles bulged over the edges of some battered blue bedroom slippers. Nevertheless she was very light on her feet and she moved slowly, so that her progress seemed to be a weightless drift—no mean feat considering she must have topped twelve stone.

A mass of fine light brown hair hung in an amorphous cloud around her head, from which a pair of dreamy eyes surveyed the world as though she were half asleep.

Her face was soft and rounded, not young, but still in a way immature. Her fantasy life, I guessed uncharitably, was more real to her than the present. She had been far away in the past hour, much farther than upstairs.

"I didn't know you were in," she said to Roncey.

He stood up several seconds after me. "Madge, this is James Tyrone. I told you he was coming."

"Did you?" She transferred her vague gaze to me. "Carry on, then."

"Where have you been?" Roncey said. "Didn't you hear me calling?"

"Calling?" She shook her head. "I was making the beds, of course." She stood in the center of the room, looking doubtfully around at the mess. "Why didn't you light the fire?"

I glanced involuntarily at the heap of ashes in the grate, but she saw them as no obstacle at all. From a scratched oak box beside the hearth, she produced three firelighters and a handful of sticks. These went on top of the ashes, which got only a desultory poke. She struck a match, lit the firelighters, and made a wigwam of coal. The new fire flared up good-temperedly on the body of the old while Madge took the hearth brush and swept a few cinders out of sight behind a pile of logs.

Fascinated, I watched her continue with her housework. She drifted across to the dead flowers, opened the window, and threw them out. She emptied the water from the vase after them, then put it back on the window sill and shut the window.

From behind the sofa where Roncey and I sat, she pulled out a large brown cardboard box. On the outside was stenciled "KELLOGG'S CORNFLAKES, 12 x 12 FAMILY SIZE," and on the inside it was half filled with the same sort of jumble which was lying around the room. She wafted methodically around in a large circle, taking everything up and throwing it just as it was into the box, a process which took approximately three minutes. She then pushed the box out of sight again behind the sofa and plumped up the seat cushions of two armchairs on her way back to the door. The room, tidy and with the brightly blazing fire, looked staggeringly different. The cobwebs were still there but one felt it might be their turn tomorrow. Peter was right. Ma had got the time-and-motion kick completely buttoned up, and what did it matter if the motive was laziness?

Roncey insisted that I should stay to lunch and filled in the time beforehand with a brisk but endless account of all the horses he had ever owned. Over lunch—cold beef and pickles and cheese and biscuits served at two-thirty on the kichen table—it was still he who did all the talking. The boys ate steadily in silence and Madge contemplated the middle distance with eyes which saw only the scenes going on in her head.

When I left shortly afterward, Pat asked for a lift into Bishop's Stortford and braved his father's frown to climb into the front seat of the van. Roncey shook hands firmly, as before, and said he hoped to receive a free copy of *Tally*. "Of course," I said. But *Tally* was notoriously mean; I would have to send it myself.

He waved me out of the yard and told Pat brusquely to come straight back on the four-o'clock bus, and we were barely out through the sagging gateposts before Pat unburdened himself of a chunk of bottled resentment.

"He treats us like children. . . . Ma's no help, she never listens. . . ."

"You could leave here," I pointed out. "You're what—nineteen?"

"Next month. But I can't leave and he knows it. Not if I want to race. I can't turn professional yet; I'm not well enough known and no one would put me up on their horses. I've got to start as an amateur and make a name for myself, Pa says so. Well, I couldn't be an amateur if I left home and got an ordinary job somewhere, I couldn't afford all the expenses and I wouldn't have any time."

"A job in a stable. . . ." I suggested.

"Do me a favor. The rules say you can't earn a salary in any capacity in a racing stable and ride as an amateur, not even if you're a secretary or an assistant or anything. It's bloody unfair. And don't say I could get a job as a lad and do my two and have a professional license—of course I could. And how many lads ever get far as jockeys doing that? None. Absolutely none. You know that."

I nodded.

"I do a lad's work now, right enough. Six horses we've got, and I do the bloody lot. Old Joe's the only labor we've got on the whole farm, except us, believe it or not. Pa's always got a dozen jobs lined up for him. And I wouldn't mind the work, and getting practically no pay, I really wouldn't, if Pa would let me ride in anything except point-to-points, but he won't; he says I haven't enough experience, and if you ask me he's making bloody sure I never get enough experience. . . . I'm absolutely fed up, I'll tell you straight."

He brooded over his situation all the way into Bishop's Stortford. A genuine grievance, I thought. Victor Roncey was not a father to help his sons get on.

FOUR

They held the inquest on Bert Checkov on that Monday afternoon. Verdict: Misadventure. Dead drunk he was, said the girl typists who saw him fall. Dead drunk.

And after he hit the pavement, just dead.

When I went into the office on Tuesday morning, Luke-John and Derry were discussing whether or not to go to the funeral on the Wednesday.

"Croxley," Derry said. "Where's that?"

"Near Watford," I said. "On the Metropolitan line. A straight run in to Farringdon Street."

"What Fleet Street needs," said Derry gloomily, "is a tube station a lot nearer than blooming Farringdon. It's three-quarters of a mile if it's an inch."

"If you're right, Ty, we can manage it easily," Luke-John said authoritatively. "We should all go, I think."

Derry squinted at the small underground map in his diary. "Croxley. Next to Watford. What do you know?"

I'd had a girl in Watford once. The second one. I'd spent a lot of time on the Metropolitan line while Elizabeth was under the impression I was extra busy at the *Blaze*. Guilt and deceit were old familiar traveling companions. From Watford, from Virginia Water, from wherever.

"Ty," Luke-John was saying sharply.

"Huh?"

"The funeral is at two-thirty. An hour, say, to get there?"

"Not me," I said. "There's this *Tally* article to be done. It'll take me at least another two days in interviews."

He shrugged. "I'd have thought . . ."

"What depths have you plumbed so far?" Derry asked. He was sitting with his feet up on the desk. No work in a Sunday paper on Tuesday.

"The Roncey family," I said. "Tiddely Pom."

Derry sniffed. "Antepost favorite."

"Will he be your tip?" I asked with interest.

"Shouldn't think so. He's won a few races but he hasn't beaten much of any class."

"Bert tipped him strongly. Wrote a most emphatic piece about catching the odds now before they shorten. He wrote it last Thursday; it must have been straight after the handicap was published in the racing calendar, and it was in his paper on Friday. Roncey showed me the clipping. He said Bert was drunk when he rang up."

Luke-John sighed. Derry said decisively, "That does it, then. If Bert tipped him, I'm not going to."

"Why not?"

"Bert's heavy long-distance tips were nearly always nonstarters."

Luke-John stretched his neck until the tendons stood out like strings, and massaged his nobbly larynx. "Always the risk of that, of course. It happens to everyone."

"Do you mean that seriously?" I asked Derry.

"Oh, sure. Sorry about your *Tally* article and all that."
He grinned. "But I'd say just about the time it's
published you'll find Tiddely Pom has been taken out
of the Lamplighter."

Derry twiddled unconcernedly with a rubber band
and Luke-John shuffled absent-mindedly through some
papers. Neither of them felt the shiver traveling down
my spine.

"Derry," I said, "are you sure?"

"Of what?"

"That Bert always tipped nonstarters for big races."

Derry snapped the band twice in his fingers. "To be
precise, if you want me to be precise, Bert tipped a higher
percentage of big-race nonstarters than anyone else in
the street, and he has been at his best in this direction,
or worst—or, at any rate, his most consistent—during the
past year. He'd blow some horse up big, tell everyone
to back it at once, and then, wham, a day or two before
the race it would be scratched."

"I've never noticed," said Luke-John forbiddingly,
as if it couldn't have happened without.

Derry shrugged. "Well, it's a fact. Now, if you want to
know something equally useless about that puffed-up
Connersley of the *Sunday Hemisphere,* he has a weird
habit of always tipping horses which start with his own
initial, C. Delusions of grandeur, I imagine."

"You're having us on," Luke-John said.

Derry shook his head. "Uh-uh. I don't just sit here
with my eyes shut, you know; I read the newspapers."

"I think," I said suddenly, "I will fetch my
typewriter."

"Where is it?"

Over my shoulder on the way to the door I said,
"Being cleaned."

This time the typewriter was ready. I collected it and
went farther along the street, to Bert's paper. Up in the
lift, to Bert's department. Across the busy floor to the
sports desk. Full stop beside the assistant sports editor,
a constant racegoer, a long-known bar pal.

"Ty! What's the opposition doing here?"

"Bert Checkov," I said.

We discussed him for a while. The assistant sports editor was hiding something. It showed in half looks, unfinished gestures, an unsuccessfully smothered embarrassment. He said he was shocked, shattered, terribly distressed by Bert's death. He said everyone on the paper would miss him, the paper would miss him, they all felt his death was a great loss. He was lying.

I didn't pursue it. Could I, I asked tentatively, have a look at Bert's clippings book? I would very much like to reread some of his articles.

The assistant sports editor said kindly that I had little to learn from Bert Checkov, or anyone else for that matter, but to go ahead. While he got back to work, I sorted out the records racks at the side of the room and eventually found three brown paper clippings books with Bert's work stuck into the pages.

I took my typewriter out of its carrying case and left it lying on an inconspicuous shelf. The three clippings books went into the carrying case, though I had to squeeze to get it shut, and I walked quietly and unchallenged out of the building with my smuggled goods.

Luke-John and Derry goggled at the books of cuttings.

"How on earth did you get them out? And why on earth do you want them?"

"Derry," I said, "can now set about proving that Bert always tipped nonstarters in big races."

"You're crazy," Luke-John said incredulously.

"No," I said regretfully. "If I'm right, the *Blaze* is on the edge of the sort of scandal it thrives on. A circulation explosion. And all by courtesy of the sports section."

Luke-John's interest sharpened instantly from nil to needles.

"Don't waste time then, Derry. If Ty says there's a scandal, there's a scandal."

Derry gave me a sidelong look. "Our truffle hound on the scent, eh?" He took his feet off the desk and resignedly got to work checking what Bert had forecast against what had actually happened. More and more form books and racing calendars were brought out, and Derry's written lists slowly grew.

"All right," he said at last. "Here it is, just as I said. These books cover the last three years. Up till eighteen months ago he tipped runners and nonrunners in about the same proportion as the rest of us poor slobs. Then he went all out suddenly for horses which didn't run when it came to the point. All in big races, which had antepost betting." He looked puzzled. "It can't be just coincidence, I do see that. But I don't see the point."

"Ty?" said Luke-John.

I shrugged. "Someone has been working a fiddle."

"Bert wouldn't." His voice said it was unthinkable.

"I'd better take these books back before they miss them," I said, packing again into the typewriter case.

"Ty!" Luke-John sounded exasperated.

"I'll tell you when I come back," I said.

There was no denunciation at Bert's office. I returned the books to their shelf and retrieved my typewriter, and thanked the assistant sports editor for his kindness.

"You still here? I thought you'd gone." He waved a friendly hand. "Any time."

"All right," said Luke-John truculently when I got back to the *Blaze*. "I won't believe Bert Checkov was party to any fiddle."

"He sold his soul," I said plainly. "Like he told me not to."

"Rubbish."

"He sold his column. He wrote what he was told to write."

"Not Bert. He was a newspaperman, one of the old school."

I considered him. His thin face looked obstinate and pugnacious. Loyalty to an old friend was running very strong.

"Well, then," I said slowly, "Bert wrote what he was forced to write."

A good deal of the Morton tension subsided and changed course. He wouldn't help to uncover a scandal an old friend was responsible for, but he'd go the whole way to open up one he'd been the victim of.

"Clever beast," said Derry under his breath.

"Who forced him?" Luke-John said.

"I don't know. Not yet. It might be possible to find out."

"And *why?*"

"That's much easier. Someone has been making an antepost book on a certainty. What Bert was doing—being forced to do—was persuading the public to part with their money."

They both looked contemplative. I started again, explaining more fully. "Say a villain takes up bookmaking. It can happen, you know."

Derry grinned. "Say one villain hits on a jolly scheme for making illegal gains in a foolproof way with very little effort. He only works it on big races which have antepost betting, because he needs at least three weeks to rake in enough to make it worth the risk. He chooses a suitable horse, and he forces Bert to tip it for all his column's worth. Right? So the public put their money on, and our villain sticks to every penny that comes his way. No need to cover himself against losses. He knows there won't be any. He knows he isn't going to have to pay out on that horse. He knows it's going to be scratched at or after the four-day forfeits. Very nice fiddle."

After a short silence Derry said, "How does he know?"

"Ah, well," I said, shrugging, "that's another thing we'll have to find out."

"I don't believe it," Luke-John said skeptically. "All that just because Bert tipped a few nonstarters."

Derry looked dubiously at the lists he had made. "There were too many nonstarters. There really were."

"Yes," I said.

"But you *can't* have worked out all that just from what I said, from just that simple casual remark. . . ."

"No," I said. "There was something else, of course. It was something Bert himself said, last Friday, when

I walked back with him from lunch. He wanted to give me a piece of advice."

"That's right," Derry said. "He never came out with it."

"Yes, he did. He did indeed. With great seriousness. He told me not to sell my soul. Not to sell my column."

"No," Luke-John said.

"He said, 'First they buy you and then they blackmail you.'"

Luke-John said "No" again, automatically.

"He was very very drunk," I said. "Much worse than usual. He called the advice he was giving me his famous last words. He went up in the lift with a half bottle of whiskey, he walked right across his office, he drank from the bottle, and without a pause he fell straight out of the window."

Luke-John put his freckled fingers on his thin mouth, and when he spoke his voice was low, protesting, and thick: "No. . . . My *God.*"

After leaving the *Blaze* I collected the van and drove down to a racing stable in Berkshire to interview the girl who looked after the best-known horse in the Lamplighter.

Zig Zag was a household name, a steeplechaser of immense reputation and popularity, automatic headline material; but any day the cracks would begin to show, since he would be turning eleven on January 1st. The Lamplighter, to my mind, would be his last bow as grand old man before the younger brigade shouldered him out. Until Bert Checkov had rammed home the telling difference in weights, Zig Zag, even allotted a punitive twelve stone ten pounds, had been the automatic choice for antepost favorite.

His girl groom was earnest and devoted to him. In her twenties, unsophisticated, of middling intelligence, Sandy Willis's every sentence was packed with pithy stable language which she used unself-consciously and which contrasted touchingly with her essential innocence. She showed me Zig Zag with proprietary pride and could recite, and did, his every race from the day he was foaled. She had looked after him always, she said, ever since he came into the yard as a leggy untried three-year-old. She didn't know what she'd do when he was retired; racing wouldn't be the same without him somehow.

I offered to drive her into Newbury to have tea in a café or a hotel, but she said no, thank you, she wouldn't have time because the evening work started at four. Leaning against the door of Zig Zag's box, she told about her life, hesitantly at first, and then in a rush. Her parents didn't get on, she said. There were always rows at home, so she'd cleared out pretty soon after leaving school, glad to get away; her old man was so mean with the housekeeping and her mum did nothing but screech, nag, nag, at him mostly but at her, too, and her two kid sisters, right draggy the whole thing was, and she hoped Zig Zag would be racing at Kempton on Boxing Day so she'd have a good excuse not to go home for Christmas. She loved her work, she loved Zig Zag, the racing world was the tops, and no, she wasn't in any hurry to get married; there were always boys around if she wanted them and honestly whoever would swap Zig Zag for a load of draggy housework, especially if it turned out like her mum and dad. . . .

She agreed with a giggle to have her photograph taken if Zig Zag could be in the picture, too, and said she hoped that *Tally* magazine would send her a free copy.

"Of course," I assured her, and decided to charge all free copies against expenses.

When I left her, I walked down through the yard and called on the trainer, Norton Fox, whom I saw almost every time I went racing. A businesslike man in his fifties, with no airs and few illusions.

"Come in, Ty," he said. "Did you find Sandy Willis?"

"Thank you, yes. She was very helpful."

"She's one of my best lads." He waved me to an armchair and poured some oak-colored tea out of a silver pot. "Sugar?" I shook my head. "Not much in the up-

stairs department, but her horses are always jumping
out of their skins."

"A spot of transferred mother love," I said. I tasted
the tea. My tongue winced at the strength of the tannin.
Norton poured himself another cup and took three deep
swallows.

"If I write her up for *Tally*," I said, "you won't do
the dirty on me and take Zig Zag out of the Lamplighter
at the last minute?"

"I don't plan to."

"Twelve stone is a prohibitive weight," I suggested.

"He's won with twelve thirteen." He shrugged. "He'll
never come down the handicap."

"As a matter of interest," I said, "what happened
to Brevity just before the Champion Hurdle?"

Norton clicked his tongue in annoyance. "You can
rely on it, Zig Zag will *not* be taken out at the last minute. At least not for no reason, like Brevity."

"He was favorite, wasn't he?" I knew he was; I'd
checked carefully from Derry's list. "What exactly happened?"

"I've never been so furious about anything." The eight-
month-old grievance was still vivid in his voice. "I trained
that horse to the minute. To the minute. We always had
the Champion Hurdle as his main target. He couldn't
have been more fit. He was ready to run for his life.
And then what? Do you know what? I declared him at
the four-day stage, and the owner—the *owner,* mark you
—went and telephoned Weatherbys two days later and
canceled the declaration. Took the horse out of the race.
I ask you! And on top of that he hadn't even the
courtesy—or the nerve, probably—to tell me what he'd
done, and the first I knew of it was when Brevity wasn't
in the overnight list of runners. Of course I couldn't
believe it and rang up Weatherbys in a fury and they
told me old Dembley himself had struck his horse out.
And I still don't know why. I had the most God-almighty
row with him about it and all he would say was that he
had decided not to run, and that was that. He never once
gave me a reason. Not one, after all that planning and

all that work. I told him to take his horses away, I was so angry. I mean, how can you train for a man who's going to do that to you? It's impossible."

"Who trains for him now?" I asked sympathetically.

"No one. He sold all three of his horses, including Brevity. He said he'd had enough of racing; he was finished with it."

"You wouldn't still have his address?" I asked.

"Look here, Ty, you're not putting all that in your wretched paper!"

"No," I assured him. "Just one day I might write an article on owners who've sold out."

"Well . . . yes, I still have it." He copied the address from a ledger and handed it to me. "Don't cause any trouble."

"Not for you," I said. Trouble was always Luke-John's aim, and often mine. The only difference was that I was careful my friends shouldn't be on the receiving end. Luke-John had no such difficulties. He counted no one, to that extent, a friend.

Mrs. Woodward and Elizabeth were watching the news on television when I got back. Mrs. Woodward took a quick look at her watch and made an unsuccessful attempt at hiding her disappointment. I had beaten her to six o'clock by thirty seconds. She charged overtime by the half hour, and was a shade over-businesslike about it. I never got a free five minutes: five past six and it would have cost me the full half hour. I understood that it wasn't sheer miserliness. She was a widow whose teen-age son had a yearning to be a doctor, and as far as I could see it would be mainly Tyrone who put him through medical school.

The timekeeping war was conducted with maximum politeness and without acknowledgment that it existed. I simply synchronized our two clocks and my watch with the B.B.C. time signal every morning, and paid up with a smile when I was late. Mrs. Woodward gave me a warmer welcome at ten past six than at ten to, but never arrived a minute after nine-thirty in the mornings. Neither of us had let on to Elizabeth how acutely the clock was watched.

Mrs. Woodward was spare and strong, with a little of her native Lancashire in her voice and a lot in her character. She had dark hair going gray, rich brown eyes, and a determined jaw line which had seen her through a jilting fiancé and a work-shy husband. Unfailingly gentle to Elizabeth, she had never yet run out of patience, except with the vacuum cleaner, which occasionally regurgitated where it should have sucked.

In our flat she wore white nylon uniforms which she knew raised her status to nurse from home help in the eyes of visitors, and I saw no reason to think any worse of her for it. She took off the uniform and hung it up, and I helped her into the dark blue coat she had been wearing every single day for at least three years.

"Night, Mr. Tyrone. Night luv," she said, as she always said. And as always I thanked her for coming, and she said I'd see her in the morning.

"Did you have a good day?" Elizabeth asked when I kissed her forehead. Her voice sounded tired. The Spiroshell tugged her chest up and down in steady rhythm, and she could only speak easily on the outgoing breaths.

"I went to see a girl about a horse," I said, smiling, and told her briefly about Sandy Willis and Zig Zag. She liked to know a little of what I'd been doing, but her interest always flagged pretty soon, and after so many years I could tell the exact instant by the microscopic relaxation in her eye muscles. She rarely said she was tired and had had enough of anything, because she was afraid I would think her complaining and querulous and find her too much of a burden altogether. I couldn't persuade her to say flatly, "Stop, I'm tired." She agreed each time I mentioned it that she would, and she never did.

"I've seen three of the people for the *Tally* article," I said. "Owners, owner-trainer, and stable girl. I'm afraid after supper I'd better make a start on the writing. Will you be all right watching television?"

"Of course." She gave me a sweet brilliant smile which made every chore for her possible. Occasionally I spotted her manufacturing it artificially, but no amount of reassurance seemed able to convince her that she needn't perform tricks for me, that I wouldn't shove her back into hospital if she lost her temper, and that I didn't need her to be angelic, that she was safe with me, and loved, and, in fact, very much wanted.

"Like a drink?" I said.

"Love one."

I poured us both a J & B with Malvern water, and took hers over and fastened it into a holder I'd rigged up, with the bent drinking straw near to her mouth. Using that, she could drink in her own time, and a lot less got spilt on the sheets. I tasted appreciatively the pale fine Scotch, slumping into the big armchair beside her bed, sloughing off the day's traveling with a comfortable feeling of being at home. The pump's steady soft thumping had its usual soporific effect. It sent most of our visitors fast asleep.

We watched a brain-packed quiz game on television and companionably answered most of the questions wrong. After that I went into the kitchen and looked at what Mrs. Woodward had put out for supper. Plaice coated in bread crumbs, a bag of frozen chips, one lemon. Stewed apples, custard. Cheddar cheese, square crackers. The Woodward views on food didn't entirely coincide with my own. Stifling thoughts of underdone steak, I cooked the chips in oil and the plaice in butter, and left mine to keep hot while I helped Elizabeth. Even with the new pulley gadget, some foods were difficult; the plaice broke up too easily and her wrist got tired, and we ended up with me feeding her as usual.

While I washed the dishes, I made coffee in mugs, fixed Elizabeth's into the holder, and took mine with my typewriter into the little room which could have been a child's bedroom if we'd ever had a child.

The *Tally* article came along slowly, its price tag reproaching me for every sloppy phrase. The Huntersons, the Ronceys, Sandy Willis. Dissect without hurting, probe but leave whole. Far easier, I thought resignedly, to pick them to bits. Good for *Tally*'s sales, too. Bad for the conscience, lousy for the Huntersons, the Ronceys, Sandy Willis. To tell all so that the victim liked it. . . . This is what took the time.

After two hours I found myself staring at the wall, thinking only of Gail. With excruciating clearness I went through in my mind every minute of that uninhibited lovemaking, felt in all my limbs and veins an echo of passion. Useless to pretend that once was enough, that the tormenting hunger had been anesthetized for more than a few days. With despair at my weakness I thought about how it would be on the next Sunday. Gail with no clothes on, graceful and firm. Gail smiling with my hands on her breasts, Gail fluttering her fingers at the base of my spine.

The bell rang sharply above my head. One ring: not urgent. I stood up slowly, feeling stupid and ashamed. Daydreaming like Madge Roncey. Just as bad. Probably much worse.

Elizabeth was apologetic. "Ty, I'm so sorry to interrupt you. . . ."

How can I do it, I thought. And I knew I would.

"My feet are awfully cold."

I pulled out the hot-water bottle, which had no heat left. Her feet were warm enough to touch, but that meant nothing. Her circulation was so poor that her ankles and feet ached with cold if they were not constantly warmed from outside.

"You should have said," I protested.

"Didn't want to disturb you."

"Any time," I said fiercely. "Any time." And preferably twenty minutes ago. For twenty minutes she'd suffered her cold feet and all I'd done was think of Gail.

I filled her bottle and we went through her evening routine. Rubs with surgical spirit. Washing. Bedpan.

Her muscles had nearly all wasted to nothing so that her bones showed angularly through the skin, and one had to be careful when lifting her limbs, as pressure in some places hurt her. That day Mrs. Woodward had painted her toenails for her instead of only her fingernails as usual.

"Do you like it?" she said. "It's a new color, Tawny Pink."

"Pretty," I nodded. "It suits you."

She smiled contentedly. "Sue Davis brought it for me. She's a pet, that girl."

Sue and Ronald Davis lived three doors away: married for six months and it still showed. They had let their euphoria spill over onto us. Sue brought things in to amuse Elizabeth and Ronald used his Rugger-bred strength to carry the pump downstairs when we went out in the van.

"It matches my lipstick better than the old color."

"Yes, it does," I said.

When we married, she had had creamy skin and hair as glossy as new peeled chestnuts. She had had sun-browned agile limbs and a pretty figure. The transition to her present and forever state had been as agonizing for her mentally as it had been physically, and at one point of that shattering progress I was aware she would have killed herself if even that freedom hadn't been denied her.

She still had a good complexion, fine eyebrows, and long-lashed eyes, but the russet lights had turned to gray in both her irises and her hair, as if the color had drained away with the vitality. Mrs. Woodward was luckily expert with shampoo and scissors and I, too, had long grown accurate with a lipstick, so that Elizabeth always turned a groomed and attractive head to the world and could retain at least some terrifically important feminine assurance.

I settled her for the night, slowing the rate of the breathing pump a little and tucking the covers in firmly around her chin to help with the draft. She slept in the same half-sitting propped-up position as she spent the days; the Spiroshell was too heavy and uncomfortable if she lay down flat, besides not dragging as much air into her lungs.

She smiled when I kissed her cheek. "Good night, Ty."

"Good night, honey."

"Thanks for everything."

"Be my guest."

Lazily I pottered round the flat, tidying up, brushing my teeth, rereading what I'd written for *Tally,* and putting the cover on the typewriter. When I finally made it to bed, Elizabeth was asleep, and I lay between the lonely sheets and thought about Bert Checkov and the non-starters like Brevity in the Champion Hurdle, planning in detail the article I would write for the *Blaze* on Sunday.

Sunday.

Inevitably, inexorably, every thought led back to Gail.

FIVE

I telephoned to Charles Dembley, the ex-owner of Brevity, on Wednesday morning, and a girl answered, bright fresh voice, carefree and inexperienced.

"Golly, did you say Tyrone? *James* Tyrone? Yes, we do have your perfectly frightful paper. At least we used to. At least the gardener does, so I often read it. Well, of course come down and see Daddy, he'll be frightfully pleased."

Daddy wasn't.

He met me outside his house, on the front step, a smallish man nearing sixty with a gray mustache and heavy pouches under his eyes. His manner was courteous stone-wall.

"I am sorry you have had a wasted journey, Mr. Tyrone. My daughter Amanda is only fifteen and is apt to rush into things. . . . I was out when you telephoned, as I expect she told you. I hope you will forgive her.

I have absolutely nothing to say to you. Nothing at all. Good afternoon, Mr. Tyrone."

There was a tiny twitch in one eyelid and the finest of dews on his forehead. I let my gaze wander across the front of his house (genuine Georgian, not too large, unostentatiously well kept) and brought it gently back to his face.

"What threat did they use?" I asked. "Amanda?"

He winced strongly and opened his mouth.

"With a fifteen-year-old daughter," I commented, "one is dangerously vulnerable."

He tried to speak but achieved only a croak. After clearing his throat with difficulty he said, "I don't know what you're talking about."

"How did they set about it?" I asked. "By telephone? By letter? Or did you actually see them face to face?"

His expression was a full giveaway, but he wouldn't answer.

I said, "Mr. Dembley, I can write my column about the last-minute unexplained withdrawal of favorites, mentioning you and Amanda by name, or I can leave you out of it."

"Leave me out," he said forcefully. "Leave me out."

"I will," I agreed, "if in return you will tell me what threat was made against you, and in what form."

His mouth shook with a mixture of fear and disgust. He knew blackmail when he heard it. Only too well.

"I can't trust you."

"Indeed you can," I said.

"If I keep silent, you will print my name and they will think I told you anyway—" He stopped dead.

"Exactly," I said mildly.

"You're despicable."

"No," I said. "I'd simply like to stop them doing it to anyone else."

There was a pause. Then he said, "It *was* Amanda. They said someone would rape her. They said I couldn't guard her twenty-four hours a day for years on end. They said to make her safe all I had to do was call Weatherbys and take Brevity out of the Champion Hur-

dle. Just one little telephone call, against my daughter's—
my daughter's health. So I did. Of course I did. I had to.
What did running a horse in the Champion Hurdle matter compared with my daughter?"

What indeed.

"Did you tell the police?"

He shook his head. "They said . . ."

I nodded. They would.

"I sold all my horses, after," he said. "There wasn't
any point going on. It could have happened again,
anytime."

"Yes."

He swallowed. "Is that all?"

"No. . . . Did they telephone, or did you see them?"

"It was one man. He came here, driven by a chauffeur.
In a Rolls. He was, he seemed to me, an educated man.
He had an accent; I'm not sure what it was, perhaps
Scandinavian, or Dutch, something like that. Maybe even
Greek. He was civilized . . . except for what he said."

"Looks?"

"Tall. About your height. Much heavier, though.
Altogether thicker, more flesh. Not a crook's face at all.
I couldn't believe what I was hearing him say. It didn't
fit the way he looked."

"But he convinced you," I commented.

"Yes." He shuddered. "He stood there watching me
while I telephoned to Weatherbys. And when I'd finished
he simply said, 'I'm sure you've made a wise decision,
Mr. Dembley,' and he just walked out of the house and
the chauffeur drove him away."

"And you've heard no more from him at all?"

"No more. You will keep your bargain, too, like
him?"

My mouth twisted. "I will."

He gave me a long look. "If Amanda comes to any
harm through you, I will see it costs you—costs you—"
He stopped.

"If she does," I said, "I will pay."

An empty gesture. Harm couldn't be undone, and

paying wouldn't help. I would simply have to be careful.

"That's all," he said. "That's all." He turned on his heel, went back into his house, and shut the front door decisively between us.

For light relief on the way home, I stopped in Hampstead to interview the man who had done the handicap for the Lamplighter. Not a well-timed call. His wife had just decamped with an American colonel.

"Damn her eyes," he said. "She's left me a bloody note." He waved it under my nose. "Stuck up against the clock, just like some ruddy movie."

"I'm sorry," I said.

"Come in, come in. What do you say to getting pissed?"

"There's the unfortunate matter of driving home."

"Take a taxi, Ty, be a pal. Come on."

I looked at my watch. Four-thirty. Half an hour to home, counting rush-hour traffic. I stepped over the threshold and saw from his relieved expression that company was much needed. He already had a bottle out with a half-full glass beside it, and he poured me one the same size.

Major Colly Gibbons, late forties, trim, intelligent, impatient, and positive. Never suffered fools gladly and interrupted rudely when his thoughts leaped ahead, but was much in demand as a handicapper, as he had a clear comprehensive view of racing as a whole, like a master chess player winning ten games at once. He engineered more multiple dead heats than anyone else in the game; the accolade of his profession and a headache to the interpreters of photo finishes.

"A bloody colonel," he said bitterly. "Outranked, too."

I laughed. He gave me a startled look and then an unwilling grin.

"I suppose it *is* funny," he said. "Silly thing is, he's very like me. Looks, age, character, everything. I even like the guy."

"She'll probably come back," I said.

"Why?"

"If she chose a carbon copy of you, she can't hate you all that much."

"Don't know as I'd have her," he said aggressively. "Going off with a bloody colonel, and a Yank at that."

His pride was bent worse than his heart: nonetheless painful. He sloshed another stiff whiskey into his glass and asked me why, as a matter of interest, I had come. I explained about the *Tally* article, and, seeming to be relieved to have something to talk about besides his wife, he loosened up with his answers more than I would normally have expected. For the first time I understood the wideness of his vision and the grasp and range of his memory. He knew the form book for the past ten years by heart.

After a while I said, "Can you remember about antepost favorites which didn't run?"

He gave me a quick glance which would have been better focused three drinks earlier. "Is this for *Tally*, still?"

"No," I admitted.

"Didn't think so. Question like that's got the *Blaze* written all over it."

"I won't quote you."

"Too right you won't." He drank deeply, but seemed no nearer oblivion. "Put yourself some blinkers on and point in another direction."

"Read what I say on Sunday," I said mildly.

"Ty," he said explosively. "Best to keep out."

"Why?"

"Leave it to the authorities."

"What are they doing about it? What do they know?"

"You know I can't tell you," he protested. "Talk to the *Blaze?* I'd lose my job."

"Mulholland went to jail rather than reveal his sources."

"All journalists are not Mulholland."

"Same secretive tendencies."

"Would you," he said seriously, "go to jail?"

"It's never cropped up. But if my sources want to stay unrevealed, they stay unrevealed. If they didn't, who would tell me anything?"

He thought it over. "Something's going on," he said at last.

"Quite," I said. "And what are the authorities doing about it?"

"There's no evidence. . . . Look, Ty, there's nothing you can put your finger on. Just a string of coincidences."

"Like Bert Checkov's articles?" I suggested.

He was startled. "All right, then. Yes. I heard it on good authority that he was going to be asked to explain them. But then he fell out of the window. . . ."

"Tell me about the nonrunners," I said.

He looked gloomily at the note from his wife, which he still clutched in his hand. He took a deep swallow and shrugged heavily. The caution barriers were right down.

"There was this French horse, Polyxenes, which they made favorite for the Derby. Remember? All last winter and spring there was a stream of information about it, coming out of France—how well he was developing, how nothing could stay with him on the gallops, how he made all the three-year-olds look like knock-kneed yearlings? Every week, something about Polyxenes."

"I remember," I said. "Derry Clark wrote him up for the *Blaze.*"

Colly Gibbons nodded. "So there we are. By Easter, six-to-one favorite for the Derby. Right? They leave him in through all the forfeit stages. Right? They declare him at the four-day declarations. Right? Two days later he's taken out of the race. Why? He knocked himself out at exercise and his leg's blown up like a football. Can't run a lame horse. Too bad, everybody who'd backed him. Too bad. All their money down the drain. All right. Now I'll tell you something, Ty. That Polyxenes, I'll never believe he was all that good. What had he ever done? Won two moderate races as a two-year-old at Saint-Cloud. He didn't run this year before the Derby. He didn't run the whole season in the end. They said his leg was still bad. I'll tell you what I think. He never was good enough to win the Derby, and from the start they never meant him to run."

"If he were as bad as that, they could have run him anyway. He wouldn't have won."

"Would you risk it if you were them? The most fantastic outsiders *have* won the Derby. Much more certain not to run at all."

"Someone must have made thousands," I said slowly.

"More like hundreds of thousands."

"If they know it's going on, why don't the racing authorities do something about it?"

"What *can* they do? I told you, no evidence. Polyxenes *was* lame, and he stayed lame. He was seen by dozens of vets. He had a slightly shady owner, but no shadier than some of ours. Nothing, absolutely nothing, could be proved."

After a pause I said, "Do you know of any others?"

"God, Ty, you're a glutton. Well . . . yes. . . ."

Once started, he left little out. In the next half hour I listened to the detailed case histories of four more antepost favorites who hadn't turned up on the day. All could have been bona-fide hard-luck stories. But all, I knew well, had been over-praised by Bert Checkov.

He ran down, in the end, with a faint look of dismay.

"I shouldn't have told you all this."

"No one will know."

"You'd get information out of a deaf-mute."

I nodded. "They can usually read and write."

"Go to hell," he said. "Or, rather, don't. You're four behind me; you aren't trying." He waved the bottle in my general direction and I went over and took it from him. It was empty.

"Got to go home," I said apologetically.

"What's the hurry?" He stared at the letter in his hand. "Will your wife give you gip if you're late? Or will she be running off with some bloody Yankee colonel?"

"No," I said unemotionally. "She won't."

He was suddenly very sober. *"Christ,* Ty . . . I forgot."

He stood up, as steady as a rock. Looked forlornly around his comfortable wifeless sitting room. Held out his hand.

"She'll come back," I said uselessly.

He shook his head. "I don't think so." He sighed deeply. "Anyway, I'm glad you came. Needed someone to talk to, you know. Even if I've talked too much . . . better than getting drunk alone. And I'll think of you, this evening. You . . . and your wife."

I got hung up in a jam at Swiss Cottage and arrived home at eight minutes past seven. An hour and a half overtime. Mrs. Woodward was delighted.

"Isn't she sweet?" Elizabeth said when she had gone. "She never minds when you are late. She never complains about having to stay. She's so nice and kind."

"Very," I said.

As usual I spent most of Thursday at home, writing Sunday's article. Mrs. Woodward went out to do the week's shopping and to take and collect the laundry. Sue Davis came in and made coffee for herself and Elizabeth. Elizabeth's mother telephoned to say she might not come on Sunday; she thought she could be getting a cold.

No one came near Elizabeth with a cold. With people on artificial respiration, colds too often meant pneumonia, and pneumonia too often meant death.

If Elizabeth's mother didn't come on Sunday, I couldn't go to Virginia Water. I spent much of the morning unproductively trying to persuade myself it would be better if the cold developed, and knowing I'd be wretched if it did.

Luke-John galloped through the article on nonstarting favorites, screwed his eyes up tight, and leaned back in his chair with his face to the ceiling. Symptoms of extreme emotion. Derry reached over, twitched up the typewritten sheets, and read them in his slower, intense, shortsighted-looking way. When he'd finished, he took a deep breath.

"Wowee," he said. "Someone's going to love this."

"Who?" said Luke-John, opening his eyes.

"The chap who's doing it."

Luke-John looked at him broodingly. "As long as he can't sue, that's all that matters. Take this down to the lawyers and make sure they don't let it out of their sight."

Derry departed with a folded carbon copy of the article and Luke-John permitted himself a smile.

"Up to standard, if I may say so."

"Thanks," I said.

"Who told you all this?"

"Couple of little birds."

"Come off it, Ty."

"Promised," I said. "They could get their faces pushed in, one way or another."

"I'll have to know. The editor will want to know."

I shook my head. "Promised."

"I could scrub the article altogether. . . ."

"Tut, tut," I said. "Threats, now?"

He rubbed his larynx in exasperation. I looked around the vast busy floor space, each section, like the sports desk, collecting and sorting out its final copy. Most of the feature stuff went down to the compositors on Fridays, some even on Thursdays, to be set up in type. But anything like a scoop stayed under wraps upstairs until after the last editions of the Saturday evening papers had all been set up and gone to press. The compositors were apt to make the odd ten quid by selling a red-hot story to reporters on rival newspapers. If the legal department and the editor both cleared my article, the printshop wouldn't see it until too late to do them any good. The *Blaze* held its scandalous disclosures very close to its chest.

Derry came back from the lawyers without the article.

"They said they'd have to work on it. They'll ring through later."

The *Blaze* lawyers were of Counsel standard on the libel laws. They needed to be. All the same they were true *Blaze* men with "publish and be damned" engraved on their hearts. The *Blaze* accountants allowed for damages in their budget as a matter of course. The *Blaze*'s owner looked upon one or two court cases a year as splendid free advertising, and watched the sales graphs rise. There had, however, been four actions in the past six months and two more were pending. A mild memo had gone around, saying to cool it just a fraction. Loyal forever, Luke-John obeyed even where he disapproved.

"I'll take this to the editor," he remarked. "See what he says."

Derry watched his retreating back with reluctant admiration.

"Say what you like, the sports pages sell this paper to people who otherwise wouldn't touch it with gloves on. Our Luke-John, for all his stingy little ways, must be worth his weight in gumdrops."

Our Luke-John came back and went into a close huddle with a soccer correspondent. I asked Derry how the funeral had been, on the Wednesday.

"A funeral's a funeral." He shrugged. "It was cold. His wife wept a lot. She had a purple nose, blue from cold and red from crying."

"Charming."

He grinned. "Her sister told her to cheer up. Said how lucky it was Bert took out all that extra insurance."

"He did what?"

"Yeah. I thought you'd like that. I chased the sister up a bit. Two or three weeks ago Bert trebled his life insurance. Told his wife they'd be better off when he retired. Sort of self-help pension scheme."

"Well, well," I said.

"So it had to be an accident." Derry nodded. "In front of witnesses. The insurance company might not have paid up if he'd fallen out of the window with no one watching."

"I wonder if they'll contest it."

"Don't see how they can, when the inquest said misadventure."

The editor's secretary came back with my piece. The editor's secretary was an expensive package tied up with barbed wire. No one, reputedly, had got past the prickles to the goodies.

The editor had scrawled "O.K. on the lawyers' say-so" across the top of the page. Luke-John stretched out a hand for it, nodded in satisfaction, and slid it into the lockable top drawer of his desk, talking all the while to the soccer man. There was no need for me to stay longer. I told Derry I'd be at home most of the day if they wanted me and sketched a goodbye.

I was halfway to the door when Luke-John called after me.

"Ty . . . I forgot to tell you. A woman phoned, wanted you."

"Mrs. Woodward?"

"Uh-uh. Let's see, I made a note. . . . Oh, yes, here it is. A Miss Gail Pominga. Would you ring her back. Something about *Tally* magazine."

He gave me the slip of paper with the telephone number. I went across to the underpopulated news desk and picked up the receiver. My hands were steady. My pulse wasn't.

"The Western School of Art. Can I help you?"

"Miss Pominga."

Miss Pominga was fetched. Her voice came on the line, as cool and uninvolved as at the railway station.

"Are you coming on Sunday?" Crisp. Very much to the point.

"I want to." Understatement. "It may not be possible to get away."

"Well . . . I've been asked out to lunch."

"Go, then," I said, feeling disappointment lump in my chest like a boulder.

"Actually, if you are coming I will stay at home."

Damn Elizabeth's mother, I thought. Damn her and her cold.

"I want to come. I'll come if I possibly can," I said.

There was a short silence before she said, "When can you let me know for sure?"

"Not until Sunday, really. Not until I go out to catch the train."

"Hmm." She hesitated, then said decisively, "Ring me in any case, whether you can come or whether you can't. I'll fix it so that I can still go to lunch if you aren't coming."

"That's marvelous," I said with more feeling than caution.

She laughed. "Good. Hope to see you then. Anytime after ten. That's when Harry and Sarah go off to golf."

"It would be eleven-thirty or so."

She said "All right," and "Goodbye," and disconnected. I went home to write up Colly Gibbons for *Tally* and to have lunch with Elizabeth and Mrs. Woodward. It was fish again, unspecified variety and not much flavor. I listened to Elizabeth's sporadic conversation and returned her smiles and hoped fiercely not to be there with her forty-eight hours later. I ate automatically, sightlessly. By the end of that meal, treachery tasted of salt.

SIX

Time was running short, *Tally*-wise. With their deadline only two days ahead I went to Heathbury Park races on Saturday to meet Dermot Finnegan, an undistinguished jockey with an undistinguished mount in the Lamplighter.

For a while I couldn't understand a word he said, so impenetrable was his Irish accent. After he had sipped unenthusiastically at a cup of lunch-counter coffee for ten minutes, he relaxed enough to tell me he always spoke worse when he was nervous, and after that we got by with him having to repeat some things twice, but not four or five times, as at the beginning.

Once past the language barrier, Dermot unveiled a resigned wit and an accepting contented way of life. Although by most standards his riding success was small, Dermot thought it great. His income, less than a dustman's, seemed to him princely compared with the conditions of his childhood. His father had fed fourteen children on the potatoes he had grown on two and a half exhausted acres. Dermot, being neither the strong eldest nor the spoilt youngest, had usually had to shove for his share and hadn't always got it. At nineteen he tired of the diet and took his underdeveloped physique across the sea to Newmarket, where an Irish accent, irrespective of previous experience, guaranteed him an immediate job in the labor-hungry racing industry.

He had "done his two" for a while in a flat-racing stable, but couldn't get a ride in a flat race because he hadn't been apprenticed. Philosophically he moved down the road to a stable which trained jumpers as well, where the "Governor" gave him a chance in a couple of hurdle races. He still worked in the same stable on a part-time basis, and the Governor still put him up as his second-string jockey. How many rides? He grinned, showing spaces instead of teeth. Some seasons maybe thirty. Two years ago, of course, it was only four, thanks to breaking his leg off a brainless divil of a knock-kneed spalpeen.

Dermot Finnegan was twenty-five, looked thirty. Broken-nosed and weather-beaten, with bright sharp blue eyes. His ambition, he said, was to take a crack at Aintree. Otherwise he was all right with what he had: he wouldn't want to be a classy top jockey; it was far too much responsibility. "If you only ride the scrubbers round the gaffs at the back end of the season, see, no one expects much. Then they gets a glorious surprise if you come in."

He had ridden nineteen winners in all, and he could remember each of them in sharp detail. No, he didn't think he would do much good in the Lamplighter, not really, as he was only in it because his stable was running three. "I'll be on the pacemaker, sure. You'll see me right up there over the first, and maybe for a good while longer, but then my old boy will run out of steam and drop out of the back door as sudden as an interrupted burglar, and if I don't have to pull him up it'll be a bloody miracle."

Later in the afternoon I watched him start out on some prospective ten-year-old dogmeat in a novice chase. Horse and rider disappeared with a flurry of legs into the second open ditch, and when I went to check on his injuries some time after the second race, I met Dermot coming out of the ambulance room wearing a bandage and a grin.

"It's only a scratch," he assured me cheerfully. "I'll be there for the Lamplighter sure enough."

Further investigation led to the detail of a fingernail hanging on by a thread. "Some black divil" had leant an ill-placed hoof on the Finnegan hand.

To complete the *Tally* roundup, I spent the last half of the afternoon in the Clerk of the Course's office, watching him in action.

Heathbury Park, where the Lamplighter was to be held a fortnight later, had become under his direction one of the best-organized courses in the country. Like the handicapper, he was ex-forces, in this case R.A.F., which was unusual in that the racing authorities as a rule leant heavily toward the Army and the Navy for their executives.

Wing Commander Willy Ondroy was a quiet effective shortish man of forty-two who had been invalided out after fracturing his skull in a slight mishap with a Vulcan bomber. He still, he said, suffered from blackouts, usually at the most inconvenient, embarrassing, and even obscene moments.

It wasn't until after racing had finished for the day that he was really ready to talk, and even then he dealt with a string of people calling into his office with statistics, problems, and keys.

The Lamplighter was his own invention, and he was modestly proud of it. He'd argued the Betting Levy

Board into putting up most of the hefty stake money, and then drawn up entry conditions exciting enough to bring a gleam to the hardest-headed trainer's eye. Most of the best horses would consequently be coming. They should draw an excellent crowd. The gate receipts would rise again. They'd soon be able to afford to build a warm modern nursery room, their latest project, to attract young parents to the races by giving them somewhere to park their kids.

Willy Ondroy's enthusiasm was of the enduring, not the bubbling, kind. His voice was as gentle as the expression in his amber eyes, and only the small self-mockery in his smile gave any clue to the steel within. His obvious lack of need to assert his authority in any forceful way was finally explained after I'd dug, or tried to dig, into his history. A glossed-over throwaway phrase about a spot of formation flying turned out to be his version of three years as a Red Arrow, flying two feet away from the jet pipe of the aircraft in front. "We did two hundred displays one year," he said apologetically. "Entertaining at air shows. Like a concert party on Blackpool pier—no difference, really."

He had been lucky to transfer to bombers when he was twenty-six, he said. So many R.A.F. fighter and formation pilots were grounded altogether when their reaction times began to slow. He'd spent eight years on bombers, fifteen seconds knowing he was going to crash, three weeks in a coma, and twenty months finding himself a civilian job. Now he lived with his wife and twelve-year-old twins in a house on the edge of the racecourse, and none of them wanted to change.

I caught the last train when it was moving and made a start on Dermot and Willy Ondroy on the way back to London.

Mrs. Woodward departed contentedly at a quarter to seven, and I found she had for once left steaks ready in the kitchen. Elizabeth was in good spirits. I mixed us a drink each and relaxed in the armchair, and only after a strict ten minutes of self-denial asked her casually if her mother had telephoned.

"No, she hasn't." She wouldn't have.

"So you don't know if she's coming?"

"I expect she'll ring, if she doesn't."

"I suppose so," I said. Damn her eyes, couldn't she at least settle it, one way or another?

Trying to shut my mind to it, I worked on the *Tally* article; cooked the supper; went back to *Tally;* stopped to settle Elizabeth for the night; and returned to the typewriter until I'd finished. It was then half past two. A pity, I thought, stretching, that I wrote so slowly, crossed out so much. I put the final version away in a drawer with only the fair copy to be typed the next day. Plenty of time for that even if I spent the rest of it on the primrose path making tracks for Gail.

I despised myself. It was five before I slept.

Elizabeth's mother came. Not a sniffle in sight.

I had spent all morning trying to reconcile myself to her nonappearance at ten-fifteen, her usual time of arrival. As on past occasions, I had turned a calm and everyday face to Elizabeth and found I had consciously to stifle irritation at little tasks for her that normally I did without thought.

At ten-seventeen the doorbell rang, and there she was, a well-groomed good-looking woman in her mid-fifties with assisted tortoise-shell hair and a health-farm figure. When she showed surprise at my greeting, I knew I had been too welcoming. I damped it down a little to more normal levels and saw that she felt more at home with that.

I explained to her, as I already had to Elizabeth, that I still had people to interview for *Tally,* and by ten-thirty I was walking away down the mews feeling as though a safety valve were blowing fine. The sun was shining, too. After a sleepless night, my conscience slept.

Gail met me at Virginia Water, waiting outside the station wagon. "The train's late," she said calmly as I sat beside her. No warm, loving, kissing hello. Just as well, I supposed.

"They work on the lines on Sunday. There was a delay at Staines."

She nodded, let in the clutch, and cruised the three-quarters of a mile to her uncle's house. There she led the way into the sitting room and without asking poured two beers.

"You aren't writing today," she said, handing me the glass.

"No."

She gave me a smile that acknowledged the purpose of my visit. More businesslike about sex than most women. Certainly no tease. I kissed her mouth lightly, savoring the knowledge that the deadline of the Huntersons' return was three full hours ahead.

She nodded as if I'd spoken. "I approve of you," she said.

"Thanks."

She smiled, moving away. Her dress that day was of a pale cream color which looked wonderful against the gilded coffee skin. She was no darker, in fact, than many southern Europeans or heavily suntanned English; her mixed origin was distinct only in her face. A well-proportioned, attractive face, gathering distinction from the self-assurance within. Gail, I imagined, had had to come to terms with herself much earlier and more basically than most girls. She had done almost too good a job.

A copy of the *Sunday Blaze* lay on the low table, open at the sports page. Editors or subeditors write all the headlines, and Luke-John had come up with a beauty. Across the top of my page, big and bold, it said, "DON'T BACK TIDDELY POM—YET." Underneath, he'd left in word for word every paragraph I'd written. This didn't necessarily mean he thought each word was worth its space in print, but was quite likely because there weren't too many advertisements that week. Like all newspapers, the *Blaze* lived on advertising; if an advertiser wanted to pay for space, he got it, and out went the deathless prose of the columnists. I'd lost many a worked-on sentence to the late arrival of spiels on Whosit's cough syrup or Whammo's hair tonic. It was nice to see this intact.

I looked up at Gail. She was watching me.

"Do you always read the sports page?" I asked.

She shook her head. "Curiosity," she said. "I wanted to see what you'd written. That article—it's disturbing."

"It's meant to be."

"I mean, it leaves the impression that you know a great deal more than you've said, and it's all bad, if not positively criminal."

"Well," I said, "it's always nice to hear one has done exactly what one intended."

"What usually happens when you write in this way?"

"Repercussions? They vary from a blast from the racing authorities about minding my own business to abusive letters from nut cases."

"Do wrongs get righted?"

"Very occasionally."

"Sir Galahad," she mocked.

"No. We sell more papers. I apply for a raise."

She laughed with her head back, the line of her throat leading tautly down into her dress. I put out my hand and touched her shoulder, suddenly wanting no more talk.

She nodded at once, smiling, and said, "Not on the rug. More comfortable upstairs."

Her bedroom furnishings were pretty but clearly Sarah's work. Fitted cupboards, a cozy armchair, bookshelves, a lot of pale blue carpet, and a single bed.

At her insistence, I occupied it first. Then while I watched, like the time before, she took off her clothes. The simple, undramatized, unself-conscious undressing was more ruthlessly arousing than anything one could ever pay to see. When she had finished, she stood still for a moment near the window, a pale bronze naked girl in a shaft of winter sun.

"Shall I close the curtains?"

"Whichever you like."

She screwed my pulse rate up another notch by

stretching up to close them, and then in the midday dusk she came to bed.

At three she drove me back to the station, but a train pulled out as we pulled in. We sat in the car for a while, talking, waiting for the next one.

"Do you come home here every night?" I asked.

"Quite often not. Two of the other teachers share a flat, and I sleep on their sofa a night or two every week, after parties, or working late, or a theatre, maybe."

"But you don't want to live in London all the time?"

"D'you think it's odd that I stay with Harry and Sarah? Quite frankly, it's because of money. Harry won't let me pay for living here. He says he wants me to stay. He's always been generous. If I had to pay for everything myself in London, my present standard of living would go down with a reverberating thump."

"Comfort before independence," I commented mildly.

She shook her head. "I have both." After a considering pause she said, "Do you live with your wife? I mean, have you separated, or anything?"

"No, we've not separated."

"Where does she think you are today?"

"Interviewing someone for my *Tally* article."

She laughed. "You're a bit of a bastard."

Nail on the head. I agreed with her.

"Does she know you have—er—outside interests? Has she ever found you out?"

I wished she would change the subject. However, I owed her quite a lot, at least some answers, which might be the truth and nothing but the truth, but would certainly not be the whole truth.

"She doesn't know," I said.

"Would she mind?"

"Probably."

"But if she won't—sleep with you—well, why don't you leave her?"

I didn't answer at once. She went on, "You haven't

any children, have you?" I shook my head. "Then what's to stop you? Unless, of course, you're like me."

"How do you mean?"

"Staying where the living is good. Where the money is."

"Oh . . ." I half laughed, and she misunderstood me.

"How can I blame you"—she sighed—"when I do it myself? So your wife is rich. . . ."

I thought about what Elizabeth would have been condemned to without me: to hospital ward routine, hospital food, no privacy, no gadgets, no telephone, lights out at nine and lights on at six, no free will at all, forever and ever.

"I suppose you might say," I agreed slowly, "that my wife is rich."

Back in the flat I felt split in two, with everything familiar feeling suddenly unreal. Half my mind was still down in Surrey. I kissed Elizabeth and thought of Gail. Depression had clamped down in the train like drizzle and wouldn't be shaken off.

"Some man wants to talk to you," Elizabeth said. "He telephoned three times. He sounded awfully angry."

"Who?"

"I couldn't understand much of what he said. He was stuttering."

"How did he get our number?" I was irritated, bored; I didn't want to have to deal with angry men on the telephone. Moreover our number was ex-directory, precisely so that Elizabeth should not be bothered by this sort of thing.

"I don't know. But he did leave his number for you to ring back; it was the only coherent thing he said."

Elizabeth's mother handed me a note pad on which she had written down the number.

"Victor Roncey," I said.

"That's right," agreed Elizabeth with relief. "That sounds like it."

I sighed, wishing that all problems, especially those

of my own making, would go away and leave me in peace.

"Maybe I'll call him later," I said. "Right now I need a drink."

"I was just going to make some tea," said Elizabeth's mother reprovingly, and in silent fury I doubled the quantity I would normally have taken. The bottle was nearly empty. Gloomy Sunday.

Restlessly I took myself off into my writing room and started the clean unscribbled-on retype for *Tally,* the mechanical task eventually smoothing out the rocky tensions of my guilt-ridden return home. I couldn't afford to like Gail too much, and I did like her. To come to love someone would be too much hell altogether. Better not to visit Gail again. I decided definitely not to. My body shuddered in protest, and I knew I would.

Roncey rang again just after Elizabeth's mother had left.

"What the devil do you mean about this—this trash in the paper? Of course my horse is going to run. How dare you—how dare you suggest there's anything shady going on?"

Elizabeth had been right; he was stuttering still, at seven in the evening. He took a lot of calming down to the point of admitting that nowhere in the article was it suggested that he personally had anything but good honest upright intentions.

"The only thing is, Mr. Roncey, as I said in the article, that some owners have in the past been pressured into not running their horses. This may even happen to you. All I was doing was giving punters several good reasons why they would be wiser to wait until half an hour before big races to put their money on. Better a short starting price than losing their money in a swindle."

"I've read it," he snapped. "Several times. And no one, believe me, is going to put any pressure on *me.*"

"I very much hope not," I said. I wondered whether his antipathy to his elder sons extended to the smaller ones; whether he would risk their safety or happiness for the sake of running Tiddely Pom in the Lamplighter.

Maybe he would. The stubborn streak ran through his character like iron in granite.

When he had calmed down to somewhere near reason, I asked him if he'd mind telling me how he'd got my telephone number.

"I had the devil's own job, if you want to know. All that ex-directory piffle. The inquiries people refused point-blank to tell me, even though I said it was urgent. Stupid, I call it, but I wasn't to be put off by that. If you want to know, your colleague on the paper told me. Derrick Clark."

"I see," I said resignedly, thinking it unlike Derry to part so easily with my defenses. "Well, thank you. Did the *Tally* photographer find you all right?"

"He came on Friday. I hope you haven't said anything in *Tally* about—" His anger was on its way up again.

"No," I said decisively. "Nothing like that at all."

"When can I be sure?" He sounded suspicious.

"That edition of *Tally* is published on the Tuesday before the Lamplighter."

"I'll ask for an advance copy from the editor. Tomorrow. I'll demand to see what you've written."

"Do that," I agreed. Divert the buck to Arnold Shankerton. Splendid.

He rang off still not wholly pacified. I dialed Derry's number and prepared to pass the ill temper along to him.

"Roncey?" He said indignantly. "Of course I didn't give your number to Roncey." His baby girl was exercising her lungs loudly in the background. "What did you say?"

"I said, who *did* you give it to?"

"Your wife's uncle."

"My wife hasn't got any uncles."

"Oh Christ. Well, he said he was your wife's uncle, and that your wife's aunt had had a stroke, and that he wanted to tell you but he'd lost your number."

"Lying crafty bastard," I said with feeling. "And he accused me of misrepresenting facts."

"I'm sorry, Ty."

"Never mind. Only check with me first, next time, huh? Like we arranged."

"Yeah. Sure. Sorry."

"How did he get hold of your number, anyway?"

"It's in the *Directory of the British Turf,* unlike yours. My mistake."

I put the receiver back in its special cradle near to Elizabeth's head and transferred to the armchair, and we spent the rest of the evening as we usually did, watching the shadows on the goggle box. Elizabeth never tired of it, which was a blessing, though she complained often about the shutdowns in the daytime between all the child-oriented programs. Why couldn't they fill them, she said with interesting things for captive adults?

Later I made some coffee and did the alcohol rubs and other jobs for Elizabeth, all with a surface of tranquil domesticity, going through my part with my thoughts somewhere else, like an actor at the thousandth performance.

On the Monday morning I took my article to the *Tally* offices and left the package at the reception desk, virtuously on the deadline.

After that I caught the race train to Leicester, admitting to myself that although it was technically my day off I did not want to stay in the flat. Also the Hunterson's raffle horse Egocentric was to have its pre-Lamplighter warm-up, which gave me an excellent overt reason for the journey.

Raw near-mist was doing its best to cancel the proceedings and only the last two fences were visible. Egocentric finished fourth without enough steam left to blow a whistle, and the jockey told the trainer that the useless bugger had made a right bloody shambles of three fences on the far side and couldn't jump for peanuts. The trainer didn't believe him and engaged a different jockey for the Lamplighter. It was one of those days.

The thin Midland crowd of cloth caps and mufflers strewed the ground with betting slips and newspapers and ate a couple of hundredweight of jellied eels out of little paper cups. I adjourned to the bar with a colleague from the *Sporting Life,* and four people commented on my nonstarters with varying degrees of belief. Not much of a day. One, on the whole, to forget.

The journey home changed all that. When I forget it, I'll be dead.

SEVEN

Thanks to having left before the last race, I had a chance in the still empty and waiting train for a forward-facing window seat in a nonsmoker. I turned the heating to "hottest," and opened the newspaper to see what "Spyglass" had come up with in the late editions.

"Tiddely Pom will run, trainer says. But is your money really safe?"

Amused, I read to the end. He'd cribbed most of my points and rehashed them. Complimentary. Plagiarism is the sincerest form of flattery.

The closed door to the corridor slid open and four bookmakers' clerks lumbered in, stamping their feet with cold and discussing some luckless punter who had lost an argument over a betting slip.

"I told him to come right off it, who did he think he was kidding? We may not be archangels, but we're not the ruddy mugs he takes us for."

They all wore navy-blue overcoats, which after a while they shed onto the luggage racks. Two of them shared a large packet of stodgy-looking sandwiches and the other two smoked. They were all in the intermediate thirty-forties, with London Jewish accents in which they next discussed their taxi drive to the station in strictly non-Sabbath-day terms.

"Evening," they said to me, acknowledging I existed,

and one of them gestured with his cigarette to the nonsmoking notice on the window and said, "O.K. with you, chum?"

I nodded, hardly taking them in. The train rocked off southward, the misty day turned to foggy night, and five pairs of eyelids fell gently shut.

The door to the corridor opened with a crash. Reluctantly I opened one eye a fraction, expecting the ticket collector. Two men filled the opening, looking far from bureaucratic. Their effect on my four fellow travelers was a spine-straightening mouth-opening state of shock. The larger of the newcomers stretched out a hand and pulled the blinds down on the inside of the corridor-facing windows. Then he gave the four clerks a contemptuous comprehensive glance, jerked his head toward the corridor, and said with simplicity, "Out."

I still didn't connect any of this as being my business, not even when the four men meekly took down their navy-blue overcoats and filed out into the train. Only when the large man pulled out a copy of the *Blaze* and pointed to an article did I have the faintest prickle on the spine.

"This is unpopular in certain quarters," remarked the larger man. Thick sarcastic Birmingham accent. He pursed his lips, admiring his own heavy irony. "Unpopular."

He wore grubby overalls from shoes to throat, with above that a thick neck, puffy cheeks, a small wet mouth, and slicked-down hair. His companion, also in overalls, was hard and stocky with wide eyes and a flat-topped head.

"You shouldn't do it, you shouldn't really," the large man said. "Interfering and that."

He put his right hand into his pocket and it reappeared with a brass ridge across the knuckles. I glanced at the other man. Same thing.

I came up with a rush, grabbing for the communication cord. Penalty for improper use, twenty-five pounds. The large man moved his arm in a professional short jab and made havoc of my intention.

They had both learned their trade in the ring; that much was clear. Not much else was. They mostly left my head alone, but they knew where and how to hit to hurt on the body, and if I tried to fight off one of them, the other had a go. The most I achieved was a solid kick on the smaller man's ankle, which drew from him four letters and a frightening kidney punch. I collapsed onto the seat. They leant over me and broke the Queensberry rules.

It crossed my mind that they were going to kill me, that maybe they weren't meaning to, but they were killing me. I even tried to tell them so, but if any sound came out they took no notice. The larger one hauled me bodily to my feet and the small one broke my ribs.

When they let go, I crumpled slowly onto the floor and lay with my face against cigarette butts and the screwed-up wrappings of sandwiches. Stayed quite motionless, praying to a God I had no faith in not to let them start again.

The larger one stooped over me.

"Will he cough it?" the smaller one said.

"How can he? We ain't ruptured nothing, have we? Careful, aren't I? Look out the door, time we was off."

The door slid open and presently shut, but not for a long time was I reassured that they had completely gone. I lay on the floor breathing in coughs and jerky shallow breaths, feeling sick. For some short time it seemed in a weird transferred way that I had earned such a beating not for writing a newspaper article but because of Gail; and to have deserved it, to have sinned and deserved it, turned it into some sort of expurgation. Pain flowed through me in a hot red tide, and only my guilt made it bearable.

Sense returned, as sense does. I set about the slow task of picking myself up and assessing the damage. Maybe they had ruptured nothing; I had only the big man's word for it. At the receiving end it felt as though they had ruptured pretty well everything, including self-respect.

I made it up to the seat, and sat vaguely watching the lights flash past, fuzzy and yellow from fog. Eyes half shut, throat closing with nausea, hands nerveless and weak. No one focus of pain, just too much. Wait, I thought, and it will pass.

I waited a long time.

The lights outside thickened and the train slowed down. London. All change. I would have to move from where I sat. Dismal prospect. Moving would hurt.

The train crept into King's Cross and stopped with a jerk. I stayed where I was, trying to make the effort to stand up and not succeeding, telling myself that if I didn't get up and go I could be shunted into a siding for a cold uncomfortable night, and still not raking up the necessary propulsion.

Again the door slid open with a crash. I glanced up, stifling the beginnings of panic. No heavy man with overalls and knuckle-duster. The guard.

Only when I felt the relief wash through me did I realize the extent of my fear, and I was furious with myself for being so craven.

"The end of the line," the guard was saying.

"Yeah," I said.

He came into the compartment and peered at me. "Been celebrating, have you, sir?" He thought I was drunk.

"Sure," I agreed. "Celebrating."

I made the long-delayed effort and stood up. I'd been quite right about it. It hurt.

"Look, mate, do us a favor and don't throw up in here," said the guard urgently.

I shook my head. Reached the door. Rocked into the corridor. The guard anxiously took my arm and helped me down onto the platform, and as I walked carefully away I heard him behind me say to a bunch of porters, half laughing, "Did you see that one? Greeny gray and sweating like a pig. Must have been knocking it back solid all afternoon."

I went home by taxi and took my time up the stairs to the flat. Mrs. Woodward for once was in a hurry for me to come, as she was wanting to get home in case the fog thickened. I apologized. "Quite all right, Mr. Tyrone.

You know I'm usually glad to stay. . . ." The door closed behind her and I fought down a strong inclination to lie on my bed and to groan.

Elizabeth said, "Ty, you look terribly pale," when I kissed her. Impossible to hide it from her completely.

"I fell," I said. "Tripped. Knocked the breath out of myself, for a minute or two."

She was instantly concerned, with the special extra anxiety for herself apparent in her eyes.

"Don't worry," I comforted her. "No harm done."

I went into the kitchen and held on to the table. After a minute or two I remembered Elizabeth's pain-killing tablets and took the bottle out of the cupboard. Only two left. There would be. I swallowed one of them, tying a mental knot to remind me to ring the doctor for another prescription. One wasn't quite enough, but better than nothing. I went back into the big room and, with a fair try at normality, poured out evening drinks.

By the time I had done the supper and the jobs for Elizabeth and got myself undressed and into bed, the main damage had resolved itself into two or possibly three cracked ribs low down on my left side. The rest slowly subsided into a blanketing ache. Nothing had ruptured, like the man said.

I lay in the dark breathing shallowly and trying not to cough, and at last took time off from simply existing to consider the who and why of such a drastic roughing up, along with the pros and cons of telling Luke-John. He'd make copy of it, put it on the front page, plug it for more than it was worth, write the headlines himself. My feelings would naturally be utterly disregarded as being of no importance compared with selling papers. Luke-John had no pity. If I didn't tell him and he found out later, there would be frost and fury and a permanent atmosphere of distrust. I couldn't afford that. My predecessor had been squeezed off the paper entirely as a direct result of having concealed from Luke-John a red-hot scandal in which he was involved. A rival paper got hold of it and scooped the *Blaze*. Luke-John never forgave, never forgot.

I sighed deeply. A grave mistake. The cracked ribs stabbed back with unnecessary vigor. I spent what could not be called a restful, comfortable, sleep-filled night, and in the morning could hardly move. Elizabeth watched me get up and the raw anxiety twisted her face.

"Ty!"

"Only a bruise or two, honey, I told you, I fell over."

"You look . . . hurt."

I shook my head. "I'll get the coffee."

I got the coffee. I also looked with longing at Elizabeth's last pill, which I had no right to take. She still suffered sometimes from terrible cramp, and on these occasions had to have the pills in a hurry. I didn't need any mental knots to remind me to get some more. When Mrs. Woodward came, I went.

Dr. Antonio Perelli wrote the prescription without hesitation and handed it across.

"How is she?"

"Fine. Same as usual."

"It's time I went to see her."

"She'd love it," I said truthfully. Perelli's visits acted on her like champagne. I'd met him casually at a party three years earlier, a young Italian doctor in private practice in Welbeck Street. Too handsome, I'd thought at once. Too feminine, with those dark, sparkling eyes. All bedside manner and huge fees, with droves of neurotic women patients paying to have their hands held.

Then, just before the party broke up, someone told me he specialized in chest complaints and not to be put off by his youth and beauty, he was brilliant; and by coincidence we found ourselves outside on the pavement together, hailing the same taxi, and going the same way.

At the time I had been worried about Elizabeth. She had to return to hospital for intensive nursing every time she was ill, and with the virtual stamping out of polio the hospitals geared to care for patients on artificial respiration were becoming fewer and fewer. We had just been told she could not expect to go back any more to the hospital that had always looked after her.

I shared the taxi with Perelli and asked him if he knew of anywhere I could send her quickly if she ever needed it. Instead of answering directly he invited me into his tiny bachelor flat for another drink, and before I left he had acquired another patient. Elizabeth's general health had improved instantly under his care and I paid his moderate fees without a wince.

I thanked him for the prescription and put it in my pocket.

"Ty . . . are the pills for Elizabeth or for you?"

I looked at him, startled. "Why?"

"My dear fellow, I have eyes. What I see in your face is . . . severe."

I smiled wryly. "All right. I was going to ask you. Could you put a bit of strapping on a couple of ribs?"

He stuck me up firmly and handed me a small medicine glass containing, he said, Disprins dissolved in nepenthe, which worked like a vanishing trick: now you feel it, now you don't.

"You haven't told Elizabeth?" he said anxiously.

"Only that I fell and winded myself."

He relaxed, moving his head in a gesture of approval. "Good."

It had been his idea to shield her from worries which ordinary women could cope with in their stride. I had thought him unduly fussy at first, but the strict screening he had urged had worked wonders. She had become far less nervous, much happier, and even put on some badly needed weight.

"And the police? Have you told the police?"

I shook my head and explained about Luke-John.

"Difficult. Um. Suppose you tell this Luke-John simply that those men threatened you. You'll not be taking your shirt off in the office." He smiled in the way that made Elizabeth's eyes shine. "These two men, they will not go about saying they inflicted so much damage."

"They might," I frowned, considering. "It could be a good idea if I turned up in perfect health at the races today and gave them the lie."

With an assenting gesture he mixed me a small bottleful

of Disprin and nepenthe. "Don't eat much," he said, handing it over. "And only drink coffee."

"O.K."

"And do nothing that would get you another beating like this."

I was silent.

He looked at me with sad understanding. "That is too much to give up for Elizabeth?"

"I can't just . . . crawl away," I protested. "Even for Elizabeth."

He shook his head. "It would be best for her. But . . ." He shrugged, and held out his hand in good-bye. "Stay out of trains, then."

I stayed out of trains. For ninety-four minutes. Then I caught the race train to Plumpton and traveled down safely with two harmless strangers and a man I knew slightly from the B.B.C.

Thanks to Tonio's mixture, I walked about all day and talked and laughed much the same as usual. Once I coughed. Even that caused only an echo of a stab. For maximum effect, I spent a good deal of my time walking about the bookmakers' stalls, inspecting both their prices and their clerks. The fraternity knew something had happened. Their heads swiveled as I passed and they were talking behind my back, nudging each other. When I put ten shillings on a semi-outsider with one of them, he said, "You feeling all right, chum?"

"Why not?" I said in surprise. "It's a nice enough day."

He looked perplexed for a second, and then shrugged. I walked on, looking at faces, searching for a familiar one. The trouble was I paid the four clerks in the compartment so little attention that I wasn't sure I'd recognize any of them again, and I wouldn't have done if he hadn't given himself away. When he saw me looking at him, he jerked, stepped down off his stand, and bolted.

Running was outside my repertoire. I walked quietly

up behind him an hour later when he had judged it safe
to go back to his job.

"A word in your ear," I said at his elbow.

He jumped six inches. "It was nothing to do with
me."

"I know that. Just tell me who the two men were.
Those two in overalls."

"Do me a favor. Do I want to end up in hospital?"

"Twenty quid?" I suggested.

"I dunno about that. . . . How come you're here
today?"

"Why not?"

"When those two've seen to someone, they stay seen
to."

"Is that so? They seemed pretty harmless."

"No, straight up," he said curiously, "didn't they touch
you?"

"No."

He was puzzled.

"A pony. Twenty-five quid," I said. "For their names,
or who they work for."

He hesitated. "Not here, mate. On the train."

"Not on the train." I was positive. "In the press box.
And now."

He got five minutes off from his grumbling employer
and went in front of me up the stairs to the aerie allotted
to newspapers. I gave a shove-off sign to the only press
man up there, and he obligingly disappeared.

"Right," I said. "Who were they?"

"They're Brummies," he said cautiously.

"I know that. You could cut their accents."

"Bruisers" he ventured.

I stopped myself just in time from telling him I knew
that, too.

"They're Charlie Boston's boys" It came out in a
nervous rush.

"That's better. Who's Charlie Boston?"

"So who hasn't heard of Charlie Boston? Got some
betting shops, hasn't he, in Birmingham and Wolver-
hampton and such like."

"And some boys on race trains?"

He looked more puzzled than ever. "Don't you owe Charlie no money? So what did they want, then? It's usually bad debts they're after."

"I've never heard of Charlie Boston before, let alone had a bet with him." I took out my wallet and gave him five fivers. He took them with a practiced flick and stowed them away in a pocket like Fort Knox under his left armpit. "Dirty thieves," he explained. "Taking precautions, aren't I?"

He scuttled off down the stairs, and I stayed up in the press box and took another swig at my useful little bottle, reflecting that when Charlie Boston unleashed his boys on me he had been very foolish indeed.

Luke-John reacted predictably with a bridling "They can't do that to the *Blaze*" attitude.

Wednesday morning. Not much doing in the office. Derry with his feet up on the blotter, Luke-John elbow deep in the dailies' sports pages, the telephone silent, and every desk in the place exhibiting the same feverish inactivity.

Into this calm I dropped the pebble of news that two men, adopting a threatening attitude, had told me not to interfere in the nonstarters racket. Luke-John sat up erect like a belligerent bullfrog, quivering with satisfaction that the article had produced tangible results. With a claw hand he pounced on the telephone.

"Manchester office? Give me the sports desk. . . . That you, Andy? Luke Morton. What can you tell me about a bookmaker named Charlie Boston? Has a string of betting shops around Birmingham."

He listened to a lengthy reply with growing intensity.

"That adds up. Yes. Yes. Fine. Ask around and let me know."

He put down the receiver and rubbed his larynx. "Charlie Boston changed his spots about a year ago. Before that he was apparently an ordinary Birmingham bookmaker with about six shops and a reasonable reputation. Now, Andy says, he's expanded a lot and

become a bully. He says he's been hearing too much
about Charlie Boston lately. Seems he hires two ex-
boxers to collect unpaid debts from his credit customers,
and as a result of all this he's coining it."

I thought it over. Charlie Boston of Birmingham with
his betting shops and bruisers didn't jell at all with the
description Dembley had given me of a quiet gentleman
in a Rolls with a chauffeur and a Greek, Dutch, or Scandinavian accent. They even seemed an unlikely pair as
shoulder-to-shoulder partners. There might of course be
two separate rackets going on, and if so, what happened
if they clashed? And by which of them had Bert Checkov
been seduced? But if they were all one outfit, I'd settle
for the Rolls gent as the brains and Charlie Boston the
muscles. Setting his dogs on me had been classic muscle-
bound thinking.

Luke-John's telephone rang and he reached out a hand.
As he listened, his eyes narrowed and he turned his head
to look straight at me.

"What do you mean he was pulped? He certainly
was not. He's here in the office at this moment and he
went to Plumpton races yesterday. What your paper needs
is a little less imagination. . . . If you don't believe me,
talk to him yourself." He handed me the receiver, saying
with a grimace, "Connersley. Bloody man."

"I heard," said the precise malicious voice on the
phone, "that some Birmingham heavies took you to
pieces on the Leicester race train."

"A rumor," I said with boredom. "I heard it myself
at Plumpton."

"According to my informant, you couldn't have gone
to Plumpton."

"Your informant is unreliable. Scrap him."

A small pause. Then he said, "I can check if you were
there."

"Check away." I put the receiver down with a brusque
crash and thanked my stars I had reached Luke-John
with my version first.

"Are you planning a follow-up on Sunday?" he was
asking. Connersley had planted no suspicions: was

already forgotten. "Hammer the point home. Urge the racing authorities to act. Agitate. You know the drill."

I nodded. I knew the drill. My bruises gave me a protesting nudge. No more, they said urgently. Write a nice mild piece on an entirely different, totally innocuous subject.

"Get some quotes," Luke-John said.

"O.K."

"Give with some ideas," he said impatiently. "I'm doing all your ruddy work."

I sighed. Shallowly and carefully. "How about us making sure Tiddely Pom starts in the Lamplighter? Maybe I'll go fix it with the Ronceys. . . ."

Luke-John interrupted, his eyes sharp. "The *Blaze* will see to it that Tiddely Pom runs. Ty, that's genius. Start your piece with that. The *Blaze* will see to it. . . . Splendid. Splendid."

Oh God, I thought. I'm the world's greatest bloody fool. Stay out of race trains, Tonio Perelli had said. Nothing about lying down on the tracks.

EIGHT

Nothing much had changed at the Ronceys'. Dead leaves, cobwebs still in place. No dripping meat on the kitchen table; two unplucked pheasants sagged with limp necks there instead. The sink overflowed with unwashed dishes and the Wellington smell had intensified.

I arrived unannounced at two-thirty and found Roncey himself out in the yard watching Pat and the old man saw up a large hunk of dead tree. He received me with an unenthusiastic glare but eventually took me through into the sitting room with a parting backward instruction to his son to clean out the tack room when he'd finished the logs.

Madge was lying on the sofa, asleep. Still no stockings, still the blue slippers, still the yellow dress, very dirty now down the front. Roncey gave her a glance of complete indifference and gestured me to one of the armchairs.

"I don't need help from the *Blaze*," he said, as he'd said outside the yard. "Why should I?"

"It depends on how much you want Tiddely Pom to run in the Lamplighter."

"Of course he's going to run." Roncey looked aggressive and determined. "I told you. Anyone who tries to tell me otherwise has another think coming."

"In that case," I said mildly, "one of two things will happen. Either the man operating the racket will abandon the idea of preventing Tiddely Pom from running, as a result of all the publicity they've been getting. Or they will go ahead and stop him. If they've any sense, they'll abandon the idea. But I don't see how one can count on them having any sense."

"They won't stop him." Pugnacious jaw, stubborn eyes.

"You can be sure they will, one way or another, if they want to."

"I don't believe you."

"But would you object to taking precautions, just in case? The *Blaze* will foot the bills."

He stared at me long and hard. "This is not just a publicity stunt to cover your sensation-hunting paper with glory?"

"Dual purpose," I said. "Half for you and the betting public. Half for us. But only one object: to get Tiddely Pom safely off in the Lamplighter."

He thought it over.

"What sort of precautions?" he said at last.

I sighed inwardly with mixed feelings, a broken-ribbed skier at the top of a steep and bumpy slope, with only myself to thank.

"There are three main ones," I said. "The simplest is a letter to Weatherbys, stating your positive intention to run in the Lamplighter, and asking them to check carefully with you if they should receive any instructions to strike out the horse either before or after the four-day declaration stage next Tuesday. You do realize, don't you, that I or anyone else could send a telegram or telex striking out the horse, and nothing you could do would get him put back again?"

His mouth dropped open. *"Anyone?"*

"Anyone signing your name. Of course. Weatherbys receive hundreds of cancellations a week. They don't check to make sure the trainer really means it. Why should they?"

"Good God," he said, stunned. "I'll write at once. In fact I'll ring them up." He began to stand up.

"There won't be that much urgency," I said. "Much more likely a cancellation would be sent in at the last moment, in order to allow as much time as possible for antepost bets to be made."

"Oh . . . quite." A thought struck him as he sat down again. "If the *Blaze* declares it is going to make Tiddely Pom safe and then he *doesn't* run for some reason, you are going to look very silly."

I nodded. "A risk. Still . . . We'll do our best. But we do need your wholehearted cooperation, not just your qualified permission."

He had made up his mind. "You have it. What next?"

"Tiddely Pom will have to go to another stable."

That rocked him. "Oh, no."

"He's much too vulnerable here."

He swallowed. "Where, then?"

"To one of the top trainers. He will still be expertly prepared for the race. He can have the diet he's used to. We'll give you a report on him every day."

He opened and shut his mouth several times, speechless.

"Thirdly," I said, "your wife and at least your three youngest sons must go away for a holiday."

"They can't," he protested automatically.

"They must. If one of the children were kidnapped, would you set his life against running Tiddely Pom?"

"It isn't possible," he said weakly.

"Just the threat might be enough."

Madge got up and opened her eyes. They were far from dreamy. "Where and when do we go?" she said.

"Tomorrow. You will know where after you get there."

She smiled with vivid delight. Fantasy had come to life. Roncey himself was not enchanted.

"I don't like it," he said, frowning.

"Ideally, you should all go. The whole lot of you," I said.

Roncey shook his head. "There are the other horses, and the farm. I can't leave them. And I need Pat here, and Peter."

I agreed to that, having gained the essentials. "Don't tell the children they are going," I said to Madge. "Just keep them home from school in the morning, and someone will call for you at about nine. You'll need only country clothes. And you'll be away until after the race on Saturday week. Also, please do not on any account write any letters straight to here, or let the children send any. If you want to write, send the letters to us at the *Blaze,* and we will see that Mr. Roncey gets them."

"But Vic can write to us?" Madge said.

"Of course . . . but also via the *Blaze.* Because he won't know where you are."

They both protested, but in the end saw the sense of it. What he didn't know, he couldn't give away, even by accident.

"It won't only be people working the racket who might be looking for them," I explained apologetically. "But one or two of our rival newspapers will be hunting for them, so as to be able to black the *Blaze's* eye. And they are quite skilled at finding people who want to stay hidden."

I left the Ronceys looking blankly at each other and drove the van back to London. It seemed a very long way, and too many aches redeveloped on the journey. I'd finished Tonio's mixture just before going into the office in the morning and was back on Elizabeth's pills,

ich were not as good. By the time I got home, I was
ed, thirsty, hurting, and apprehensive.

Dealt with the first three: armchair and whiskey.
ontemplated the apprehension, and didn't know which
ould be worse, another encounter with the Boston boys
a complete failure with Tiddely Pom. It would likely
e one or the other. Could even be both.

"What's the matter, Ty?" Elizabeth looked and
ounded worried.

"Nothing." I smiled at her. "Nothing at all, honey."

The anxious lines relaxed in her face as she smiled
ack. The pump hummed and thudded, pulling air into
er lungs. My poor, poor Elizabeth. I stretched my hand
ver and touched her cheek in affection, and she turned
er head and kissed my fingers.

"You're a fantastic man, Ty," she said. She said
omething like it at least twice a week. I twitched my
ose and made the usual sort of answer, "You're not
o bad yourself." The disaster that a virus had made of
ur lives never got any better. Never would. For her it
as total and absolute; for me there were exits, like Gail.
Vhen I took them, the guilt I felt was not just the
rdinary guilt of an unfaithful husband, but that of a
eserter. Elizabeth couldn't leave the battlefield; but when
got too much for me, I just slid out and left her.

At nine o'clock the next morning Derry Clark collected
Iadge and the three Roncey boys in his own Austin
nd drove them down to Portsmouth and straight on
the Isle of Wight car ferry.

At noon I arrived at the farm with a car and Rice
ailer borrowed from the city editor, whose daughters
ent in for show jumping. Roncey showed great reluc-
nce at parting with Tiddely Pom, and loaded the sec-
nd stall of the trailer with sacks of feed and bales of
ay, adding to these the horse's saddle and bridle, and
so three dozen eggs and a crate of beer. He had written
it the diet and training regime in four-page detail scat-
red with emphatic underlinings. I assured him six times

I would see that the new trainer followed the instruction to the last full stop.

Pat helped with the loading with a twisting smile, no unhappy that his father was losing control of the horse He gave me a quick look full of ironic meaning when he saw me watching him, and said under his breath a he humped past with some hay, "Now he knows wha it feels like."

I left Victor Roncey standing disconsolately in the center of his untidy farmyard watching his one treasur depart, and drove carefully away along the Essex lanes heading west to Berkshire. About five miles down the road I stopped at a telephone box and rang up the Western School of Art.

Gail said, "Surprise, surprise."

"Yes," I agreed. "How about Sunday?"

"Um." She hesitated. "How about tomorrow?"

"Won't you be teaching?"

"I meant," she explained, "tomorrow night."

"Tomorrow . . . all night?"

"Can you manage it?"

I took so deep a breath that my sore ribs jumped. I depended on whether Mrs. Woodward could stay, a she sometimes did.

"Ty?" she said. "Are you still there?"

"Thinking."

"What about?"

"What to tell my wife."

"You slay me," she said. "Is it yes or no?"

"Yes," I said with a sigh. "Where?"

"A hotel, I should think."

"All right," I agreed. I asked her what time she finished work, and arranged a meeting point at King': Cross railway station.

When I called the flat, Elizabeth answered.

"Ty! Where are you?"

"On the road. There's nothing wrong. It's just tha I forgot to ask Mrs. Woodward before I left if she coul stay with you tomorrow night . . . so that I could go up to Newcastle ready for the races on Saturday." Louse

I thought. Mean, stinking louse. Lying, deceiving louse. I listened miserably to the sounds of Elizabeth asking Mrs. Woodward and found no relief at all in her answer.

"She says yes, Ty, she could manage that perfectly. You'll be home again on Saturday?"

"Yes, honey. Late, though."

"Of course."

"See you this evening."

"Bye, Ty," she said with a smile in her voice. "See you."

I drove all the way to Norton Fox's stable wishing I hadn't done it. Knowing that I wouldn't change it. Round and round the mulberry bush and a thumping headache by Berkshire.

Norton Fox looked curiously into the trailer parked in the private front drive of his house.

"So that's the great Tiddely Pom. Can't say I think much of him from this angle."

"Nor from any other," I added. "It's good of you to have him."

"Happy to oblige. I'm putting him in the box next to Zig Zag, and Sandy Willis can look after both of them."

"You won't tell her what he is?" I asked anxiously.

"Of course not." He looked resigned at my stupidity. "I've recently bought a chaser over in Kent. I've just postponed collecting it a while, but Sandy and all the other lads think Tiddely Pom is him."

"Great."

"I'll just get my head lad to drive the trailer into the yard and unload. You said on the phone that you wanted to stay out of sight. . . . Come inside for a cuppa?"

Too late, after I'd nodded, I remembered the near-black tea of my former visit. The same again. Norton remarked that his housekeeper had been economizing; he never could get her to make it strong enough.

"Did the *Tally* photographer get here all right?" I asked as he came in from the yard, filling his cup, and sat down opposite me.

He nodded. "Took dozens of pics of Sandy Willis and thrilled her to bits." He offered me a slice of dry-looking fruitcake and, when I said no, ate a large chunk himself, undeterred. "That article of yours last Sunday," he said past the currants. "That must have been a bombshell in certain quarters."

I said, "Mmm, I hope so."

"Brevity—that Champion Hurdler of mine—that was definitely one of the nonstarters you were talking about, wasn't it? Even though you didn't mention it explicitly by name?"

"Yes, it was."

"Ty, did you find out *why* Dembley struck his horse out, and then sold out of racing altogether?"

"I can't tell you why, Norton," I said.

He considered this answer with his head on one side and then nodded as if satisfied. "Tell me one day, then."

I smiled briefly. "When and if the racket is extinct."

"You go on the way you are, and it will be. If you go on exposing it publicly, the antepost market will be so untrustworthy that we'll find ourselves doing as the Americans do, only betting on a race on the day of the race, and never before. They don't have any off-the-course betting at all over there, do they?"

"Not legally."

He drank in big gulps down to the tea leaves. "Might shoot our attendances up if punters had to go to the races to have a bet."

"Which would shoot up the prize money, too. . . . Did you see that their champion jockey earned well over three million dollars last year? Enough to make Gordon Richards weep."

I put down the half-finished tea and stood up. "Must be getting back, Norton. Thank you again for your help."

"Anything to prevent another Brevity."

"Send the accounts to the *Blaze*."

He nodded. "And ring the sports desk every day to give a report, and don't speak to anyone except you or

Derry Clark or a man called Luke-John Morton. Right?"

"Absolutely right," I agreed. "Oh, and here are Victor Roncey's notes. Eggs and beer in Tiddely Pom's food every night."

"I've one owner," Norton said, "who sends his horse champagne."

I drove the trailer back to the city editor's house, swapped it for my van, and went home. Ten to seven on the clock. Mrs. Woodward was having a grand week for overtime and had cooked a chicken à la king for our supper, leaving it ready and hot. I thanked her. "Not at all, Mr. Tyrone, a pleasure I'm sure. Ta-ta, luv, see you tomorrow. I'll bring my things for stopping the night."

I kissed Elizabeth, poured the drinks, ate the chicken, watched a TV program, and let a little of the day's tension trickle away. After supper there was my Sunday article to write. Enthusiasm for the project: way below zero. I went into the writing room determined to put together a calm played-down sequel to the previous week, with a sober let's-not-rush-our-fences approach. Somewhere along the line most of these good intentions vanished. Neither Charlie Boston nor the foreign gent in the Rolls was going to like the result.

Before setting off to the office in the morning I packed an overnight bag, with Elizabeth reminding me to take my alarm clock and a clean shirt.

"I hate it when you go away," she said. "I know you don't go often, probably not nearly as much as you ought to. I know you try not to get the faraway meetings. Derry nearly always does them, and I feel so guilty because his wife has those tiny children to look after all alone. . . ."

"Stop worrying," I said, smiling. "Derry likes to go." I had almost convinced myself that I really was taking the afternoon train to Newcastle. Gail was hours away, unreal. I kissed Elizabeth's cheek three times and dearly regretted leaving her. Yet I left.

Luke-John and Derry were both out of the office when I arrived. Luke-John's secretary handed me a large envelope which she said had come for me by hand just after I left on Wednesday. I opened it. The galley proofs of my *Tally* article: please would I read and O.K. immediately.

"*Tally* telephoned for you twice yesterday," Luke-John's secretary said. "They go to press today. They wanted you urgently."

I read the article. Arnold Shankerton had changed it about here and there and had stamped his own slightly pedantic views of grammar all over it. I sighed. I didn't like the changes, but a hundred and fifty guineas plus expenses softened the impact.

Arnold Shankerton said in his perfectly modulated tenor, with a mixture of annoyance and apology, "I'm afraid we've had to go ahead and print, as we hadn't heard from you."

"My fault. I've only just picked up your letter."

"I see. Well, after I'd worked on it a little I think it reads very well, don't you? We're quite pleased with it. We think it will be a success with our readers. They like that sort of intimate human touch."

"I'm glad," I said politely. "Will you send me a copy?"

"I'll make a note of it," he said suavely. I thought I would probably have to buy one on a bookstall. "Let me have your expenses. Small, I hope?"

"Sure," I agreed. "Tiny."

Luke-John and Derry came back as I disconnected and Luke-John without bothering to say good morning stretched out a hand for my Sunday offering. I took it out of my pocket and he unfolded it and read it.

"Hmph," he said. "I expected a bit more bite."

Derry took one of the carbon copies from me and read it.

"Any more bite and he'd have chewed up the whole page," he said.

"Couldn't you emphasize a bit more that only the

Blaze knows where Tiddely Pom is?" Luke-John said. "You've only implied it."

"If you think so."

"Yes, I do think so. As the *Blaze* is footing the bills, we want all the credit we can get."

"Suppose someone finds him—Tiddely Pom?" I asked mildly. "Then we'd look right nanas, hiding him, boasting about it, and then having him found."

"No one will find him. The only people who know where he is are us three and Norton Fox. To be more precise, only you and Fox know *exactly* where he is. Only you and Fox know which in that yardful of sixty horses is Tiddely Pom. Neither of you is going to tell anyone else. So how is anyone going to find him? No, no, Ty. You make that article absolutely definite. The *Blaze* is keeping the horse safe, and only the *Blaze* knows where he is."

"Charlie Boston may not like it," Derry observed to no one in particular.

"Charlie Boston can stuff it," Luke-John said impatiently.

"I meant," Derry explained, "that he might just send his thug-uglies to take Ty apart for so obviously ignoring their keep-off-the-grass."

My pal. Luke-John considered the possibility for two full seconds before shaking his head. "They wouldn't dare."

"And even if they did," I said, "it would make a good story if you could sell more papers."

"Exactly." Luke-John started nodding and then looked at me suspiciously. "That was a joke?"

"A feeble one." I sighed, past smiling.

"Change the intro, then, Ty. Make it one hundred per cent specific." He picked up a pencil and put a line through the first paragraph. Read the next, rubbed his larynx thoughtfully, let that one stand. Axed the next. Turned the page.

Derry watched sympathetically as the pencil marks grew. It happened to him, too, often enough. Luke-John scribbled his way through to the end and then returned to the beginning, pointing out each alteration that he wanted made. He was turning my moderately hard-hitting original into a bulldozing battering ram.

"You'll get me slaughtered," I said, and I meant it.

I worked on the rewrite most of the morning, fighting a rear-guard action all the way. What Luke-John finally passed was a compromise between his view and mine, but still left me so far out on a limb as to be balancing on twigs. Luke-John took it in to the editor, stayed there while he read it, and brought it triumphantly back.

"He liked it. Thinks it's great stuff. He liked Derry's piece yesterday, too, summing up the handicap. He told me the sports desk is a big asset to the paper."

"Good," Derry said cheerfully. "When do we get our next raise?"

"Time for a jar at the Devereux," Luke-John suggested, looking at his watch. "Coming today, Ty?"

"Norton Fox hasn't rung through yet."

"Call him, then."

I telephoned to Fox. Tiddely Pom was fine, ate his feed the previous evening, had settled in well, had done a mile at a working canter that morning, and no one had looked at him twice. I thanked him and relayed the news to Roncey, who sounded both agitated and depressed.

"I don't like it," he said several times.

"Do you want to risk having him at home?"

He hesitated, then said, "I suppose not. No. But I don't like it. Don't forget to ring tomorrow evening. I'll be at Kempton races all afternoon."

"The sports editor will ring," I assured him. "And don't worry."

He put the receiver down saying an explosive "Huh." Luke-John and Derry were already on the way to the door and I joined them to go to lunch.

"Only a fortnight since Bert Checkov died," observed Derry, sitting on a bar stool. "Only ten days since we spotted the nonstarters. Funny."

Hilarious. And eight more days to go to the Lamplighter. This Monday, I decided, I would stay safely tucked away at home.

"Don't forget," I said to Derry. "Don't tell anyone my phone number."

"What brought that on all of a sudden?"

"I was thinking about Charlie Boston. My address isn't in the phone book. . . ."

"Neither Derry nor I will give your address to anyone," Luke-John said impatiently. "Come off it, Ty, anyone would think you were frightened."

"Anyone would be so right," I agreed, and they both laughed heartily into their pints.

Derry was predictably pleased that I wanted to go to Newcastle instead of Kempton, leaving the London meeting for once for him.

"Is it all right," he said, embarrassed. "With your wife, I mean?"

I told him what Elizabeth had said, but as usual anything to do with her made him uncomfortable. Luke-John said dutifully "How is she?" and I said "Fine."

I kicked around the office all the afternoon, arranging a travel warrant to Newcastle, putting in a chit for expenses for Heathbury Park, Leicester, and Plumpton, and collecting the cash from Accounts. Luke-John was busy with a football columnist and the golfing correspondent, and Derry took time off from working out his tips for every meeting in the following week to tell me about taking the Roncey kids to the Isle of Wight.

"Noisy little devils," he said disapprovingly. "Their mother has no control over them at all. She seemed to be in a dream most of the time. Anyway, none of them actually fell off the ferry, which was a miracle considering Tony—that was the eldest one—was trying to lean over far enough to see the paddles go round. I told him they were under the water. Made no difference."

I made sympathetic noises, trying not to laugh out of pity for my ribs. "They were happy enough, then?"

"Are you kidding? No school and a holiday at the sea? Tony said he was going to bathe, November or no November. His mother showed no signs of stopping him. Anyway, they settled into the boarding house all right, though I should think we shall get a whacking bill for damage, and they thought it tremendous fun to change their names to Robinson—no trouble there. They thought Robinson was a smashing choice; they would all pretend they were cast away on a desert island. . . . Well, I tell you, Ty, by the time I left them I was utterly exhausted."

"Never mind. You can look forward to bringing them back."

"Not me," he said fervently. "Your turn for that."

At four I picked up my suitcase and departed for King's Cross. The Newcastle train left at five. I watched it go.

At five-forty-eight she came up from the underground, wearing a beautifully cut darkish-blue coat and carrying a creamy white suitcase. Several heads turned to look at her, and a nearby man who had been waiting almost as long as I had watched her steadfastly until she reached the corner where I stood.

"Hallo," she said. "Sorry I'm late."

"Think nothing of it."

"I gather," she said with satisfaction, "that you fixed your wife."

NINE

She moved against me in the warm dark and put her mouth on the thin skin somewhere just south of my neck. I tightened my arms around her, and buried my nose in her clean sweet-scented hair.

"There's always something new," she said sleepily. "Broken ribs are quite a gimmick."

"I didn't feel them."

"Oh, yes, you did."

I stroked my hands slowly over her smooth skin and didn't bother to answer. I felt relaxed and wholly content. She had been kind to my ribs, gentle to my bruises. They had even in an obscure way given her pleasure.

"How did it happen?"

"What?"

"The black-and-blue bit."

"I lost an argument."

She rubbed her nose on my chest. "Must have been quite a debate."

I smiled in the dark. The whole world was inside the sheets, inside the small private cocoon wrapping two bodies in intimate primeval understanding.

"Ty?"

"Mmm?"

"Can't we stay together all weekend?"

I said through her hair, "I have to phone in a report from Newcastle. Can't avoid it."

"Damn the *Blaze*."

"There's Sunday, though."

"Hurrah for the golf club."

We lay quiet for a long while. I felt heavy with sleep and fought to stay awake. There were so few hours like this. None to waste.

For Gail time was not so precious. Her limbs slackened and her head slid down onto my arm, her easy breath fanning softly against my chest. I thought of Elizabeth lying closely curled against me like that when we were first married, and for once it was without guilt, only with regret.

Gail woke of her own accord a few hours later and pulled my wrist around to look at the luminous hands on my watch.

"Are you awake?" she said. "It's ten to six."

"Do you like it in the morning?"

"With you, Ty, anytime." Her voice smiled in the darkness. "Any old time you care to mention."

I wasn't that good. I said, "Why?"

"Because you're normal, maybe. Nice bread-and-butter

love." She played the piano down my stomach. "Some men want the weirdest things. . . ."

"Let's not talk about them."

"O.K.," she said. "Let's not."

I caught the Newcastle express at eight o'clock with ten seconds in hand. It was a raw cold morning with steam hissing up from under the train. Hollow clanking noises and unintelligible station announcements filled the ears, and bleary-eyed shivering passengers hurried grayly through the British Standard dawn.

I took my shivering bleary-eyed self into the dining car and tried some strong black coffee, but nothing was going to shift the dragging depression which had settled in inexorably as soon as I left Gail. I imagined her as I had left her, lying warm and luxuriously lazy in the soft bed and saying Sunday was tomorrow, we could start again where we'd left off. Sunday was certainly tomorrow, but there was Saturday to get through first. From where I sat it looked like a very long day.

Four and a half hours to Newcastle. I slept most of the way, and spent the rest remembering the evening and night which were gone. We had found a room in a small private hotel near the station and I had signed the register "Mr. and Mrs. Tyrone." No one there had shown any special interest in us; they had presently shown us to a clean uninspiring room and given us the key, had asked if we wanted early tea, had said they were sorry they didn't do dinners, there were several good restaurants round about. I paid them in advance, explaining that I had an early train to catch. They smiled, thanked me, withdrew, asked no questions, made no comment. Impossible to know what they guessed.

We talked for a while and then went out to a pub for a drink and from there to an Indian restaurant where we took a long time eating little, and an even longer time drinking coffee. Gail wore her usual air of businesslike poise and remained striking-looking even when surrounded by people of her own skin color. I, with my pale face, was in a minority.

Gail commented on it. "London must be the best place
in the world for people like me."

"For anyone."

She shook her head. "Especially for people of mixed
race. In so many countries I'd be on the outside looking
in. I'd never get the sort of job I have."

"It never seems to worry you, being of mixed race,"
I said.

"I accept it. In fact I wouldn't choose now to be
wholly white or wholly black, if I could alter it. I am
used to being me. And with people like you, of course,
it is easy, because you are unaffected by me."

"I wouldn't say that, exactly," I said grinning.

"Damn it, you know what I mean. You don't mind
me being brown."

"You're brown and you're beautiful. A shattering
combination."

"You're not being serious," she complained.

"And you're glossy to the bone."

Her lips curved in amusement. "If you mean I've a
hard core instead of a soft center, then I expect you're
right."

"And one day you'll part from me without a twinge."

"Will we part?" No anxiety, no involvement.

"What do you think?"

"I think you wouldn't leave your wife to live with
me."

Direct, no muddle, no fluffy wrappings.

"Would you?" she asked when I didn't quickly
answer.

"I'll never leave her."

"That's what I thought. I like to get things straight.
Then I can enjoy what I have, and not expect more."

"Hedging your bets."

"What do you mean?" she asked.

"Insuring against disappointment."

"When people desperately want what they can never
have, they *suffer*. Real grinding misery. That's not for
me."

"You will be luckier than most," I said slowly, "i you can avoid it altogether."

"I'll have a damned good try."

One day uncontrollable emotion would smash up al that organized levelheadedness. Not while I was around if I could help it. I prized it too much. Needed her to stay like that. Only while she demanded so little could I go on seeing her, and since she clearly knew it we had a good chance of staying safely on the tightrope for a long as we wanted.

With the coffee we talked, as before, about money Gail complained that she never had enough.

"Who has?" I said sympathetically.

"Your wife, for one." There was a faint asperity i her voice, which made me stifle my immediate impuls to deny it.

"Sorry," she said almost at once. "Shouldn't hav said that. What your wife has is quite irrelevant. It's wha I haven't got that we're talking about. Such as a car o my own, a sports car, and not having to borrow Harry' all the time. And a flat of my own, a sunny on overlooking a park. Never having to budget every penny Buying lavish presents for people if I feel like it. Flyin to Paris often for a few days, and having a holiday i Japan. . . ."

"Marry a millionaire," I suggested.

"I intend to."

We both laughed, but I thought she'd probably mean it. The man she finally didn't part with would have t have troubles with his surtax. I wondered what she woul do if she knew I could only afford that dinner and th hotel bill because *Tally's* fee would be plugging for while the worst holes in the Tyrone economy. Wha would she do if she knew that I had a penniless paralyze wife, not a rich one. On both counts, wave a rapi goodbye, probably. For as long as I could, I wasn't goin to give her the opportunity.

I missed the first Newcastle race altogether and onl reached the press stand halfway through the second

Delicate probes among colleagues revealed that nothing dramatic had happened in the hurdle race I had spent urging the taxi driver to go above twenty. Luke-John would never know.

After the fourth race I telephoned through a report, and another after the fifth, in which one of the top northern jockeys broke his leg. Derry came on the line and asked me to go and find out from the trainer who would be riding his horse in the Lamplighter instead, and I did his errand thanking my stars I had had the sense actually to go to Newcastle, and hadn't been tempted to watch the racing on television and phone through an "on-the-spot" account from an armchair three hundred miles away, as one correspondent of my acquaintance had been known to do.

Just before the last race someone touched my arm. I turned. Colly Gibbons, the handicapper, looking harassed and annoyed.

"Ty. Do me a favor."

"What?"

"You came by train? First class?"

I nodded. The *Blaze* wasn't mean about comfort.

"Then swap return tickets with me." He held out a slim booklet which proved to be an air ticket, Newcastle to Heathrow.

"There's some damn meeting been arranged here which I shall have to go to after this race," he explained. "And I won't be able to catch the plane. I've only just found out and—it's most annoying. There's a later train. . . . I particularly want to get to London tonight."

"Done," I said. "Suits me fine."

He smiled, still frowning simultaneously. "Thanks. And here are the keys to my car. It's in the multistory park opposite the Europa building." He told me its number and position. "Drive yourself home."

"I'll drive to your house and leave the car there," I said. "Easier than bringing it over tomorrow."

"If you're sure. . . ." I nodded, giving him my train ticket.

"A friend who lives up here was going to run me

back to the airport," he said. "I'll get him to take you instead."

"Have you heard from your wife?" I asked.

"That's just it. She wrote to say we'd have a trial reconciliation and she'd be coming home today. If I stay away all night, she'll never believe I had a good reason. She'll be gone again."

"Miss the meeting," I suggested.

"It's too important, especially now I've got your help. I suppose you couldn't explain to her, if she's there, that I'm on my way?"

"Of course," I said.

So the friend whisked me off to the airport, and I flew to Heathrow, collected the car, drove to Hampstead, explained to Mrs. Gibbons, who promised to wait, and arrived home two and a half hours early. Elizabeth was pleased, even if Mrs. Woodward wasn't.

Sunday morning. Elizabeth's mother didn't come.

Ten-fifteen, ten-thirty. Nothing. At eleven someone telephoned from the health farm and said they were so sorry, my mother-in-law was in bed with a virus infection, nothing serious, don't worry, she would ring her daughter as soon as she was a little better.

I told Elizabeth. "Oh, well," she said philosophically, "we'll have a nice cozy day on our own."

I smiled at her and kept the shocking disappointment out of my face.

"Do you think Sue Davis would pop along for a moment while I get us some whiskey?" I asked.

"She'd get it for us."

"I'd like to stretch my legs. . . ."

She smiled understandingly and rang Sue, who came at twelve with flour down the sides of her jeans. I hurried round corners to the nearest phone box and gave the Hunterson's number. The bell rang there again and again, but no one answered. Without much hope I got the number of Virginia Water station and rang there: no, they said, there was no young woman waiting outside in a station wagon. They hadn't seen one all morning.

I asked for the Huntersons' number again. Again, no reply.

Feeling flat, I walked back to our local pub and bought the whiskey, and tried yet again on the telephone too publicly installed in the passage there.

No answer. No Gail.

I went home.

Sue Davis had read out to Elizabeth my piece in the *Blaze*.

"Straight between the eyeballs," she observed cheerfully. "I must say, Ty, no one could connect the punch you pack in that paper with the you we know."

"What's wrong with the him you know?" asked Elizabeth with real anxiety under the surface gaiety. She hated people to think me weak for staying at home with her. She never told anyone how much nursing she needed from me, always pretended Mrs. Woodward did everything. She seemed to think that what I did for her would appear unmanly to others; she wanted in public a masculine never-touch-the-dishes husband, and since it made her happy I played that role except when we were alone.

"Nothing's wrong with him," Sue protested. She looked me over carefully. "Nothing at all."

"What did you mean, then?" Elizabeth was smiling still, but she wanted an answer.

"Oh . . . only that this Ty is so quiet, and that one"— she pointed to the paper—"bursts the eardrums." She put her head on one side, summing me up, then turned to Elizabeth with the best of motives and said, "This one is so gentle. That one is tough."

"Gentle nothing," I said, seeing the distress under Elizabeth's laugh. "When you aren't here, Sue, I throw her around the room and black her eyes regularly on Fridays." Elizabeth relaxed, liking that. "Stay for a drink," I suggested to Sue, "now that I've fetched it."

She went, however, back to her half-baked Yorkshire pudding, and I avoided discussing what she had said by going to the kitchen and rustling up some omelets for lunch. Elizabeth particularly liked them, and could eat hers with the new feeding gadget, up to a point. I helped her when her wrist tired, and made some coffee and fixed her mug in its holder.

"Do you really know where the horse is?" she asked.

"Tiddely Pom? Yes, of course."

"Where is it?"

"Dark and deadly secret, honey," I said. "I can't tell anyone, even you."

"Oh, go on," she urged. "You know I won't tell either."

"I'll tell you next Sunday."

Her nose wrinkled. "Thanks for nothing." The pump heaved away, giving her breath. "You don't think anyone would try to . . . well . . . *make* you tell. Where he is, I mean." More worry, more anxiety. She couldn't help it. She was always on the edge of a precipice, always on the distant lookout for anything which would knock her over.

"Of course not, honey. How could they?"

"I don't know," she said but her eyes were full of horrors.

"Stop fussing," I said with a smile. "If anyone threatened me with anything really nasty, I'd say quick enough where he is. No horse is worth getting in too deep for." Echoes of Dembley. The matrix which nurtured the germ. No one would sacrifice himself or his family for the sake of running a horse.

Elizabeth detected the truth in my voice and was satisfied. She switched on the television and watched some fearful old movie which bored me to death. Three o'clock came and went. Even if I'd gone to Virginia Water, I would have been on the way back again. And I'd had Friday night. Rare unexpected Friday night. Trouble was, the appetite grew on what it fed on, as someone else once said. The next Sunday was at the wrong end of the telescope.

Drinks, supper, jobs for Elizabeth, bed. No one else called, no one telephoned. It crossed my mind once or twice, as I lazed in the armchair in our customary closed-in little world, that perhaps the challenge implicit in my column had stirred up, somewhere, a hive of bees.

Buzz buzz, busy little bees. Buzz around the *Blaze*. And don't sting me.

I spent all Monday in and around the flat. Washed the van, wrote letters, bought some socks, kept off race trains from Leicester.

Derry telephoned twice, once to tell me (a) that Tiddely Pom was flourishing, and (b) the Roncey children had sent him a stick of peppermint rock.

"Big deal," I said.

"Not bad kids."

"You'll enjoy fetching them."

He blew a raspberry and hung up.

Tuesday morning I walked to the office. One of those brownish late-November days, with saturated air and a sour scowl of fog to come. Lights shone out brightly at 11 A.M. People hurried along Fleet Street with pinched mean eyes, working out whose neck to scrunch on the next rung of the ladder, and someone bought a blind man's matches with a poker chip.

Luke-John and Derry wore moods to match.

"What's the matter?" I asked mildly.

"Nothing's happened," Derry said.

"So?"

"So where's our reaction?" Luke-John inquired angrily. "Not a letter. No one's phoned, even. Unless"—he brightened—"unless Charlie Boston's boys have called on you with a few more threats?"

"They have not."

Relapse into gloom for the sports desk. I alone wasn't sorry the article had fallen with a dull thud. If it had. I thought it was too soon to be sure. I said so.

"Hope you're right, Ty," Luke-John said skeptically. "Hope it hasn't all been a coincidence—Bert Checkov and the nonstarters. Hope the *Blaze* hasn't wasted its time and money for nothing on Tiddely Pom."

"Charlie Boston's boys were not a coincidence."

"I suppose not." Luke-John sounded as though he thought I might have misunderstood what the Boston boys had said.

"Did your friend in Manchester find out any more about Charlie B.?" I asked.

Luke-John shrugged. "Only that there was some talk about his chain of betting shops being taken over by a bigger concern. But it doesn't seem to have happened. He is still there, anyway, running the show."

"Which bigger concern?"

"Don't know."

To pass the time, we dialed for the biggest London bookmaking businesses which had chains of betting shops all over the country. None of them admitted any immediate interest in buying out Charlie Boston. But one man was hesitant, and when I pressed him he said, "We did put out a feeler, about a year ago. But Boston decided to remain independent and turned down both offers."

"Thanks," I said, and Luke-John commented that that took us a long way, didn't it. He turned his attention crossly to a pile of letters which had flooded in contradicting one of the football writers, and Derry began to assess the form for the big race on Boxing Day. All over the vast office space the Tuesday picking of teeth and scratching of scabs proceeded without haste, the slow week still slumbering. Tuesday was gossip day, Wednesday, planning. Thursday, writing. Friday, editing. Saturday, printing. Sunday, *Blaze* away. And on Mondays the worked-on columns lit real fires or wrapped up fish-and-chips. No immortality for a journalist.

Tuesday was also *Tally* day. Neither at home nor at the office had a copy come for me by post. I went downstairs to the next-door magazine stand, bought one, and went back inside the *Blaze*.

The pictures were offbeat and rather good, the whole article well presented. One had to admit that Shankerton knew his stuff. I forgave him his liberties with my syntax.

I picked up Derry's telephone and got through to the

Tally dispatch department. As expected, they didn't send free copies to the subjects of any articles: not their policy. Would they send them? Oh, sure, give us the addresses, we'll let you have the bill. I gave them the six addresses, Huntersons, Ronceys, Sandy Willis, Colly Gibbons, Dermont Finnegan, Willy Ondroy.

Derry picked up the magazine and plodded through the article, reading at one-third Luke-John's wide-angled speed.

"Deep, deep," he said ironically, putting it down. "One hundred and fifty fathoms."

"Sixty will go in tax."

"A hard life." Derry sighed. "But if you hadn't picked on Roncey, we would never have cottoned on to his nonstarter racket."

Nor would I have had any cracked ribs. With them, though, the worst was over. Only coughing, sneezing, laughing, and taking running jumps were sharply undesirable. I had stopped eating Elizabeth's pills. In another week, the cracks would have knitted.

"Be seeing you," I said to Derry. Luke-John waved a freckled farewell hand. Carrying *Tally,* I went down in the lift and turned out of the front door up toward the Strand, bound for a delicatessen shop that sold Austrian apple cake which Elizabeth liked.

Bought the cake. Came out into the street. Heard a voice in my ear. Felt a sharp prick through my coat abeam the first lumbar vertebra.

"It's a knife, Mr. Tyrone."

I stood quite still. People could be stabbed to death in busy streets and no one noticed until the body cluttered up the fairway. Killers vanished into crowds with depressing regularity.

"What do you want?" I said.

"Just stay where you are."

Standing on the Fleet Steet pavement, holding a magazine and a box of apple cake. Just stay where you are. For how long?

"For how long?" I said.

He didn't answer. But he was still there, because his

knife was. We stood where we were for all of two minutes. Then a black Rolls came to a silent halt at the curb directly opposite where I stood. The door to the back seat swung open.

"Get in," said the voice behind me.

I got in. There was a chauffeur driving, all black uniform and a stolid acne-scarred neck. The man with the knife climbed in after me and settled by my side. I glanced at him, knew I'd seen him somewhere before, didn't know where. I put *Tally* and the apple cake carefully on the floor. Sat back. Went for a ride.

TEN

We turned north into the Aldwych and up Drury Lane to St. Giles' Circus. I made no move toward escape, although we stopped several times at traffic lights. My companion watched me warily, and I worked on where I had seen him before and still came up with nothing. Up Tottenham Court Road. Left, right, left again. Straight into Regent's Park and around the semicircle. Stopped smoothly at the turnstile entrance to the Zoo.

"Inside," said my companion, nodding.

We stepped out of the car, and the chauffeur quietly drove off.

"You can pay," I remarked.

He gave me a quick glance, tried to juggle the money out of his pocket one-handed, and found he couldn't manage it if he was to be of any use with his knife.

"No," he said. "You pay. For us both."

I paid, almost smiling. He was nowhere near as dangerous as he wanted to be thought.

We checked through the turnstiles. "Where now?" I said.

"Straight ahead. I'll tell you."

The Zoo was nearly empty. On that oily November Tuesday lunchtime, not even the usual busloads from schools. Birds shrieked mournfully from the aviary and a notice board said the vultures would be fed at three.

A man in a dark overcoat and black homburg hat was sitting on a seat looking toward the lions' outdoor compounds. The cages were empty. The sun-loving lions were inside under the sun lamps.

"Over there," said my companion, nodding.

We walked across. The man in the black homburg watched us come. Every line of his clothes and posture spoke of money, authority, and high social status, and his manner of irritating superiority would have done credit to the Foreign Office. As Dembley had said, his subject matter was wildly at variance with his appearance.

"Did you have any trouble?" he asked.

"None at all," said the knife man smugly.

A bleak expression crept into pale gray eyes as cold as the stratosphere. "I am not pleased to hear it."

The accent in his voice was definite but difficult. A thickening of some consonants, a clipping of some vowels.

"Go away, now," he said to the knife man. "And wait."

My nondescript abductor in his nondescript raincoat nodded briefly and walked away, and I nearly remembered where I'd seen him. Recollection floated up, but not far enough.

"You chose to come," the man in the homburg said flatly.

"Yes and no."

He stood up. My height, but thicker. Yellowish skin, smooth except for a maze of wrinkles around his eyes. What I could see of his hair was nearly blond, and I put his age down roughly as five or six years older than myself.

"It is cold outside. We will go in."

I walked around with him inside the big cats' house, where the strong feral smell seemed an appropriate background to the proceedings. I could guess what he wanted. Not to kill: that could have been done in Fleet Street or anywhere on the way. To extort. The only question was how.

"You show too little surprise," he said.

"We were waiting for some—reaction. Expecting it."

"I see." He was silent, working it out. A bored-looking tiger blinked at us lazily, claws sheathed inside rounded pads, tail swinging a fraction from side to side. I sneered at him. He turned and walked three paces and three paces back, around and around, going nowhere.

"Was last week's reaction not enough for you?"

"Very useful," I commented. "Led us straight to Charlie Boston. So kind of you to ask. That makes you a sidekick of his."

He gave me a frosty glare. "I *employ* Boston."

I looked down, not answering. If his pride was as easily stung as that, he might give me more answers than I gave him.

"When I heard about it, I disapproved of what they did on the train. Now I am not so sure." His voice was quiet again, the voice of culture, diplomacy, tact.

"You didn't order it, then?"

"I did not."

I ran my hand along the thick metal bar which kept visitors four feet away from the animals' cages. The tiger looked tame, too gentle to kill. Too indifferent to maul, to maim, to scrape to the bone.

"You know what we want," said the polite tiger by my side. "We want to know where you have hidden the horse."

"Why?" I said.

He merely blinked at me.

I sighed. "What good will it do you? Do you still seriously intend to try to prevent it from running? You would be much wiser to forget the whole thing and quietly fold your tent and steal away."

"You will leave that decision entirely to me." Again the pride stuck out a mile. I didn't like it. Few enemies were as ruthless as those who feared a loss of face. I began to consider before how wide an acquaintanceship the face had to be preserved. The wider, the worse for me.

"Where is it?"

"Tiddely Pom?" I said.

"Tiddely Pom." He repeated the name with fastidious disgust. "Yes."

"Quite safe."

"Mr. Tyrone, stop playing games. You cannot hide forever from Charlie Boston."

I was silent. The tiger yawned, showing a full set of fangs. Nasty.

"They could do more damage next time," he said.

I looked at him curiously, wondering if he seriously thought I would crumble under so vague a threat. He stared straight back and was umoved when I didn't answer. My heart sank slightly. More to come.

"I suspected," he said conversationally, "when I heard that you were seen at Plumpton races the day following Boston's ill-judged attack, that physical pressure would run us into too much difficulty in your case. I see that this suspicion was correct. I directed that a different lever should be found. We have, of course, found it. And you will tell us where the horse is hidden."

He took out the black crocodile wallet and removed from it a small sheet of paper, folded once. He gave it to me. I looked. He saw the deep shock in my face and he smiled in satisfaction.

It was a photocopy of the bill of the hotel where I had stayed with Gail. Mr. and Mrs. Tyrone, one double room.

"So you see, Mr. Tyrone, that if you wish to keep this interesting item of news from your wife, you must give us the address we ask."

My mind tumbled over and over like a dry-cleaning machine, and not a useful thought came out.

"So quiet, Mr. Tyrone? You really don't like that, do you? So you will tell us. You would not want your wife to divorce you, I am sure. And you have taken such pains to deceive her that we are certain you know she would throw you out if she discovered this. . . ." He pointed to the bill. "How would she like to know that your mistress is colored? We have other dates, too. Last Sunday week, and the Sunday before that. Your wife will be told it all. Wealthy women will not stand for this sort of thing, you know."

I wondered numbly how much Gail had sold me for.

"Come along, Mr. Tyrone. The address."

"I need time," I said dully.

"That's right," he said calmly. "It takes time to sink in properly, doesn't it? Of course you can have time. Six hours. You will telephone to us at precisely seven o'clock this evening." He gave me a plain white card with numbers on it. "Six hours is all, Mr. Tyrone. After that, the information will be on its way to your wife, and you will not be able to stop it. Do you clearly understand?"

"Yes." I said. The tiger sat down and shut its eyes. Sympathetic.

"I thought you would." He moved away from me toward the door. "Seven o'clock precisely. Good day, Mr. Tyrone."

With erect easy assurance he walked straight out of the cat house, turned a corner, and was gone. My feet seemed to have become disconnected from my body. I was going through the disjointed floating feeling of irretrievable disaster. A disbelieving part of my mind said that if I stayed quite still the nutcracker situation would go away.

It didn't, of course. But after a while I began to think normally instead of in emotional shock waves; began to look for a hole in the net. I walked slowly away from the tiger, out into the unwholesome air, and down toward the gate, all my attention turned inward. Out of the corner of my eye I half caught sight of my abductor in his raincoat standing up a side path looking into an apparently empty wire-netted compound, and when I'd gone out of the turnstile onto the road it hit me with a thump where I'd seen him before. So significant a thump that I came to a rocking halt. Much had urgently to be understood.

I had seen him at King's Cross station while I waited for Gail. He had been standing near me; had watched her all the way from the underground until she had reached me. Looking for a lever. Finding it.

To be watching me at King's Cross, he must have followed me from the *Blaze*.

Today he had picked me up outside the *Blaze*.

I walked on slowly, thinking about it. From King's Cross in the morning I had gone on the train to Newcastle, but I hadn't come back on my train ticket. Colly Gibbons had. I'd taken that unexpected roundabout route home, and somewhere, maybe back at Newcastle races, I'd shaken off my tail.

Someone also must either have followed Gail or have gone straight into the hotel to see her after I left. I balked at thinking she would sell me out with my imprint still on our shared sheets. But maybe she would. It depended on how much they had offered her, I supposed. Five hundred would have tempted her mercenary heart too far.

No one but Gail could have got a receipt from the hotel. No one but Gail knew of the two Sunday afternoons. No one but Gail thought my wife was rich. I coldly faced the conclusion that I had meant little to her. Very little indeed. My true desserts. I had sought her out because she could dispense sex without involvement. She had been consistent. She owed me nothing at all.

I reached the corner and instinctively turned my plodding steps toward home. Not for twenty paces did I realize that this was a desperate mistake.

Gail didn't know where I lived. She couldn't have told them. They didn't know the facts about Elizabeth; they thought she was a rich woman who would divorce me. *They picked me up this morning outside the* Blaze. . . . At the same weary pace I turned right at the next crossing.

If the man in the black homburg didn't know where I lived, the raincoat would be following to find out. Around the next corner I stopped and looked back through the thick branches of a may bush, and there he was, hurrying. I went on slowly as before, heading imperceptibly toward Fleet Street.

The Homburg Hat had been bluffing. He couldn't tell Elizabeth about Gail, because he didn't know where to find her. Ex-directory telephone. My address in none of the reference books. By sheer luck I twice hadn't led them straight to my own front door.

All the same, it couldn't go on forever. Even if I fooled them until after the Lamplighter, one day, somehow, they would tell her what I'd done.

First they buy you, then they blackmail, Bert Checkov had said. Buy Gail, blackmail me. All of a piece. I thought about blackmail for three long miles back to the *Blaze*.

Luke-John and Derry were surprised to see me back. They made no comment on a change in my appearance. I supposed the inner turmoil didn't show.

"Have any of the crime reporters a decent pull with the police?" I asked.

Derry said, "Jimmy Sienna might have. What do you want?"

"To trace a car number."

"Someone bashed that ancient van of yours?" Luke-John asked uninterestedly.

"Hit and run," I agreed with distant accuracy.

"We can always try," Derry said with typical helpfulness. "Give me the number, and I'll go and ask him."

I wrote down for him the registration number of Homburg Hat's Silver Wraith.

"A London number," Derry remarked. "That might make it easier." He took off across the room to the crime desk and consulted a mountainous young man with red hair.

I strolled over to the deserted news desk and, with a veneer of unconcern over a thumping heart, dialed the number Homburg Hat had told me to ring at seven. It was three-eighteen. More than two hours gone out of six.

A woman answered, sounding surprised.

"Are you sure you have the right number?" she said.

I read it out to her.

"Yes, that's right. How funny."

"Why is it funny?"

"Well, this is a public phone box. I had just shut the door and was going to make a call when the phone started ringing. . . . Are you *sure* you have the right number?"

"I can't have," I said. "Where is this phone box, exactly?"

"It's one of a row in Piccadilly underground station."

I thanked her and rang off. Not much help.

Derry came back and said Jimmy Sienna was doing what he could; good job it was Tuesday, he was bored and wanted something to pass the time with.

I remembered that I had left my copy of *Tally* and Elizabeth's apple cake on the floor of the Rolls. Debated whether or not to get replacements. Decided there was no harm in it, and went out and bought them. I didn't see Raincoat, but that didn't mean he wasn't there, or that they hadn't swapped him for someone I wouldn't know.

Derry said Jimmy Sienna's police friend was checking the registration number but would use his discretion as to whether it was suitable to pass on to the *Blaze*. I sat on the side of Derry's desk and bit my nails.

Outside, the fog which had been threatening all day slowly cleared right away. It would. I thought about unobserved exits under the bright Fleet Street lights.

At five Luke-John said he was going home, and Derry apologetically followed. I transferred myself to Jimmy Sienna's desk and bit my nails there instead. When he, too, was lumbering to his feet to leave, his telephone finally rang. He listened, thanked, scribbled.

"There you are," he said to me. "And good luck with the insurance. You'll need it."

I read what he'd written. The Silver Wraith's number

had been allocated to an organization called Hire Cars
Lucullus.

I left the *Blaze* via the roof. *Tally,* apple cake, and
mending ribs complicated the journey, but after circum-
venting ventilation shafts and dividing walls I walked
sedately through the fire door of the next-door newspaper,
a popular daily in the full flood of going to press.

No one asked me what I was doing. I went down in
the lift to the basement and out to the huge garage to
the rear where rows of yellow vans stood ready to take
the wet-ink bundles off to the trains. I knew one of the
drivers slightly, and asked him for a lift.

"Sure, if you want Paddington."

"I do." I wanted anywhere he was going.

"Hop in, then."

I hopped in, and after he was loaded he drove briskly
out of the garage, one indistinguishable van among a
procession. I stayed with him to Paddington, thanked
him, and backtracked home on the underground, as
certain as I could be that no one had followed.

I beat Mrs. Woodward to six by two minutes but had
no heart for the game.

From six-thirty to seven I sat in the armchair holding
a glass of whiskey and looking at Elizabeth, trying to
make up a beleaguered mind.

"Something's worrying you, Ty," she said, with her
ultra-sensitive feeling for trouble.

"No, honey."

The hands galloped around the clock. At seven o'clock
precisely I sat absolutely still and did nothing at all. At
five past I found I had clenched my teeth so hard that
I was grinding them. I imagined the telephone box in
Piccadilly Circus, with Homburg Hat or Raincoat or
the chauffeur waiting inside it. Tiddely Pom was nothing
compared with Elizabeth's peace of mind, and yet I
didn't pick up the receiver. From seven onward the clock
hands crawled.

At half past Elizabeth said again, with detectable fear.

"Ty, there *is* something wrong. You never look so—so bleak."

I made a great effort to smile at her as usual, but she wasn't convinced. I looked down at my hands and said with hopeless pain, "Honey, how much would it hurt you if I went—and slept with a girl?"

There was no answer. After an unbearable interval I dragged my head up to look at her. Tears were running down her cheeks. She was swallowing, trying to speak.

From long, long habit I pulled a tissue out of the box and wiped her eyes, which she couldn't do for herself.

"I'm sorry," I said uselessly. "I'm sorry."

"Ty . . ." She never had enough breath for weeping. Her mouth strained open in her need for more air

"Honey, don't cry. Don't cry. Forget I said it. You know I love you, I'd never leave you, Elizabeth, honey, dear Elizabeth, don't cry."

I wiped her eyes again and cursed the whim which had sent me down to the Huntersons' for *Tally.* I could have managed without Gail. Without anyone. I had managed without for most of eleven years.

"Ty." The tears had stopped. Her face looked less strained. "Ty." She gulped, fighting for more breath. "I can't bear to think about it."

I stood beside her, holding the tissue, wishing she didn't have to.

"We never talk about sex," she said. The Spiroshell heaved up her chest, let it drop, rhythmically. "I don't want it any more . . . you know that . . . but sometimes I remember . . . how you taught me to like it. . . ." Two more tears welled up. I wiped them away. She said, "I haven't ever asked you . . . about girls. . . . I couldn't, somehow."

"No," I said slowly.

"I've wondered sometimes . . . if you ever have, I mean . . but I didn't really want to know. . . . I know I would be too jealous. . . . I decided I'd never ask you . . . because I wouldn't want you to say yes . . . and yet I know that's selfish. . . . I've always been told men are different, they need women more . . . is it true?"

"Elizabeth," I said helplessly.

"I didn't expect you ever to say anything . . . after all these years. . . . Yes, I would be hurt, if I knew. . . . I couldn't help it. . . . Why did you ask me? I wish you hadn't."

"I would never have said anything," I said with regret, "but someone is trying to blackmail me."

"Then . . . you *have*. . . ."

"I'm afraid so."

"Oh." She shut her eyes. "I see."

I waited, hating myself. The tears were over. She never cried for long. She physically couldn't. If she progressed into one of her rare bursts of rebellious anger, she would utterly exhaust herself. Most wives could scream and throw things. Elizabeth's furies were the worse for being impotent. It must have been touch and go, because when she spoke her voice was low, thick, and deadly quiet.

"I suppose you couldn't afford to be blackmailed."

"No one can."

"I know it's unreasonable of me to wish you hadn't told me. To wish you hadn't done it at all. Any man who stays with a paralyzed wife ought to have something. . . . So many of them pack up and leave altogether. . . . I know you say you never will and I do mostly believe it, but I must be such an unbearable burden to you. . . ."

"That," I said truthfully, "is just not true."

"It must be. Don't tell me . . . about the girl."

"If I don't, the blackmailer will."

"All right . . . get it over quickly. . . ."

I got it over quickly. Briefly. No details. Hated myself for having to tell her, and knew that if I hadn't, Homburg Hat wouldn't have stopped his leverage with the whereabouts of Tiddely Pom. Blackmailers never did. Don't sell your soul, Bert Checkov said. Don't sell your column. Sacrifice your wife's peace instead.

"Will you see her again?" she asked.

"No."

"Or . . . anyone else?"

"No."

"I expect you will," she said. "Only if you do . . . don't tell me. . . . Unless of course someone tries to blackmail you again. . . ."

I winced at the bitterness in her voice. Reason might tell her that total lifelong celibacy was a lot to demand, but emotion had practically nothing to do with reason, and the tearing emotions of any ordinary wife on finding her husband unfaithful hadn't atrophied along with her muscles. I hadn't expected much else. She would have to have been a saint or a cynic to have laughed it off without a pang, and she was neither of those things, just a normal human being trapped in an abnormal situation. I wondered how suspicious she would be in the future of my most innocent absences; how much she would suffer when I was away. Reassurance, always tricky, was going to be doubly difficult.

She was very quiet and depressed all evening. She wouldn't have any supper, wouldn't eat the apple cake. When I washed her and did the rubs and the other intimate jobs, I could almost feel her thinking about the other body my hands had touched. Hands, and much else. She looked sick and strained and, for almost the first time since her illness, embarrassed. If she could have done without me that evening, she would have.

I said, meaning it, "I'm sorry, honey."

"Yes." She shut her eyes. "Life's just bloody, isn't it."

ELEVEN

The uncomfortable coolness between Elizabeth and myself persisted in the morning. I couldn't go on begging for a forgiveness she didn't feel. At ten I said I was going out, and saw her make the first heart-rending effort not to ask where.

Hire Cars Lucullus hung out in a small plushy office
in Stratton Street, off Piccadilly. Royal-blue Wilton
carpet, executive-type acre of polished desk, tasteful
prints of vintage cars on dove-gray walls. Along one side
a wide gold upholstered bench for wide gold upholstered
clients. Behind the desk, a deferential young man with
Uriah Heep eyes.

For him I adopted a languid voice and my best
imitation of the Homburg Hat manners. I had, I explained, left some property in one of his firm's cars, and
I hoped he could help me get it back.

We established gradually that no, I had not hired one
of their cars, and no, I did not know the name of the
man who had; he had merely been so kind as to give
me a lift. Yesterday.

Ah. Then had I any idea which car. . . ?

A Rolls-Royce, a Silver Wraith.

They had four of those. He briefly checked a ledger
though I suspected he didn't need to. All four had been
out on hire yesterday. Could I describe the man who
had given me a lift?

"Certainly. Tallish, blondish, wearing a black homburg.
Not English. Possibly South African."

"Ah. Yes." He had no need to consult the ledger this
time. He put his spread fingertips carefully down on the
desk. "I regret, sir, I cannot give you his name."

"But surely you keep records?"

"This gentleman puts great store on privacy. We have
been instructed not to give his name or address to
anyone."

"Isn't that a bit odd?" I said, raising eyebrows.

He considered judicially. "He is a regular customer.
We would, of course, give him any service he asked for
without question."

"I suppose it wouldn't be possible to—um—purchase
the information?"

He tried to work some shock into his deference. It
was barely skin-deep.

"Was your lost property very valuable?" he asked.

Tally and apple cake. "Very," I said.

"Then I am sure our client will return it to us. If you would let us have your own name and address, perhaps we could let you know?"

I said the first name I thought of, which nearly came out as Kempton Park. "Kempton Jones. 31 Cornwall Street."

He wrote it down carefully on a scratch pad. When he had finished, I waited. We both waited.

After a decent interval he said, "Of course, if it is really important, you could ask in the garage. . . . They would let you know as soon as the car comes in, whether your property is still in it."

"And the garage is where?" The only listed number and address of the Lucullus cars had been the office in Stratton Street.

He studied his fingertips. I produced my wallet and resignedly sorted out two fivers. The twenty-five for the bookmaker's clerk's information about Charlie Boston's boys I had put down to expenses and the *Blaze* had paid. This time I could be on my own. Ten pounds represented six weeks' whiskey, a month's electricity, three and a half days of Mrs. Woodward, one and a half weeks' rent.

He took it greedily, nodded, gave me a hypocritical obsequious smile, and said, "Radnor Mews, Lancaster Gate."

"Thanks."

"You do understand, sir, that it's more than my job is worth to give you our client's name?"

"I understand," I said. "Principles are petty things."

Principles were luckily not so strongly held in Radnor Mews. The foreman sized me up and another tenner changed hands. Better value for money this time.

"The chauffeur comes here to collect the car, see? We never deliver it or supply a driver. Unusual, that. Still, the client is always right, as long as he pays for it, I always say. This foreigner, see, he likes to travel in style when he comes over here. Course, most of our trade is like that. Americans, mostly. They hire a car and a driver for a week, two weeks, maybe three. We drive them all

over, see, Stratford, Broadway, the Cotswold run mo
often, and Scotland a good deal, too. Never have all th
cars in here at once; there'd hardly be room see, fo
Silver Wraiths for a start, and then two Austin Princesse
and three Bentleys and a couple of large Wolseleys."

I brought him back gently to the Silver Wraith i
question.

"I'm telling you, aren't I?" he protested. "This foreig
chap, he takes a car—always a Rolls, mind you, thoug
of course not always the same one—whenever he's ov
here. Started coming just over a year ago, I'd say. Bee
back several times, usually just for three or four day
Longer this time, I'd say. Let's see, the chauffeur cam
for a car last week. I could look it up. . . .Wednesday
Yes, that's right. What they do, see, is the chauffeur fli
over first, picks up the car, and then drives out t
Heathrow to fetch his gent off the next flight. Neat, tha
Shows money, that does."

"Do you know where they fly from?"

"From? Which country? Not exactly. Mind, I thin
it varies. I know once it was Germany. But usually furthe
than that, from somewhere hot. The chauffeur isn't exactl
chatty, but he's always complaining how cold it i
here."

"What is the client's name?" I asked patiently.

"Oh, sure, hang on a minute. We always put th
booking in the chauffeur's name, see; it's easier, bein
Ross. His gent's name is something chronic. I'll hav
to look back."

He went into his little boarded cubicle of an office and
looked back. It took him nearly twenty minutes, by whic
time he was growing restive. I waited, making it plai
I would wait all day. For ten pounds he could keep o
looking. He was almost as relieved as I was when h
found it.

"Here it is, look." He showed me a page in a ledger
pointing to a name with a black-rimmed fingernail. "Tha
one."

There was a pronunciation problem, as he'd said.

Vjoersterod.

"Ross is easier," the foreman repeated. "We always put Ross."

"Much easier," I agreed. "Do you know where I could find them, or where they keep the car while they're in England?"

He sniffed meditatively, shutting the ledger with his finger in the page.

"Can't say as I do, really. Always a pretty fair mileage on the clock, though. Goes a fair way in the three or four days, see? But then that's regular with our cars, most times. Mind you, I wouldn't say that this Ross and his gent go up to Scotland, not as far as that."

"Birmingham?" I suggested.

"Easily. Could be, easily. Always comes back immaculate, I'll say that for Ross. Always clean as a whistle. Why don't you ask in the front office, if you want to find them?"

"They said they couldn't help me."

"That smarmy crumb," he said disgustedly. "I'll bet he knows, though. Give him his due, he's good at that job, but he'd sell his grandmother if the price was right."

I started to walk in the general direction of Fleet Street, thinking. Vjoersterod had to be the real name of Homburg Hat. Too weird to be an alias. Also, the first time he had hired a Silver Wraith from Hire Cars Lucullus he would have to have produced cast-iron references and a passport at least. The smarmy crumb was no fool. He wouldn't let five thousand pounds' worth of machinery be driven away without being certain he would get it back.

Vjoersterod. South African of Afrikaner stock.

Nothing like Fleet Street if one wanted information. The only trouble was, the man who might have heard of Vjoersterod worked on the racing page of a deadly rival to the *Blaze*. I turned in to the first telephone box and rang his office. Sure, he agreed cautiously, he would meet me in the Devereux for a pint and a sandwich. He coped manfully with stifling any too open speculation about what I wanted. I smiled, and crossed the road to catch a bus. A case of who pumped who. He would be trying to find out what story I was working on, and Luke-John would be slightly displeased if he was successful and scooped the *Blaze*.

Luke-John and Derry were both among the crowd in the Devereux. Not so, Mike de Jong. I drank a half pint while Luke-John asked me what I planned to write for Sunday.

"An account of the Lamplighter, I suppose."

"Derry can do that."

I lowered my glass, shrugging. "If you like."

"Then you," said Luke-John, "can do another follow-up to the Tiddely Pom business. Whether he wins or loses, I mean. Give us a puff for getting him to the starting gate."

"He isn't there yet," I pointed out.

Luke-John sniffed impatiently. "There hasn't been a vestige of trouble. No reaction at all. We've frightened them off, that's what's happened."

I shook my head, wishing we had. Asked about the reports on Tiddely Pom and the Roncey children.

"All O.K.," said Derry cheerfully. "Everything going smoothly."

Mike de Jong appeared in the doorway, a quick dark intense man with double-strength glasses and a fringe of black beard outlining his jaw. Caution rolled over him like a sea mist when he saw who I was with, and most of the purposefulness drained out of his stride. It took much maneuvering to get Luke-John and Derry to go into the farther bar to eat without me, and Luke-John left looking back over his shoulder with smoldering suspicion, wanting to know why.

Mike joined me, his sharp face alight with appreciation. "Keeping secrets from the boss, eh?"

"Sometimes he's butterfingered with other people's TNT."

Mike laughed. The cogs whirred around in his high-speed brain. "So what you want is private? Not for the *Blaze*?"

I dodged a direct answer. "What I want is very simple. Just anything you may have heard about a fellow countryman of yours."

"Who?" His accent was a carbon copy, clipped and flat.

"A man called Vjoersterod."

There was a tiny pause while the name sank in, and then he choked on his beer. Recovered, and pretended someone had jogged his elbow. Made a playing-for-time fuss about brushing six scattered drops off his trouser leg. Finally he ran out of alibis and looked back at my face.

"Vjoersterod?" His pronunciation was subtly different from mine. The real thing.

"That's right," I agreed.

"Yes. . . . Well, Ty—why do you ask me about him?"

"Just curiosity."

He was silent for thirty seconds. Then he said carefully again, "Why are you asking about him?" Who pumped who.

"Oh, come on," I said in exasperation. "What's the big mystery? All I want is a bit of gen on a harmless chap who goes racing occasionally."

"Harmless? You must be mad."

"Why?" I sounded innocently puzzled.

"Because he's—" He hesitated, decided I wasn't on to a story, and turned thoroughly helpful. "Look here, Ty, I'll give you a tip, free, gratis, and for nothing. Just steer clear of anything to do with that man. He's poison."

"In what way?"

"He's a bookmaker, back home. Very big business, with branches in all the big cities and a whole group of them round Johannesburg. Respectable enough on the surface. Thousands of perfectly ordinary people bet with him. But there have been some dreadful rumors. . . ."

"About what?"

"Oh, blackmail, extortion, general high-powered thuggery. Believe me, he is not good news."

"Then why don't the police. . . ?" I suggested tentatively.

"Why don't they? Don't be so naïve, Ty. They can' find anyone to give evidence against him, of course."

I sighed. "He seemed so charming."

Mike's mouth fell open and his expression becam acutely anxious.

"You've *met* him?"

"Yeah."

"Here . . . in England?"

"Well, yes, of course."

"Ty, for God's sake, keep away from him."

"I will," I said with feeling. 'Thanks a lot, Mike I'm truly grateful."

"I'd hate anyone I liked to tangle with Vjoersterod,' he said, the genuine friendship standing out clear in hi eyes, unexpectedly affecting. Then, with a born newspa perman's instinct for the main chance, a look of intens curiosity took over.

"What did he want to talk about with you?" h asked.

"I don't really know," I said, sounding puzzled.

"Is he going to get in touch with you again?"

"I don't know that, either."

"Hmm. . . . Give me a ring if he does, and I'll tel you something else."

"Tell me now." I tried hard to make it casual.

He considered, shrugged, and friendship won agai over journalism. "All right. It's nothing much. Just tha I, too, saw him here in England; must have been nin or ten months ago, back in the spring." He paused.

"In that case," I said, "whyever were you so horrifie when I said I'd met him?"

"Because when I saw him he was in the buffet ba on a race train, talking to another press man. Ber Checkov."

With an enormous effort, I kept my mildly puzzle face intact.

Mike went on without a blink. "I warned Bert abo

him later, just like I have you. In here, actually. Bert
was pretty drunk. He was always pretty drunk after
that."

"What did he say?" I asked.

"He said I was three months too late."

Mike didn't know any more. Bert had clammed up
after that one indiscretion and had refused to elaborate
or explain. When he fell out of the window, Mike had
wondered. Violent and often unexplained deaths among
people who had had dealings with Vjoersterod were not
unknown, he said. When I said I had met Vjoersterod,
it had shocked him. He was afraid for me. Afraid I could
follow Bert down onto the pavement.

I put my mind at rest. After what he'd told me, I
would be forewarned, I said.

"I wonder why he got his hooks into Bert," Mike said,
his eyes on the middle distance, all the cogs whirring.

"I've no idea," I said, sighing, and distracted his
attention to another half pint and a large ham sandwich.
Luke-John's thin freckled face loomed over his shoulder,
and he turned to him with a typical bounce, as if all his
body were made of springs.

"So how's the Gospel Maker? What's cooking on the
Blaze?"

Luke-John gave him a thin smile. He didn't care for
his Fleet Street nickname, or for puns in general. Or,
it seemed, for Mike de Jong's puns in particular. Mike
received the message clearly, sketched me a farewell,
and drifted over to another group.

"What did he want?" Luke-John asked sharply.

"Nothing," I said mildly. "Just saying hello."

Luke-John gave me a disillusioned look, but I knew
very well that if I told him at that stage about Vjoersterod
he would dig until he stumbled on the blackmail, dig
again quite ruthlessly to find out how I could have been
blackmailed, and then proceed to mastermind all sub-
sequent inquiries with a stunning absence of discretion.
Vjoersterod would hear his steamroller approach clean
across the country. Luke-John was a brilliant sports

editor. As a field marshal his casualty list would have
been appalling.

He and Derry drank around to closing time at three, by
which time the crowd had reduced to Sunday writers
only. I declined their invitation to go back with them
to the doldrums of the office, and on reflection telephoned
to the only member of the racing authorities I knew well
enough for the purpose.

Eric Youll at thirty-seven was the youngest and newest
of the three Stewards of the National Hunt Committee,
the ruling body of steeplechasing. In two years, by natural
progression, he would be Senior Steward. After that,
reduced to the ranks until re-elected for another three-
year term. As a Steward he made sense because until
recently he had himself ridden as an amateur, and knew
at first hand all the problems and mechanics of racing.
I had written him up in the *Blaze* a few times and we
had been friendly acquaintances for years. Whether he
either could or would help me now was nonetheless open
to doubt.

I had a good deal of trouble getting through to him,
as he was a junior sprig in one of the grander merchant
banks. Secretaries with bored voices urged me to make
an appointment.

"Right now," I said, "will do very well."

After the initial shock the last voice conceded that
right now Mr. Youll could just fit me in. When I got
there, Mr. Youll was busily engaged in drinking a cup
of tea and reading the *Sporting Life*. He put them both
down without haste, stood up, and shook hands.

"This is unexpected," he said. "Come to borrow a
million?"

"Tomorrow, maybe."

He smiled, told his secretary on the intercom to bring
me some tea, offered me a cigarette, and leaned back
in his chair, his manner throughout one of indecision
and uncertainty. He was wary of me and of the purpose
of my visit. I saw that uneasy expression almost every
day of my life: the screen my racing friends erected when
they weren't sure what I was after, the barrier that kept

their secrets from publication. I didn't mind that sort
of withdrawal. Understood it. Sympathized. And never
printed anything private, if I could help it. There was
a very fine edge to be walked when one's friends were
one's raw material.

"Off the record," I assured him. "Take three deep
breaths and relax."

He grinned and tension visibly left his body. "How
can I help you, then?"

I waited until the tea had come and been drunk, and
the latest racing news chewed over. Then, without making
much of it, I asked him if he'd ever heard of a bookmaker
called Vjoersterod.

His attention pinpointed itself with a jerk.

"Is that what you've come to ask?"

"For openers."

He drummed his fingers on the desk. "Someone showed
me your column last week and the week before. . . . Stay
out of it, Ty."

"If you racing bigwigs know what's going on and who
is doing it, why don't you stop him?"

"How?"

The single word hung in the air, cooling. It told me
a lot about the extent of their knowledge. They should
have known how.

"Frankly," I said at last, "that's your job, not mine.
You could of course ban all antepost betting, which
would knock the fiddle stone dead."

"That would be highly unpopular with the Great
British Public. Anyway, your articles have hit the antepost
market badly enough as it is. One of the big firms was
complaining to me bitterly about you a couple of hours
ago. Their Lamplighter bets are down by more than
twenty per cent."

"Then why don't they do something about Charlie
Boston?"

He blinked. "Who?"

I took a quiet breath. "Well, now. . . . Just what do
the Stewards know about Vjoersterod?"

"Who is Charlie Boston?"

"You first," I said.

"Don't you trust me?" He looked hurt.

"No," I said flatly. "You first."

He sighed and told me that all the Stewards knew about Vjoersterod was hearsay, and scanty at that. None of them had ever actually seen him, and wouldn't know him if they did. A member of the German horse-racing authorities had sent them a private warning that Vjoersterod was suspected of stage-managing a series of nonstarting antepost favorites in big races in Germany, and that they had heard rumors he was beginning to operate in England. Pursuit had almost cornered him in Germany. He was now moving on. The British Stewards had noted the alarming proportion of non-starters in the past months and were sure the German authorities were right, but although they had tried to find out the facts from various owners and trainers, they had been met with only a brick wall of silence everywhere.

"It's a year since Vjoersterod came here first," I remarked. "A year ago he bought out Charlie Boston's string of betting shops round Birmingham and started raking in the dough. He also found a way to force Bert Checkov to write articles which persuaded antepost punters to believe they were on to a good thing. Vjoersterod chose a horse, Checkov wrote it up, Vjoersterod stopped it running, and, bingo, the deed was done."

His face was a mixture of astonishment and satisfaction. "Ty, are you sure of your facts?"

"Of course I am. If you ask me, both the bookmakers and the authorities have been dead slow on the trail."

"And how long exactly have you been on it?"

I grinned, conceding the point. I said, "I met Vjoersterod yesterday. I referred to Charlie Boston being his partner and he told me he owned Charlie Boston. Vjoersterod wanted to know where Tiddely Pom was."

He stared. "Would you—um—well, if necessary, testify to that?"

"Certainly. But it would be only my word against his. No corroboration."

"Better than anything we've had before."

"There might be a quicker way to get results, though."

"How?" he asked again.

"Find a way to shut Charlie Boston's shops, and you block off Vjoersterod's intakes. Without which there is no point in him waiting around to stop any favorites. If you can't get him convicted in the Courts, you might at least freeze him out, back to South Africa."

There was another long pause, during which he thought complicated thoughts. I waited, guessing what was in his mind. Eventually, he said it.

"How much do you want for your help?"

"An exclusive for the *Blaze*."

"As if I couldn't guess. . . ."

"It will do," I said, "if the *Blaze* can truthfully claim to have made the antepost market safe for punters to play in. No details. Just a few hints that but for the libel laws, all would and could be revealed."

"Whyever do you waste your time with that dreadful rag?" he exclaimed in exasperation.

"Good pay," I said. "It's a good paper to work for. And it suits me."

"I'll promise you one thing," he said, smiling. "If through you personally we get rid of Vjoersterod, I'll take it regularly."

From Eric Youll's bank, I went home. If the youngest Steward did his stuff, Vjoersterod's goose was on its way to the oven and would soon be cooked. He might of course one day read the *Blaze* and send someone to carve up the chef. It didn't trouble me much. I didn't believe it would happen.

Elizabeth had had Mrs. Woodward put her favorite rose-pink, white-embroidered sheets on the bed. I looked at her searchingly. Her hair had been done with particular care. Her make-up was flawless.

"You look pretty," I said tentatively.

Her expression was a mixture of relief and misery. I understood with a sudden rocking wince what had led her to such scenery painting: the increased fear that if she was bitchy I would leave her. No matter if I'd earned and deserved the rough side of her tongue; I had to be placated at all costs, to be held by the best she could do to appear attractive, to be obliquely invited, cajoled, entreated to stay.

"Did you have a good day?" Her voice sounded high and near to cracking point.

"Quite good. . . . How about a drink?"

She shook her head, but I poured her one all the same, and fixed it in the clip.

"I've asked Mrs. Woodward to find someone to come and sit with me in the evenings," she said. "So that you can go out more."

"I don't want to go out more," I protested.

"You must do."

"Well, I don't." I sat down in the armchair and took a hefty mouthful of nearly neat whiskey. At best, I thought, in an unbearable situation alcohol offered post-ponement. At worst, aggravation. And anyway it was too damned expensive, nowadays, to get drunk.

Elizabeth didn't answer. When I looked at her, I saw she was quietly crying again. The tears rolled down past her ears and into her hair. I took a tissue out of the box and dried them. Had she but known it, they were harder for me to bear than any amount of fury.

"I'm getting old," she said. "And you still look so young. You look . . . strong . . . and dark . . . and young"

"And you look pale and pretty and about fifteen. So stop fretting."

"How old is . . . that girl?"

"You said you didn't want to hear about her."

"I suppose I don't, really."

"Forget her," I said. 'She is of no importance. She means nothing to me. Nothing at all." I sounded con-vincing, even to myself. I wished it were true. In spite of the scope of her betrayal, in a weak inner recess I ached to be able to sleep with her again. I sat with the whiskey glass in my hand and thought about her on the white rug and in her own bed and in the hotel, and suffered dismally from the prospect of the arid future.

After a while I pushed myself wearily to my feet and went to fix the supper. Fish again. Mean little bits of frozen plaice. I cooked and ate them with aversion and fed Elizabeth when her wrist tired on the gadget. All evening she kept up the pathetic attempt to be nice to me, thanking me exaggeratedly for every tiny service, apologizing for needing me to do things for her which we had both for years taken for granted, trying hard to keep the anxiety, the embarrassment, and the unhappiness out of her eyes and voice, and nowhere near succeeding.

She couldn't have punished me more if she had tried.

Late that evening Tiddely Pom developed violent colic.

Norton Fox couldn't get hold of Luke-John or Derry, who had both long gone home. The *Blaze* never divulged home addresses, however urgent the inquiry. Norton didn't know my telephone number, either; didn't know anyone who did.

In a state of strong anxiety, and on his vet's advice, he rang up Victor Roncey and told him where his horse was, and what they were doing to save its life.

TWELVE

I heard about it in the morning. Roncey telephoned at ten-thirty, when I was sitting in the writing room looking vacantly at the walls and trying to drum up some preliminary gems for my column on Sunday. Mrs.

Woodward had gone out to the launderette, and Elizabeth
called me with two rings on the bell over my head: two
rings for come at once but not an emergency. Three rings
for 999. Four for panic.

Roncey had calmed down from the four ring stage
he had clearly been in the night before. He was calling,
he said, from Norton Fox's house, where he had driven
at once after being given the news. I sorted out that he
had arrived at 2 A.M. to find that the vet had got Tiddely
Pom over the worst, with the stoppage in the horse's gut
untangling into normal function. Norton Fox had given
Roncey a bed for the rest of the night, and he had just
come in from seeing Tiddely Pom walk and trot out at
morning exercise. The horse was showing surprisingly
few ill effects from his rocky experience, and it was quite
likely he would be fit enough to run in the Lamplighter
on Saturday.

I listened to his long, brisk, detailed saga with uncomfortable alarm. There were still two whole days before
the race. Now that Roncey knew where he was, Tiddely
Pom's safety was halved. When he had come to the end
of his tale, I asked him whether anyone had tried to find
out from him at home where his horse had gone.

"Of course they did," he said. "Exactly as you said.
Several other newspapers wanted to know. Most of them
telephoned. Three or four actually turned up at the farm,
and I know they asked Peter and Pat as well as me. Some
of their questions were decidedly tricky. I thought at the
time you'd been quite right, we might have let it slip
if we'd known ourselves."

"When did these people come to the farm? What did
they look like?"

"They didn't look like anything special. Just nondescript. One of them was from the *Evening Peal*, I
remember. All the inquiries were on Sunday and Monday, just after your article came out."

"No one turned up in a Rolls?" I asked.

He laughed shortly. "They did not."

"Were any of your visitors tallish, thickish, blondish,
with a faintly yellow skin and a slightly foreign accent?"

"None that I saw were like that. One or two saw only the boys, because they called while I was in Chelmsford. You could ask them, if you like."

"Maybe I will," I said. "No one tried any threats?"

"No. I told your sports editor that. No one has tried any pressure of any sort. To my mind, all your elaborate precautions have been a waste of time. And now that I know where Tiddely Pom is, you may as well tell me where my family is, too."

"I'll think about it," I said. "Would you ask Norton Fox if I could have a word with him?"

He fetched Norton, who apologized for bursting open the secrecy, but said he didn't like the responsibility of keeping quiet when the horse was so ill.

"Of course not. It can't be helped," I said. "As long as it goes no further than Roncey himself, it may not be too bad, though I'd prefer—"

"His sons know, of course," Norton interrupted. "Though I don't suppose that matters."

"What?" I said.

"Roncey told one of his sons where he was. He telephoned to him just now. He explained to me that he couldn't remember your telephone number, but he'd had it written down somewhere at home, from having rung you up before sometime. So he rang his son—Pat, I think he said—and his son found it for him. I think he, the son, asked Roncey where he was calling from, because Roncey said that as everyone had stopped inquiring about where the horse was, he didn't see any harm in his son knowing, so he told him."

"Damn it," I said. "The man's a fool."

"He might be right."

"And he might be wrong," I said bitterly. "Look, Norton, I suppose there was no question of Tiddely's colic being a misjudged case of poisoning?"

"For God's sake, Ty . . . no. It was straightforward colic. How on earth could he have been poisoned? For a start, no one knew then who he was."

"And now?" I asked. "How many of your lads know now that he is Tiddely Pom?"

There was a brief supercharged silence.

"All of them," I said flatly.

"Some of them knew Roncey by sight," he explained. "And they'd all read the *Blaze*. So they put two and two together."

One of them would soon realize he could earn a fiver by ringing up a rival newspaper. Tiddely Pom's whereabouts would be as secret as the Albert Memorial. Tiddley Pom, at the moment, was a certain nonstarter for the Lamplighter Gold Cup.

Even if Victor Roncey thought that the opposition had backed out of the project, I was certain they hadn't. In a man like Vjoersterod, pride would always conquer discretion. He wouldn't command the same respect in international criminal circles if he turned out and ran just because of a few words in the *Blaze*. He wouldn't, therefore, do it.

At the four-day declaration stage, on the Tuesday, Roncey had confirmed with Weatherbys that his horse would be a definite runner. If he now withdrew him, as he could reasonably do because of the colic, he would forfeit his entry fee, a matter of fifty pounds. If he left his horse at Norton's, still intending to run, he would forfeit a great deal more.

Because I was certain that if Tiddely Pom stayed where he was, he would be lame, blind, doped, or dead by Saturday morning.

Norton listened in silence while I outlined these facts of life.

"Ty, don't you think you are possibly exaggerating?"

"Well," I said with a mildness I didn't feel, "how many times will you need to have Brevity—or any other of your horses—taken out of the Champion Hurdle at the last moment without any explanation before you see any need to do something constructive in opposition?"

There was a short pause. "Yes," he said. "You have a point."

"If you will lend me your horse box, I'll take Tiddely Pom off somewhere else."

"Where?"

"Somewhere safe," I said noncommittally. "How about it?"

"Oh, all right." He sighed. "Anything for a quiet life."

"I'll come as soon as I can."

"I'll repel boarders until you do." The flippancy in his voice told me how little he believed in any threat to the horse. I felt a great urge to leave them to it, to let Roncey stew in his own indiscretion, to let Vjoersterod interfere with the horse and stop it running, just to prove I was right. Very childish urge indeed. It didn't last long, because in my way I was as stubborn as Vjoersterod. I wasn't going to turn and run from him, either, if I could help it.

When I put the telephone receiver back in its special cradle, Elizabeth was looking worried with a more normal form of anxiety.

"That Tiddely Pom," I said lightly, "is more trouble than a busload of eleven-year-old boys. As I expect you gathered, I'll have to go and shift him off somewhere else."

"Couldn't someone else do it?"

I shook my head. "Better be me."

Mrs. Woodward was still out. I filled in the time until her return by ringing up Luke-John and giving him the news that the best-laid plan had gone astray.

"Where are you taking the horse, then?"

"I'll let you know when I get there."

"Are you sure it's necessary—" he began.

"Are you," I interrupted, "sure the *Blaze* can afford to take any risk, after boasting about keeping the horse safe?"

"Hmm." He sighed. "Get on with it, then."

When Mrs. Woodward came back, I took the van and drove to Berkshire. With me went Elizabeth's best effort at a fond wifely farewell. She had even offered her mouth for a kiss, which she did very rarely, as mouth-to-mouth kissing interfered with her frail breathing arrangements and gave her a feeling of suffocation. She liked to kiss and be kissed on the cheek or forehead, and never too often.

I spent most of my journey worrying whether I should not after all have allowed myself to be blackmailed, whether any stand against pressure was a luxury when compared with the damage I'd done to Elizabeth's weak hold on happiness. After all the shielding, which had improved her physical condition, I'd laid into her with a bulldozer. Selfish. Just to save myself from a particularly odious form of tyranny. If she lost weight or fretted to breakdown point, it would be directly my fault; and either or both seemed possible.

A hundred and fifty guineas, plus expenses, less tax. A study in depth. *Tally* had offered me the deeps. And in I jumped.

On the outskirts of London I stopped to make a long and involved telephone call, arranging a destination and care for Tiddely Pom. Norton Fox and Victor Roncey were eating lunch when I arrived at the stables, and I found it impossible to install into either of them enough of a feeling of urgency to get them to leave their casseroled beef.

"Sit down and have some," Norton said airily.

"I want to be on my way."

They didn't approve of my impatience and proceeded to gooseberry crumble and biscuits and cheese. It was two o'clock before they agreed to amble out into the yard and see to the shifting of Tiddely Pom.

Norton had at least had his horse box made ready. It stood in the center of the yard with the ramp down. As public an exit as possible. I sighed. The horse box driver didn't like handing over to a stranger and gave me some anxious instructions about idiosyncratic gear change.

Sandy Willis led Tiddely Pom across the yard, up the ramp, and into the center stall of the three-stall box. The horse looked worse than ever, no doubt because of the colic. I couldn't see him ever winning any Lamplighter Gold Cup. Making sure he ran in it seemed a gloomy waste of time. Just as well, I reflected, that I wasn't to Tiddely Pom himself that I was committed, but to the principle that if Roncey wanted to run Tiddely Pom he should. Along the lines of "I disagree that your horse has the slightest chance, but I'll defend to the death your right to prove it."

Sandy Willis finished tying the horse into his stall and took over where the driver left off. Her instructions on how Tiddely Pom was to be managed were detailed and anxious. In her few days with the horse she had already identified herself with its well-being. As Norton had said, she was one of the best of his lads. I wished I could take her, too, but it was useless expecting Norton to let her go, when she also looked after Zig Zag.

She said, "He will be having the proper care, won't he?"

"The best," I assured her.

"Tell them not to forget his eggs and beer."

"Right."

"And he hates having his ears messed about with."

"Right."

She gave me a long searching look, a half smile, and a reluctant farewell. Victor Roncey strode briskly across to me and unburdened himself along similar lines.

"I want to insist that you tell me where you are taking him."

"He will be safe."

"Where?"

"Mr. Roncey, if you know where, he is only half as safe. We've been through all this before."

He pondered, his glance darting about restlessly, his eyes not meeting mine. "Oh, very well," he said finally, with impatience. "But it will be up to you to make sure he gets to Heathbury Park in good time on Saturday."

"The *Blaze* will arrange that," I said. "The Lamplighter is at three. Tiddely Pom will reach the racecourse stables by noon, without fail."

"I'll be there," he said. "Waiting."

I nodded. Norton joined us, and the two of them discussed this arrangement while I shut up the ramp with the help of the hovering box driver.

"What time do you get Zig Zag to Heathbury?" I asked Norton, pausing before I climbed into the cab.

"Midday," he said. "It's only thirty-two miles. He'll be setting off at about eleven."

I climbed into the driving seat and looked out of the window. The two men looked back, Roncey worried, Norton not. To Norton I said, "I'll see you this evening when I bring the horse box back." To Roncey, "Don't worry, he'll be quite safe. I'll see you on Saturday. Ring the *Blaze,* as before, if you'd like to be reassured tonight and tomorrow."

I shut the window, sorted out the eccentric gears, and drove Tiddely Pom gently out of the yard and up the land to the village. An hour later than I had intended, I thought in disgust. Another hour for Mrs. Woodward. My mind shied away from the picture of Elizabeth waiting for me to come back. Nothing would be better. Nothing would be better for a long time to come. I felt the first stirrings of resentment against Elizabeth and at least had the sense to realize that my mind was playing me a common psychological trick. The guilty couldn't stand the destruction of their self-esteem involved in having to admit they were wrong, and wriggled out of their shame by transforming it into resentment against the people who had made them feel it. I resented Elizabeth because I had wronged her. Of all the ridiculous injustices. And of all the ridiculous injustices, one of the most universal.

I maneuvered the heavy horse box carefully through the small village and set off northeastward on the road over the Downs, retracing the way I had come from London. Wide rolling hills with no trees except a few low bushes leaning sideways from the prevailing wind. No houses. A string of pylons. Black furrows in a mile of plow. A bleak early December sky, a high sheet of steel-gray cloud. Cold, dull, mood-matching landscape.

There was very little traffic on the unfenced road, which served only Norton's village and two others beyond. A blue-gray Cortina appeared on the brow of the next hill, coming toward me, traveling fast. I pulled over to give him room, and he rocked past at a stupid speed for the space available.

My attention was so involved with Elizabeth that it was several seconds before the calamity got through. With a shattering jolt the casually noticed face of the Cortina's driver kicked my memory to life. It belonged to one of Charlie Boston's boys from the train. The big one. With the brass knuckles.

December weather couldn't stop the prickly sweat that broke out on my skin. I put my foot on the accelerator and felt Tiddely Pom's weight lurch behind me from the sudden spurt. All I could hope for was that the big man had been too occupied judging the width of his car to look up and see me.

He had, of course, had a passenger.

I looked in the driving mirror. The Cortina had gone out of sight over the hill. Charlie Boston's boys hurrying toward Norton Fox's village was no wild coincidence; but Tiddely Pom's whereabouts must have been transmitted with very little delay for them to be here already, especially if they had had to come from Birmingham. Just who, I wondered grimly, had told who where Tiddely Pom was to be found? Not that it mattered much at that moment. All that mattered was to get him lost again.

I checked with the driving mirror. No Cortina. The horse box was pushing sixty-five on a road where forty would be wiser. Tiddely Pom's hoofs clattered inside his stall. He didn't like the swaying. He would have to put up with it until I got him clear of the Downs road, which was far too empty and far too visible from too many miles around.

When I next looked in the mirror, there was a pale speck on the horizon two hills behind. It might not be them, I thought. I looked again. It was them. I swore bitterly. The speedometer needle crept to sixty-eight. That was the lot. My foot was down on the floor boards. And they were gaining. Easily.

There was no town close enough to get lost in, and once on my tail they could stay there all day, waiting

to find out where I took Tiddely Pom. Even in a ca
it would have been difficult to lose them: in a lumberin
horse box impossible. Urgent appraisal of a depressin
situation came up with only a hope that Charlie Boston
boys would again be propelled by more aggression tha
sense.

They were. They came up fast behind me, leanin
on the horn. Maybe they thought I hadn't had time t
see *them* as they went past me the other way, an
wouldn't know who wanted to pass.

If they wanted to pass, they didn't want to follow
I shut my teeth. If they wanted to pass, it was now,
was here, that they meant to make certain that Tiddel
Pom didn't run in the Lamplighter. What they intende
to do about me was a matter which sent me and m
mending ribs into a tizzy. I swallowed. I didn't wan
another hammering like the last time, and this time the
might not be so careful about what they did or didn'
rupture.

I held the horse box in the center of the road so tha
there wasn't room enough for their Cortina to get by
They still went on blowing the horn. Tiddely Pom kicke
his stall. I took my foot some way off the accelerato
and slowed the proceedings down to a more manage
able forty-five. They would guess I knew who they were
I didn't see that it gave them any advantage.

A hay lorry appeared around a hill ahead with its loa
overhanging the center of the road. Instinctively I slowe
still further, and began to pull over. The Cortina's nos
showed sharply in the wing mirror, already up by m
rear axle. I swung the horse box back into the center o
the road, which raised flashing headlights from the drive
of the advancing hay lorry. When I was far too clos
to a radiator-to-radiator confrontation, he started blowin
his horn furiously as well. I swung back to my side o
the road when he was almost stationary from standin
rigidly on his brakes, and glimpsed a furious face an
a shaking fist as I swerved past. Inches to spare. Inche
were enough.

The Cortina tried to get past in the short secon

before the horse box was re-established on the crown of the road. There was a bump, this time, as I cut across its bows. It dropped back ten feet, and stayed there. It would only stay there, I thought despairingly, until Charlie Boston's boys had got what they came for.

Less than a mile ahead lay my likely Waterloo, in the shape of a crossroads. A halt sign. It was I who would have to halt. Either that or risk hitting a car speeding legitimately along the major road, risk killing some innocent motorist, or his wife, or his child. . . . Yet if I stopped, the Cortina with its faster acceleration would pass me when I moved off again, whether I turned right, as I had intended to, or left, back to London, or went straight on, to heaven knew where.

There wouldn't be anyone at the crossroads to give me any help. No police car sitting there waiting for custom. No A.A. man having a smoke. No lifesaving bystander of any sort. No troop of United States cavalry to gallop up in the nick of time.

I changed down into second to climb a steepish hill and forgot Norton's box driver's instructions. For a frightening moment the gears refused to mesh and the horse box's weight dragged it almost to a standstill. Then the cogs slid together, and with a regrettable jolt we started off again. Behind me, Charlie Boston's boys still wasted their energy and wore out their battery by almost nonstop blasts on their horn.

The horse box trundled to the top of the hill, and there already, four hundred yards down the other side, was the crossroads.

I stamped on the accelerator. The horse box leaped forward. Charlie Boston's boy had time to take in the scene below, and to realize that I must be meaning not to halt at the sign. In the wing mirror, I watched him accelerate to keep up, closing enough to stick to me whatever I did at the crossroads.

Two hundred yards before I got there, I stood on the brake pedal as if the road ended in an abyss ten yards ahead. The reaction was more than I'd bargained for. The horse box shuddered and rocked and began to spin.

It's rear slewed across the road, hit the verge, rocked again. I feared the whole high-topped structure would overturn. Instead, there was a thudding crunching anchoring crash as the Cortina bounced on and off at the rear.

The horse box screeched and slid to a juddering stop. Upright. Facing the right way.

I hauled on the hand brake and was out of the cab onto the road before the glass from the Cortina had stopped tinkling on the tarmac.

The blue-gray car had gone over onto its side and was showing its gut to the wind. It lay a good twenty yards behind the horse box, and from the dented look of the roof it had rolled completely over before stopping. I walked back toward it, wishing I had a weapon of some sort, and fighting an inclination just to drive off and leave without looking to see what had happened to the occupants.

There was only one of them in the car. The big one, the driver. Very much alive, murderously angry, and in considerable pain from having his right ankle trapped and broken among the pedals. I turned my back on him and ignored his all too audible demands for assistance. Revenge, I decided, would overcome all else if I once got within reach of his hands.

The second Boston boy had been flung out by the crash. I found him on the grass verge, unconscious and lying on his face. With anxiety I felt for his pulse; but he, too, was alive. With extreme relief I went back to the horse box, opened the side door, and climbed in to take a look at Tiddely Pom. He calmly swiveled a disapproving eye in my direction and began to evacuate his bowels.

"Nothing much wrong with you, mate," I said aloud. My voice came out squeaky with tension. I wiped my hand around my neck, tried to grin, felt both like copying Tiddely Pom's present action and being sick.

The horse really did not seem any the worse for his highly unorthodox journey. I took several deep breaths, patted his rump, and jumped down again into the road.

Inspection of the damage at the back of the horse box revealed a smashed rear light and a dent in the sturdy off-rear fender no longer than a soup plate. I hoped that Luke-John would agree to the *Blaze* paying for the repairs. Charlie Boston wouldn't want to.

His unconscious boy was beginning to stir. I watched him sit up, put his hands to his head, begin to remember what had happened. I listened to his big colleague still shouting furiously from inside the car. Then with deliberate non-haste I climbed back into the cab of the horse box, started the engine, and drove carefully away.

I had never intended to go far. I took Tiddely Pom to the safest place I could think of: the racecourse stables at Heathbury Park. There he would be surrounded by a high wall and guarded by a security patrol at night. Everyone entering racecourse stables had to show a pass; even owners were not allowed in unless accompanied by their trainers.

Willy Ondroy, consulted on the telephone, had agreed to take in Tiddely Pom, and to keep his identity a secret. The stables would in any case be open from midday and the guards would be on duty from then on; anytime after that, he said, Tiddely Pom would be just one of a number of horses arriving for the following day's racing. Horses which came from more than a hundred miles away normally traveled the day before their race and stayed overnight in the racecourse stables. A distant stable running one horse on Friday and another on Saturday would send them both down on Thursday and leave them both at the racecourse stables for two nights, or possibly even three. Tiddely Pom's two nights' stay would be unremarkable and inconspicuous. The only oddity about him was that he had no lad to look after him, an awkward detail to which Willy Ondroy had promised to find a solution.

He was looking out for me and came across the grass outside the stable block to forestall me from climbing down from the cab. Instead, he opened the door on the passenger side and joined me.

"Too many of these lads know you by sight," he said waving an arm to where two other horse boxes were unloading. "If they see you they will know you would not have brought any other horse but Tiddely Pom. And as I understand it, you don't want to land us with the security headache of a bunch of crooks trying to injure him. Right?"

"Right," I agreed thankfully.

"Drive down this road, then. First left. In through the white gateposts, fork left, park outside the read door of my house. Right?"

"Right," I said again, and followed his instructions, thankful for his quick grasp of essentials and his jet-formation pilot's clarity of decision.

"I've had a word with the racecourse manager," he said. "The stables and security are his pigeon, really. Had to enlist his aid. Hope you don't mind. He's a very sound fellow, very sound indeed. He's fixing up a lad to look after Tiddely Pom. Without telling him who the horse is, naturally."

"That's good," I said with relief.

I stopped the horse box and we both disembarked. The horse, Willy Ondroy said, could safely stay where he was until the racecourse manager came over for him. Meanwhile would I care for some tea? He looked at his watch. Three-fifty. He hesitated. Or a whiskey, he added.

"Why a whiskey?" I asked.

"I don't know. I suppose because you look as though you need it."

"You may be right," I said, dredging up a smile. He looked at me appraisingly, but how could I tell him that I'd just risked killing two men to bring Tiddely Pom safe and unfollowed to his door. That I had been ex- tremely lucky to get away with merely stopping them. That only by dishing out such violence had I avoided a second beating of proportions I couldn't contemplate. It wasn't really surprising that I looked as if I needed a whiskey. I did. It tasted fine.

THIRTEEN

Norton Fox was less than pleased when I got back.

He heard me rumble into the yard and came out of his house to meet me. It was by then full dark, but there were several external lights on, and more light flooded out of open stable doors as the lads bustled around with the evening chores. I parked, climbed stiffly down from the cab, and looked at my watch. Five-fifty. I'd spent two hours on a roundabout return journey to fool the box driver over the distance I'd taken Tiddely Pom. Heathbury Park and back was probably the driver's most beaten track: he would know the mileage to a hundred yards, recognize it instantly if he saw it on the clock, know for a certainty where the horse was, and make my entire afternoon a waste of time.

"You're in trouble, Ty," Norton said, reaching me and frowning. "What in God's name were you thinking of? First the man delivering my hay gets here in a towering rage and says my horse box drove straight at him with some maniac at the wheel and that there'd be an accident if he was any judge, and the next thing is we hear there has been an accident over by Long Barrow crossroads involving a horse box and I've had the police here making inquiries."

"Yes." I said. "I'm very sorry, Norton. Your horse box has a dent in it, and a broken rear light. I'll apologize to the hay-lorry driver. And I guess I'll have to talk to the police."

Dangerous driving. Putting it mildly. Very difficult to prove it was a case of self-preservation.

Norton looked near to explosion. "What on earth were you *doing?*"

"Playing cowboys-and-Indians," I said tiredly. "The Indians bit the dust."

He was not amused. His secretary came out to tell him he was wanted on the telephone, and I waited by the horse box until he came back, gloomily trying to remember the distinction between careless, reckless, and dangerous, and the various penalties attached. Failing to stop. Failing to report an accident. How much for those?

Norton came back less angry than he went. "That was the police," he said abruptly. "They still want to see you. However, it seems the two men involved in the crash have vanished from the casualty department in the hospital and the police have discovered that the Cortina was stolen. They are less inclined to think that the accident was your fault, in spite of what the hay-lorry driver told them."

"The men in the Cortina were after Tiddely Pom," I said flatly, "and they damn nearly got him. Maybe you could tell Victor Roncey that there is some point to our precautions, after all."

"He's gone home," he said. I began to walk across the dark stable yard to were I'd left my van, and he followed me, giving me directions about how to find the police station.

I stopped him. "I'm not going there. The police can come to me. Preferably on Monday. You tell them that."

"Why on Monday?" He looked bewildered. "Why not now?"

"Because," I spelled it out, "I can tell them roughly where to find those men in the Cortina and explain what they were up to. But I don't want the police issuing any warrants before Monday, otherwise the whole affair will be *sub judice* and I won't be able to get a squeak into the *Blaze*. After all this trouble, we've earned our story for Sunday."

"You take my breath away," he said, sounding as if I had. "And the police won't like it."

"For God's sake, don't tell them," I said in exaspera-

tion. "That was for your ears only. If and when they ask
you where I am, simply say I will be getting in touch
with them, that you don't know where I live, and that
they can reach me through the *Blaze* if they want me."

"Very well," he agreed doubtfully. "If you're sure.
But it sounds to me as though you're landing yourself
in serious trouble. I wouldn't have thought Tiddely Pom
was worth it."

"Tiddely Pom, Brevity, Polyxenes, and all the
rest—individually none of them was worth the trouble.
That's precisely why the racket goes on."

His disapproving frown lighted into a half smile.
"You'll be telling me next that the *Blaze* is more interested in justice than sensationalism."

"It says so. Often," I agreed sardonically.

"Huh," said Norton. "You can't believe everything
you read in the papers."

I drove home slowly, tired and depressed. Other times,
trouble had been a yeast lightening the daily bread. A
positive plus factor. Something I needed. But other times
trouble hadn't bitterly invaded my marriage or earned
me such a savage physical attack.

This time, although I was fairly confident that Tiddely
Pom would start in his race, the successful uncovering
and extermination of a racing scandal was bringing me
none of the usual upsurging satisfaction. This time, dust
and ashes. This time, present grief and a gray future.

I stopped on the way and rang the *Blaze*. Luke-John
had left for the day. I got him at home.

"Tiddely Pom is in the racecourse stables at Heathbury," I said. "Guarded by an ex-policeman and a large
Alsatian. The Clerk of the Course and the racecourse
manager both know who he is, but no one else does.
O.K.?"

"Very, I should think." He sounded moderately
pleased, but no more. "We can take it as certain now
that Tiddely Pom will start in the Lamplighter. It's made
a good story, Ty, but I'm afraid we exaggerated the
danger."

I disillusioned him. "Charlie Boston's boys were three miles from Norton Fox's stable by two-thirty this afternoon."

"Christ," he said. "So it's really true. . . ."

"You've looked at it so far as a stunt for the *Blaze*."

"Well. . . ."

"Well, so it is," I agreed. "Anyway, Charlie Boston's boys had a slight accident with their car, and they are now back to square one, as they don't know where I took Tiddely Pom."

"What sort of accident?"

"They ran into the back of the horse box. Careless of them. I put the brakes on rather hard, and they were following a little too close."

A shocked silence. Then he said, "Were they killed?"

"No. Hardly bent." I gave him an outline of the afternoon's events. Luke-John's reaction was typical and expected, and the enthusiasm was alive in his voice.

"Keep away from the police until Sunday."

"Sure thing."

"This is great, Ty."

"Yeah," I said.

"Knock out a preliminary version tonight and bring it in with you in the morning," he said. "Then we can discuss it tomorrow, and you can phone in the final touches from Heathbury after the Lamplighter on Saturday."

"All right."

"Oh, and give Roncey a ring, would you, and tell him the horse is only safe thanks to the *Blaze*."

"Yes," I said. "Maybe I will."

I put down the receiver and felt like leaving Roncey severely alone. I was tired and I wanted to go home. And when I got home, I thought dearly, there would be no let-off, only another dose of self-hate and remorse.

Roncey answered the telephone at the first ring and needed no telling. Norton Fox had already been through.

"Tiddely Pom is safe and well looked after," I assured him.

"I owe you an apology," he said abruptly.

"Be my guest," I said.

"Look here, there's something worrying me. Worrying me badly." He paused, swallowing a great deal of pride. "Do you—I mean, have you any idea—how those men appeared so quickly on the scene?"

"The same idea as you," I said. "Your son Pat."

"I'll break his neck," he said with real and unfatherly viciousness.

"If you've any sense, you'll let him ride your horses in all their races, not just the unimportant ones."

"What are you talking about?"

"About Pat's outsized sense of grievance. You put up anyone except him, and he resents it."

"He's not good enough," he protested.

"And how will he ever be if you don't give him the experience? Nothing teaches a jockey faster than riding a good horse in a good race."

"He might lose," he sad pugnaciously.

"He might win. When did you ever give him the chance?"

"But to give away the secret of Tiddely Pom's whereabouts. . . . What would he expect to gain?"

"He was getting his own back, that's all."

"*All!*"

"There's no harm done."

"I hate him."

"Then send him to another stable. Give him an allowance to live on and let him see if he's going to ride well enough to turn professional. That's what he wants. If you stamp on people's ambitions too hard, it's not frantically astonishing if they bite back."

"It's a son's duty to work for his father. Especially a farmer's son."

I sighed. He was half a century out of date, and no amount of telling from me was going to change him. I said I'd see him on Sunday, and disconnected.

Like his father, I took no pleasure at all in Pat Roncey's vengeful disloyalty. Understood, maybe. Admired, far from it.

One of the men who came to inquire at Roncey's farm must have sensed Pat's obvious disgruntlement and have given him a telephone number to ring if he ever found out where Tiddely Pom had gone, and wanted to revenge himself on his father. One might give Pat the benefit of enough doubt to suppose that he'd thought he was only telling a newspaperman from one of *Blaze*'s rivals; but even so he must have known that a rival paper would spread the information to every corner of the country. To the ears which waited to hear. Exactly the same in the end. But because of the speed with which Charlie Boston's boys had reached Norton Fox's village, it must have been Raincoat or the chauffeur, or even Vjoersterod himself who had talked to Pat at the farm.

It had to be Pat. Norton Fox's stable lads might have passed the word on to the newspapers, but they couldn't have told Vjoersterod or Charlie Boston because they didn't know they wanted to know, and probably didn't even know they existed.

I drove on, back to London. Parked the van in the garage downstairs. Locked up. Walked slowly and unenthusiastically up to the flat.

"Hi," said Elizabeth brightly.

"Hi yourself." I kissed her cheek.

It must have looked, to Mrs. Woodward, a normal greeting. Only the pain we could read in each other's eyes said it wasn't.

Mrs. Woodward put on her dark blue coat and checked the time again to make sure it was ten to, not ten after. She'd had three hours extra, but wanted more. I wondered fleetingly if I could charge her overtime to the *Blaze*.

"We've had our meal," Mrs. Woodward said. "I've left yours ready to warm up. Just pop it in the oven, Mr. Tyrone."

"Thanks."

"Night, then, luv," she called to Elizabeth.

"Night."

I opened the door for her and she nodded briskly,

smiled, and said she'd be there on the dot in the morning.
I thanked her appreciatively. She would indeed be there
on the dot. Kind, reliable, necessary Mrs. Woodward.
I hoped the *Tally* check wouldn't be too long coming.

Beyond that first greeting Elizabeth and I could find
little to say to each other. The most ordinary inquiries
and remarks seemed horribly brittle, like a thin sheet
of glass over a pit.

It was a relief to both of us when the doorbell rang.

"Mrs. Woodward must have forgotten something,"
I said. It was barely ten minutes since she had left.

"I expect so." Elizabeth agreed.

I opened the door without a speck of intuition. It
swung inward with a rush, weighted and pushed by a
heavy man in black. He stabbed a solid leather-gloved
fist into my diaphragm and, when my head came forward,
chopped down with something hard on the back of my
neck.

On my knees, coughing for breath, I watched
Vjoersterod appear in the doorway, take in the scene,
and walk past me into the room. A black-booted foot
kicked the door shut behind him. There was a soft
whistling swish in the air and another terrible thump high
up between my shoulder blades. Elizabeth cried out. I
staggered to my feet and tried to move in her direction.
The heavy man in black—Ross, the chauffeur—slid his
arm under mine and twisted and locked my shoulder.

"Sit down, Mr. Tyrone," Vjoersterod said calmly.
"Sit there." He pointed to the tapestry-covered stool
Mrs. Woodward liked to knit on, as there were no arms
or back to get in the way of her busy elbows.

"Ty!" Elizabeth's voice rose high with fear. "What's
happening?"

I didn't answer. I felt stupid and sunk. I sat on the
stool when Ross released my arm, and tried to work some
control into the way I looked at Vjoersterod.

He was standing near Elizabeth's head, watching me
with swelling satisfaction.

"So now we know just where we are, Mr. Tyrone.

Did you really have the conceit to think you could defy
me and get away with it? No one does, Mr. Tyrone.
No one ever does."

I didn't answer. Ross stood beside me, a pace to the
rear. In his right hand he gently swung the thing he had
hit me with, a short elongated pear-shaped truncheon.
It's weight and crushing power made a joke of Charlie
Boston's boys' knuckle-dusters. I refrained from rubbing
the aching places below my neck.

"Mr. Tyrone," Vjoersterod said conversationally,
"where is Tiddely Pom?"

When I still didn't answer immediately, he half turned,
looked down, and carefully put the toe of his shoe under
the switch of the electric outlet. From there the cable
led directly to Elizabeth's breathing pump. Elizabeth
turned her head to follow my eyes and saw what he was
doing.

"No!" she said. It was high-pitched, terrified.
Vjoersterod smiled.

"Tiddely Pom?" he said to me.

"He's in the racecourse stables at Heathbury Park."

"Ah." He took his foot away, put it down on the floor.
"You see how simple it is? It's always a matter of finding
the right lever. Of applying the right pressure. No horse,
I find, is ever worth a really serious danger to a loved
one.

I said nothing. He was right.

"Check it," Ross said from behind me.

Vjoersterod's eyes narrowed. "He couldn't risk a
lie."

"He wouldn't be blackmailed. He was out to get you,
and no messing. Check it." There was advice in Ross's
manner, not authority. More than a chauffeur. Less than
an equal.

Vjoersterod shrugged but stretched out a hand and
picked up the receiver. Telephone inquiries. Heathbury
Park racecourse. The Clerk of the Course's house? That
would do very well.

Willy Ondroy himself answered. Vjoersterod said, "Mr.

Tyrone asked me to call you to check if Tiddely Pom had settled in well. . . ."

He listened to the reply impassively, his pale yellow face immobile. It accounted for the fact, I thought inconsequentially, that his skin was unlined. He never smiled, seldom frowned. The only wrinkles were around his eyes, which I suppose he screwed up against his native sun.

"Thank you so much," he said. His best Foreign Office voice, courteous and charming.

"Ask him which box the horse is in," Ross said. "The number."

Vjoersterod asked. Willy Ondroy told him.

"Sixty-eight. Thank you. Good night."

He put the receiver carefully back in its cradle and let a small silence lengthen. I hoped that since he had got what he came for he would decently go away again. Not a very big hope to start with, and one which never got off the ground.

He said, studying his fingernails, "It is satisfactory, Mr. Tyrone, that you do at least see the need to cooperate with me." Another pause. "However, in your case I would be foolish to think that this state of affairs would last very long if I did nothing to convince you that it must."

I looked at Elizabeth. She didn't seem to have followed Vjoersterod's rather involved syntax. Her head lay in a relaxed way on the pillow and her eyes were shut. She was relieved that I had told where the horse was; she thought that everything was now all right.

Vjoersterod followed my glance and my thought. He nodded. "We have many polio victims on respirators in my country. I understand about them. About the importance of electricity. The importance of constant attendance. The razor edge between life and death. I understand it well."

I said nothing. He said, "Many men desert wives like this. Since you do not, you would care if harm came to her. Am I right? You have, in fact, just this minute proved it, have you not? You wasted so little time in telling me correctly what I wanted to know."

I made no comment. He waited a fraction, then went smoothly on. What he said, as Dembley found out, was macabrely at variance with the way he said it.

"I have an international reputation to maintain. I simply cannot afford to have pip-squeak journalists interfering with my enterprises and trying to hold me up to ridicule. I intend to make it clear to you once and for all, to impress upon you indelibly, that I am not a man to be crossed."

Ross moved a pace at my side. My skin crawled. I made as good a job as I could of matching Vjoersterod's immobility of expression.

Vjoersterod had more to say. As far as I was concerned, he could go on all night. The alternative hardly beckoned.

"Charlie Boston reports to me that you have put both his men out of action. He, too, cannot afford such affronts to his reputation. Since all you learned from his warning attentions on the train was to strike back, we will see if my chauffeur can do any better."

I tucked one foot under the stool, pivoted on it, and on the way to my feet struck at Ross with both hands, one to the stomach, one to the groin. He bent over, taken by surprise, and I wrenched the small truncheon out of his hand, raising it to clip him on the head.

"Ty!" Elizabeth's voice rose in an agonized wail. I swung around with the truncheon in my hand and met Vjoersterod's fiercely implacable gaze.

"Drop it."

He had his toe under the switch. Three yards between us.

I hesitated, boiling with fury, wanting above anything to hit him, knock him out, get rid of him—out of my life and most particularly out of the next hour of it. I couldn't risk it. One tiny jerk would cut off the current. I couldn't risk not being able to reach the switch again in time, not with Vjoersterod in front of it and Ross behind me. Under the weight of the Spiroshell she would suffocate almost immediately. If I resisted any more, I could kill her. He might really do it. Let her die. Leave me to explain her death and maybe even be accused of slaughtering her myself. The unwanted-wife bit. . . . He didn't know I knew his name or anything about him. He would think he could kill Elizabeth with reasonable safety. I simply couldn't risk it.

I put my arm down slowly and dropped the truncheon on the carpet. Ross, breathing heavily, bent and picked it up.

"Sit down, Mr. Tyrone," Vjoersterod said. "And stay sitting down. Don't get up again. Do I make myself clear?"

He still had his toe under the switch. I sat down, seething inside, rigid outside, and totally apprehensive. Twice in a fortnight was definitely too much.

Vjoersterod nodded to Ross, who hit me solidly with the truncheon on the back of the shoulder. It sounded horrible. Felt worse.

Elizabeth cried out. Vjoersterod looked at her without pity and told Ross to switch on the television. They both waited while the set warmed up. Ross adjusted the volume to medium loud and changed the channel from a news magazine to song and dance. No neighbors, unfortunately, would call to complain about the noise. The only ones who lived near enough were out working in a night club.

Ross had another go with his truncheon. Instinctively I started to stand up, to retaliate, to escape, heaven knows what.

"Sit down," Vjoersterod said.

I looked at his toe. I sat down. Ross swung his arm and that time I fell forward off the stool onto my knees.

"Sit," Vjoersterod said. Stiffly I returned to where he said.

"Don't," Elizabeth said to him in a wavering voice. "Please don't."

I looked at her, met her eyes. She was terrified. Scared to death. And something else. Beseeching. Begging me. With a flash of blinding understanding I realized she was afraid I wouldn't take any more, that I wouldn't think she was worth it, that I would somehow stop them hurting me even if it meant switching off her pump. Vjoersterod knew I wouldn't. It was ironic, I thought mordantly, that Vjoersterod knew me better than my own wife.

It didn't last a great deal longer. It had anyway reached the stage where I no longer felt each blow separately but rather as a crushing addition to an intolerable whole. It seemed as though I had the whole weight of the world across my shoulders. Atlas wasn't even in the race.

I didn't see Vjoersterod tell Ross to stop. I had the heels of my hands against my mouth and my fingertips in my hair. Some nit on the television was advising everyone to keep their sunny side up. Ross cut him off abruptly in mid-note.

"Oh God," Elizabeth said. "Oh God."

Vjoersterod's smooth voice dryly comforted her. "My dear Mrs. Tyrone, I assure you that my chauffeur knows how to be a great deal more unpleasant than that. He has, I hope you realize, left your husband his dignity."

"Dignity," Elizabeth said faintly.

"Quite so. My chauffeur used to work in the prison service in the country I come from. He knows about humiliation. It would not have been suitable, however, to apply certain of his techniques to your husband."

"Russia?" she asked. "Do you come from Russia?"

He didn't answer her. He spoke to me.

"Mr. Tyrone, should you try to cross me again, I would allow my chauffeur to do anything he liked. Anything at all. Do you understand?"

I was silent. He repeated peremptorily, "Do you understand?"

I nodded my head.

"Good, that's a start. But only a start. You will also do something more positive. You will work for me. You will write for me in your newspaper. Whatever I tell you to write, you will write."

I detached my hands slowly from my face and rested my wrists on my knees.

"I can't," I said dully.

"I think you will find that you can. In fact you will. You must. And neither will you contemplate resigning from your paper." He touched the electric switch with his brown polished toecap. "You cannot guard your wife adequately every minute for the rest of her life."

"Very well," I said slowly. "I will write what you say."

"Ah."

Poor old Bert Checkov, I thought drearily. Seven floors down to the pavement. Only I couldn't insure myself for enough to compensate Elizabeth for having to live forever in a hospital.

"You can start this week," Vjoersterod said. "You can say on Sunday that what you have written for the last two weeks turns out to have no foundation in fact. You will restore the situation to what it was before you started interfering."

"Very well."

I put my right hand tentatively over my left shoulder. Vjoersterod watched me and nodded.

"You'll remember that," he said judiciously. "Perhaps you will feel better if I assure you that many who have crossed me are now dead. You are more useful to me alive. As long as you write what I say, your wife will be safe and my chauffeur will not need to attend to you."

His chauffeur, did he but know it, had proved to be a pale shadow of the Boston boys. For all my fears, it now seemed to me that the knuckle-dusters had been worse. The chauffeur's work was a bore, a present burden, yet not as crippling as before. No broken ribs. No all-over weakness. This time I would be able to move.

Elizabeth was close to tears. "How can you?" she said. "How can you be so . . . so . . . beastly?"

Vjoersterod remained unruffled. "I am surprised you care so much for your husband after his behavior with that colored girl."

She bit her lip and rolled her head away from him

on the pillow. He stared at me calmly. "So you told her."

There was no point in saying anything. If I'd told him where Tiddely Pom had been on Tuesday, when he first tried to make me, I would have saved myself a lot of pain and trouble. I would have saved Elizabeth from knowing about Gail. I would have spared her all this fear. Some of Bert Checkov's famous last words floated up from the past: "It's the ones who don't know when to give in who get the worst clobbering . . . in the ring, I mean. . . ."

I swallowed. The ache from my shoulders was spreading down my back. I was dead tired of sitting on that stool. Mrs. Woodward could keep it, I thought. I wouldn't want it in the flat any more.

Vjoersterod said to Ross, "Pour him a drink."

Ross went over to where the whiskey bottle stood on its tray with two glasses and the Malvern water. The bottle was nearly half full. He unscrewed the cap, picked up one of the tumblers, and emptied into it all the whiskey. It was filled to the brim.

Vjoersterod nodded. "Drink it."

Ross gave me the glass. I stared at it.

"Go on," Vjoersterod said. "Drink it."

I took a breath to protest. He moved his toe toward the switch. I put the glass to my lips and took a mouthful. Jump through hoops when the man said.

"All of it," he said. "Quickly."

I had eaten little or nothing in the last twenty-four hours. Though I had a natural tolerance, a tumblerful of alcohol on an empty stomach was not my idea of fun. I had no choice. Loathing Vjoersterod, I drank it all.

"He seems to have learned his lesson," Ross said.

FOURTEEN

They stood in silence for nearly fifteen minutes, watching me. Then Vjoersterod said, "Stand up."

I stood.

"Turn round in a circle."

I turned. Lurched. Staggered. Swayed on my feet.

Vjoersterod nodded in satisfaction. "That's all, Mr. Tyrone. All for today. I expect to be pleased by what you write in the paper on Sunday. I had better be pleased."

I nodded. A mistake. My head swam violently. I overbalanced slightly. The whiskey was being absorbed into my bloodstream at a disastrous rate.

Vjoersterod and Ross let themselves out unhurriedly and without another word. As soon as the door closed behind them, I turned and made tracks for the kitchen. Behind me Elizabeth's voice called in a question, but I had no time to waste and explain. I pulled the tin of salt from the shelf, poured two inches of it into a tumbler, and splashed in an equal amount of water.

Stirred it with my fingers. No time for a spoon. Seconds counted. Drank the mixture. It tasted like the Seven Seas rolled into one. Scorched my throat. An effort to get more than one mouthful down. I was gagging over the stuff even before it did its work and came up again, bringing with it whatever of the whiskey hadn't gone straight through my stomach wall.

I leaned over the sink, retching and wretched. I had lurched for Vjoersterod more than was strictly necessary, but the alcohol had in fact taken as strong and fast a hold as I had feared it would. I could feel its effects rising in my brain, disorganizing coordination, distorting thought. No possible antidote except time.

169

Time. Fifteen minutes, maybe, since I had taken the stuff. In ten minutes more, perhaps twenty, I would be thoroughly drunk.

I didn't know whether Vjoersterod had made me drink for any special purpose or just from bloody-mindedness. I did know that it was a horrible complication to what I had planned to do.

I rinsed my mouth out with clean water and straightened up. Groaned as the heavy yoke of bruises across my shoulders reminded me I had other troubles besides drink. Went back to Elizabeth concentrating on not knocking into the walls and doors, and picked up the telephone.

A blank. Couldn't remember the number.

Think.

Out it came. Willy Ondroy answered.

"Willy," I said. "Move that horse out of box sixty-eight. That was the opposition you were talking to earlier. Put on all the guards you can, and move the horse to another box. Stake out sixty-eight and see if you can catch any would-be nobblers in the act."

"Ty! Will do."

"Can't stop, Willy. Sorry about this."

"Don't worry. We'll see no one reaches him. I think like you, that it's essential he should be kept safe until the race."

"They may be determined."

"So am I."

I put the receiver back in its cradle with his reassurance shoring me up, and met Elizabeth's horrified gaze.

"Ty," she said faintly, "what are you doing?"

I sat down for a moment on the arm of the chair. I felt terrible. Battered, sick, and drunk.

I said, "Listen, honey. Listen well. I can't say it twice. I can't put things back to where they were before I wrote the articles."

"You told them you would," she interrupted in bewilderment.

"I know I did. I had to. But I can't. I've told the

Stewards about him. I can't go back on that. In fact I won't. He's utter poison, and he's got to be stopped."

"Let someone else do it."

"That's the classic path to oppression."

"But why you?" A protesting wail, but a serious question.

"I don't know. . . . Someone has to."

"But you gave it to him. . . . You let him . . ." She looked at me with wide appalled eyes, struck by sudden realization. "He'll come back."

"Yes. When he finds out that Tiddely Pom has changed boxes and the whole stable is bristling with guards, he'll guess I warned them, and he'll come back. So I'm moving you out of here. Away. At once."

"You don't mean now?"

"I do indeed."

"But, Ty . . . all that whiskey. . . . Wouldn't it be better to leave it until the morning?"

I shook my head. The room began spinning. I held on to the chair and waited for it to stop. In the morning I would be sore and ill, much worse than at that moment; and the morning might be too late anyway. Heathbury and back would take less than three hours in a Rolls.

"Ring up Sue Davis and see if Ron can come along to help. I'm going downstairs to get the van out. O.K.?"

"I don't want to go."

I understood her reluctance. She had so little grasp on life that even a long-planned daytime move left her worried and insecure. This sudden bustle into the night seemed the dangerous course to her, and staying in a familiar warm home the safe one. Whereas they were the other way around.

"We must," I said. "We absolutely must."

I stood up carefully and concentrated on walking a straight path to the door. Made it with considerable success. Down the stairs. Opened the garage doors, started the van, and backed it out into the mews. A new set of batteries for Elizabeth's pump was in the garage. I lifted them into the van and put them in place. Waves of giddiness swept through me every time I bent my head down. I began to lose hope that I could retain any control of my brain at all. Too much whiskey sloshing about in it. Too much altogether.

I went upstairs again. Elizabeth had the receiver to her ear and her eyes were worried.

"There isn't any reply. Sue and Ron must be out."

I swore inwardly. Even at the best of times it was difficult to manage the transfer to the van on my own. This was far from the best of times.

I took the receiver out of the cradle, disconnected the Davis's vainly ringing number, and dialed that of Antonio Perelli. To my bottomless relief, he answered.

"Tonio, will you call the nursing home and tell them I'm bringing Elizabeth over?"

"Do you mean now, tonight?"

"Almost at once, yes."

"Bronchial infection?" He sounded brisk, preparing to be reassuring, acknowledging the urgency.

"No. She's well. It's a different sort of danger. I'll tell you later. Look—could you possibly down tools and come over here and help me with her?"

"I can't just now, Ty. Not if she isn't ill."

"But life and death, all the same," I said with desperate flippancy.

"I really can't, Ty. I'm expecting another patient."

"Oh. Well, just ring the nursing home, huh?"

"Sure," he said. "And—er—bring Elizabeth here on the way. Would you do that? It isn't much of a detour. I'd like just to be sure she's in good shape. I'll leave my patient for a few minutes, and just say hello to her in the van. All right?"

"All right," I said. "Thanks, Tonio."

"I'm sorry. . . ."

"Don't give it a thought," I said. "Be seeing you."

The room whirled when I put the receiver down. I held on to the bedstead to steady myself, and looked at my watch. Couldn't focus on the dial. The figures were just a blur. I made myself see. Concentrated hard. The numbers and the hands came back sharp and clear. Ten-thirty-seven. As if it mattered.

Three more trips to make up and down the stairs. Correction: five. Better start, or I'd never finish. I took the pillows and blankets off my bed, folded them as I would need them in the van, and took them down. When I'd made up the stretcher bed ready for Elizabeth, I felt an overpowering urge to lie down on it myself and go to sleep. Dragged myself back to the stairs instead.

Ridiculous, I thought. Ridiculous to try to do anything in the state I was in. Best to unscramble the eggs and go to bed. Wait till morning. Go to sleep. Sleep.

If I went to sleep, I would sleep for hours. Sleep away our margin of safety. Put it into the red time-expired section. Cost us too much.

I shook myself out of it. If I walked carefully, I could stop the world spinning around me. If I thought slowly, I could still think. There was a block now somewhere between my brain and my tongue, but if the words themselves came out slurred and wrong, I still knew with moderate clarity what I had intended them to be.

"Honey," I said to Elizabeth. "I'm going to take the pump down first. Then you and the Shiro—Spiro."

"You're drunk," she said miserably.

"Not surprising," I said. "Now, listen, love. You'll have to breathe on your own. Four minutes. You know you can do it eash—easily." She did four minutes every day, while Mrs. Woodward gave her a bed bath.

"Ty, if you drop the pump—"

"I won't," I said. "I won't . . . drop . . . the pump."

The pump was the only one we had. There was no replacement. Always we lived in the shadow of the threat that one day its simple mechanism would break down. Spares were almost impossible to find, because respirators were an uneconomical item to the manufacturers, and they had discontinued making them. If the pump needed servicing, Mrs. Woodward and I worked the bellows by hand while it was being done in the flat. Tiring for an hour. Impossible for a lifetime. If I dropped the pump and punctured the bellows, Elizabeth's future could be precisely measured.

Four minutes.

"We'd better," I said, considering, "pack some things for you first. Clean nightdress, f'rinstance."

"How long . . . how long will we be going for?" She was trying hard to keep the fear out of her voice, to treat our flight on a rational sensible basis. I admired her, understood her effort, liked her for it, loved her, had to make and keep her safe. . . . And I'd never do it, I thought, if I let my mind dribble on in that silly way.

How long? I didn't know how long. Until Vjoersterod had been jailed or deported. Even then, it would be safer to find another flat.

"A few days," I said.

I fetched a suitcase and tried to concentrate on what she needed. She began to tell me, item by item, realizing I couldn't think.

"Washing things. Hairbrush. Make-up. Bedsocks. Hot-water bottle. Cardigans. Pills. . . ." She looked with longing at the Possum machine and all the gadgets.

"I'll come soon—come back soon for those," I promised. With company, just in case.

"You'll need some things yourself," she said.

"Hmm?" I squinted at her. "Yeah."

I fetched toothbrush, comb, electric razor. I would sleep in the van, dressed, on the stretcher bed. Better take a clean shirt. And a sweater. Beyond that, I couldn't be bothered. Shoved them into a grip. Packing done.

"Could you leave a note for Mrs. Woodward?" she asked. "She'll be so worried if we aren't here in the morning."

A note for Mrs. Woodward. Found some paper. Ball-point pen in my pocket. Note for Mrs. Woodward. "Gone away for few days. Will write to you." Didn't think she would be much less worried when she read that, but didn't know what else to put. The writing straggled upward, as drunk as I felt.

"All set," I said.

The packing had postponed the moment we were both

afraid of. I looked at the pump. Its works were encased in a metal cabinet about the size of a bedside table, with a handle at each side for carrying. Like any large heavy box, it was easy enough for two to manage, but difficult for one. I'd done it often enough before, but not with a whirling head and throbbing bruises. I made a practice shot at picking it up, just to find out.

I found out.

Elizabeth said weakly, "Ty . . . you can't do it."

"Oh, yes, I can."

"Not after. . . . I mean, it's hurting you."

"The best thing about being drunk," I said carefully, "is that what you feel you don't feel, and even if you feel it you don't care."

"What did you say?"

"Live now, hurt later."

I pulled back her sheets and my fingers fumbled on the buckle which unfastened the Spiroshell. That wouldn't do, I thought clearly. If I fumbled the buckle, I'd never have a chance of doing the transfer in four minutes. I paused, fighting the chaos in my head. Sometimes in my youth I'd played a game against alcohol, treating it like an opponent, drinking too much of it and then daring it to defeat me. I knew from experience that if one concentrated hard enough it was possible to carry out quite adequately the familiar jobs one did when sober. This time it was no game. This time for real.

I started again on the buckle, sharpening every faculty into that one simple task. It came undone easily. I lifted the Spiroshell off her chest and laid it over her knees, where it hissed and sucked at the blankets.

Switched off the electricity. Unplugged the lead. Wound it into the lugs provided. Disconnected the flexible tube which led to the Spiroshell.

Committed now. I tugged the pump across the floor pulling it on its rocky old casters. Opened the door. Crossed the small landing. The stairs stretched downward. I put my hand on the wall to steady myself and turned around to go down backward.

Step by step. One foot down. Lift the pump down one step. Balance it. One foot down. Lift the pump. Balance. . . .

Normally, if Ron or Sue or Mrs. Woodward was not there to help, I simply carried it straight down. This time if I did that, I would fall. I leaned against the wall. One foot down. Lift the pump down. Balance it. . . . It overhung the steps. Only its back two casters were on the ground, the others out in space. If it fell forward, it would knock me down the stairs with it. . . .

Hurry. Four minutes. Halfway down it seemed to me with an uprush of panic that the four minutes had already gone by. That I would be still on the stairs when Elizabeth died. That I would never, never get it to the bottom unless I fell down there in a tangled heap.

Step by deliberate step, concentrating acutely on every movement, I reached the ground below. Lugged the pump across the small hall, lifted it over the threshold onto the street. Rolled it to the van.

The worst bit. The floor of the van was a foot off the ground. I climbed in, stretched down, grasped the handles, and tugged. I felt as if I'd been torn apart, like the old Chinese torture of the two trees. The pump came up, in through the door, onto the floor of the van. The world whirled violently around my head. I tripped over the end of the stretcher and fell backward still holding the pump by one handle. It rocked over, crashed on its side, broke the glass over the gauge which showed the pressures and respirations per minute.

Gasping, feeling I was clamped into a hopeless nightmare, I bent over the pump and lifted it upright. Shoved it into its place. Fastened the straps which held it. Pushed the little wedges under its wheels. Plugged in the leads to and from the batteries. Couldn't believe I had managed it all, and wasted several seconds checking through again.

If it didn't work . . . If some of the broken glass was inside . . . If it rubbed a hole in its bellows . . . I couldn't think straight, didn't know what to do about it, hoped it would be all right.

Up the stairs. Easy without the pump. Stumbled over half the steps, reached the landing on my knees.

Elizabeth was very frightened, her eyes wide and dark, looking at death because I was drunk. When she had to do her own breathing, she had no energy or air left for talking, but this time she managed one desperate word.

"Hurry."

I remembered not to nod. Picked her up, one arm under her knees, one arm around her shoulders, pulling her toward me so that she could rest her head against my shoulder. As one carries a baby.

She was feather light, but not light enough. She looked at my face and did my moaning for me.

"Hush," I said. "Just breathe."

I went down the stairs leaning against the wall, one step at a time, refusing to fall. Old man alcohol was losing the game.

The step up into the van was awful. More trees. I laid her carefully on the stretcher, putting her limp limbs straight.

Only the Spiroshell now. Went back for it, up the stairs. Like going up a down escalator, never ending, moving where it should have been still. Picked up the Spiroshell. The easiest burden. Very nearly came to grief down the stairs through tripping over the long concertina connecting tube. Stumbled into the van and thrust it much too heavily onto Elizabeth's knees.

She was beginning to labor, the tendons in her neck standing out like strings under her effort to get air.

I couldn't get the tube to screw into its connection in the pump. Cursed, sweated, almost wept. Took a deep breath, choked down the panic, tried again. The tricky two-way nut caught and slipped into a crossed thread, caught properly at last, fastened down firmly. I pressed the battery switch on the pump. The moment of truth.

The bellows nonchalantly swelled and thudded. Elizabeth gave the smallest sound of inexpressible relief. I lifted the Spiroshell gently onto her chest, slipped the strap underneath her, and couldn't do up the buckle because my fingers were finally trembling too much to control. I just knelt there holding the ends tight so that the Spiroshell was close enough for its vacuum to work. It pulled her chest safely up and down, up and down, filling her lungs with air. Some of the agonized apprehension drained out of her face, and some fragile color came back.

Sixteen life-giving breaths later I tried again with the buckle. Fixed it after two more attempts. Sat back on the floor of the van, rested my elbows on my bent knees, and my head on my hands. Shut my eyes. Everything spun in a roaring black whirl. At least, I thought despairingly, at least I had to be nearly as drunk as I was going to get. Which, thanks to having got some of the stuff up, might not now be passing-out drunk.

Elizabeth said with effortful calm, "Ty, you aren't fit to drive."

"Never know what you can do till you try."

"Wait a little while. Wait till you're better."

"Won't be better for hours." My tongue slipped on the words, fuzzy and thick. It sounded terrible. I opened my eyes, focused carefully on the floor in front of me. The swimming gyrations in my head gradually slowed down to manageable proportions. Thought about the things I still had to do.

"Got to get the shoot—suitcases."

"Wait, Ty. Wait a while."

She didn't understand that waiting would do no good. If I didn't keep moving, I would go to sleep. Even while I thought it, I could feel the insidious languor tempting me to do just that. Sleep. Sleep deadly sleep.

I climbed out of the van, stood holding on to it, waiting for some sort of balance to come back.

"Won't be long," I said. Couldn't afford to be long. She couldn't be left alone. In case.

Coordination had again deteriorated. The stairs proved worse than ever. I kept lifting my feet up far higher than was necessary, and half missing the step when I put them down. Stumbled upward, banging into the walls. In the flat, propped up the note for Mrs. Woodward so she couldn't miss it. Tucked Elizabeth's hot-water bottle under my arm, carried the suitcases to the door, switched off the light, let myself out. Started down the stairs, and dropped the lot. It solved the problem of carrying them, anyway. To prevent myself following them, I finished the journey sitting down, lowering myself from step to step.

I picked up the hot-water bottle and took it out to Elizabeth.

"I thought . . . Did you fall?" She was acutely anxious.

"Dropped the cases." I felt an insane urge to giggle. " 'S all right." Dropped the cases, but not the pump, not Elizabeth. Old man alcohol could stuff it.

I fetched the bags and put them on the floor of the van. Shut the doors. Swayed around to the front and climbed into the driving seat. Sat there trying very hard to be sober. A losing battle, but not yet lost.

I looked at Elizabeth. Her head was relaxed on the pillows, her eyes shut. She'd reached the stage, I supposed, when constant fear was too much of a burden and it was almost a relief to give up hope and surrender to disaster. She'd surrendered for nothing, if I could help it.

Eyes front. Method needed. Do things by numbers, slowly. Switched off the light inside the van. Suddenly very dark. Switched it on again. Not a good start. Start again.

Switched on the side lights. Much better. Switch on ignition. Check fuel. Pretty low after the run to Berkshire, but enough for five miles. Pull out the choke. Start engine. Turn out light inside van.

Without conscious thought I found the gear and let out the clutch. The van rolled forward up the mews.

Simple.

Stopped at the entrance, very carefully indeed. No one walking down the pavement, stepping out in front of me. Turned my head left and right, looking for traffic.

All the lights in the road swayed and dipped. I couldn't see anything coming. Took my foot off the clutch. Turned out into the road. Gently accelerated. All clear so far.

Part of my mind was stone cold. In that area, I was sharply aware that to drive too slowly was as obvious a giveaway as meandering all over the road. To drive too fast meant no margin for a sudden stop. My reaction times were a laugh. Hitting someone wouldn't be.

As long as I kept my head still and my eyes front, it wasn't impossible. I concentrated fiercely on seeing pedestrian crossings, stationary cars, traffic lights. Seeing them in time to do something about them. I seemed to be looking down a small cone of clarity: everything in my peripheral vision was a shimmering blur.

I stopped without a jerk at some red lights. Fine. Marvelous. They changed to green. A sudden hollow void in my stomach. I couldn't remember the way. Knew it well, really. The man in the car behind began flashing his headlights. Thought of the old joke. . . . What's the definition of a split second? The interval between the lights going green and the man behind hooting or flashing. Couldn't afford to sit there doing nothing. Let in the clutch and went straight on, realizing that if I strayed off course and got lost I would be sunk. The small print on my maps was for other times. Couldn't ask anyone the way; they might turn me over to the police. Breathalizers, and all that. I'd turn the crystals black.

Ten yards over the crossing I remembered the way to Welbeck Street. I hadn't gone wrong. A vote of thanks to the unconscious mind. Hip, hip, hooray. For God's sake, mind that taxi. Making U turns in front of drunken drivers ought to be banned. . . .

Too much traffic altogether. Cars swimming out of side roads like shiny half-seen fish with yellow eyes. Cars with orange rear-direction blinkers as blinding as the sun. Buses charging across to the curb and pulling up in six feet at the stops. People running where they shouldn't cross, saving the seconds and risking the years.

Fight them all. Defeat the inefficiency of crashing. Stamp on the enemy in the blood, beat the drug confus-

ng the brain. . . . Stop the world spinning, hold tight to
a straight and steady twenty miles an hour through an
imaginary earthquake. Keep death off the roads. Arrive
alive. Fasten your safety belts. London welcomes careful
drivers. . . .

I wouldn't like to do it again. Apart from the sheer
physical exertion involved in keeping control of my arms
and legs, there was also a surging recklessness trying to
conquer every care I took. An inner voice saying, "Spin
the wheel largely; go on, you can straighten out fine
round the bend," and an answer flicker saying faintly,
"Careful, careful, careful, careful. . . ."

Caution won. Mainly, I imagine, through distaste at
what would happen to me if I were caught. Only pulling
up safely at the other end could possibly justify what was
to all intents a crime. I knew that, and clung to it.

Welbeck Street had receded since I went there last.

FIFTEEN

Tonio must have been looking out for us, because he
opened the front door and came out onto the pavement
before I had climbed out of the van. True, I had been
a long time climbing out of the van. The waves of defeated intoxication had swept in as soon as I'd put on
the brakes. Not defeated after all. Just postponed.

I finally made it onto the road, put one foot in front of
the other around the front of the van, and leaned against
the near-side fender.

Tonio peered at me with absolute incredulity.

"You're drunk."

"You're so right."

"Elizabeth . . ." he said anxiously.

I nodded my head toward the van and wished I

hadn't. Hung on to the wing mirror. Still liable for drunk in charge, even on his pavement.

"Ty," he said, "for God's sake, man. Pull yourself together."

"You try," I said. "I can't."

He gave me a withering look and went around to the back of the van to open the doors. I heard him inside, talking to Elizabeth. Tried hard not to slither down the fender and fold up into the gutter. Remotely watched a man in a raincoat get out of a taxi away down the street and cross into a telephone box. The taxi waited for him. Knew I couldn't drive any farther, would have to persuade Tonio to do it, or get someone else. No use thinking any more that one could remain sober by will power. One couldn't. Old bloody man alcohol sneaked up on you just when you thought you'd got him licked.

Tonio reappeared at my elbow.

"Get in the passenger seat," he said. "And give me the keys, so that you can't be held to be in charge. I'll drive you to the nursing home. But I'm afraid you'll have to wait ten minutes or so, because I still have that patient with me and there's a prescription to write. . . . Are you taking in a word I say?"

"The lot."

"Get in, then." He opened the door for me, and put his hand on my arm when I rocked. "If Elizabeth needs me, blow the horn."

"Right."

I sat in the seat, slid down, and put my head back. Sleep began to creep in around the edges.

"You all right?" I said to Elizabeth.

Her head was behind me. I heard her murmur quietly, "Yes."

The pump hummed rhythmically, aiding and abetting the whiskey. The sense of urgency drifted away. Tonio would drive us. . . . Elizabeth was safe. My eyelids gave up the struggle. I sank into a pit, whirling and disorientated. Not an unpleasant feeling if one didn't fight it.

Tonio opened the door and shook me awake.

"Drink this," he said. A mug of coffee, black and sweet. "I'll be with you in a minute."

He went back into the house, propping the door open with a heavy wrought-iron facsimile of the Pisa Tower. The coffee was too hot. With exaggerated care I put the mug down on the floor. Straightened up wishing the load of ache across my shoulders would let up and go away, but was much too full of the world's oldest anesthetic to feel it very clearly.

I had been as drunk as that only once before, and it wasn't the night they told me Elizabeth would die, but four days later when they said she would live. I'd downed uncountable double whiskeys and I'd eaten almost nothing for a week. It was odd to remember the delicious happiness of that night because of course it hadn't after all been the end of an agony but only the beginning of the years of pain and struggle and waste. . . .

I found myself staring vacantly at the off side wing mirror. If I conshen—well, concentrated—very hard, I thought bemusedly, I would be able to see what it reflected. A pointless game. It simply irritated me that I couldn't see clearly if I wanted to. Looked obstinately at the mirror and waited for the slowed-down focusing process to come right. Finally, with a ridiculous smile of triumph, I saw what it saw down the street. Nothing much. Nothing worth the trouble. Only a silly old taxi parked by the curb. Only a silly man in a raincoat getting into it.

Raincoat.

The alarm bells rang fuzzily in my sluggish head. I opened the door and fumbled my way onto the pavement, kicking the coffee over in the process. Leaned against the side of the van and looked down toward the taxi. It was still parked. By the telephone box. Where the man in the raincoat had been ringing someone up.

They say sudden overwhelming disaster sobers you, but it isn't true. I reeled across the pavement and up the step to Tonio's door. Forgot all about blowing the car horn. Banged the solid knocker on his door, and called him loudly. He appeared at the top of the stairs which led to his consulting room on the first floor and his flat above that.

"Shut up, Ty," he said. "I won't be long."

"Shome—someone's followed us," I said. "It's dangerous." He wouldn't know what I was talking about. I didn't know where to start explaining.

Elizabeth, however, must have told him enough.

"Oh. All right, I'll be down in one minute." His head withdrew around the bend in the stairs and I swiveled unsteadily to take another look down the street. Taxi still there, in the same place. Light out, not for hire. Just waiting. Waiting to follow us again if we moved. Waiting to tell Vjoersterod where we'd gone.

I shook with futile rage. Vjoersterod hadn't after all been satisfied that Ross's truncheon and the threats against Elizabeth had been enough to insure a permanent state of docility. He'd left Raincoat outside to watch. Just in case. I hadn't spotted him. Had been much too drunk to spot anything. But there he was. Right on our trail.

I'll fix him, I thought furiously. I'll fix him properly.

Tonio started to come down the stairs, escorting a thin bent elderly man whose breath rasped audibly through his open mouth. Slowly they made it to the bottom. Tonio held his arm as they came past me, and helped him over the threshold and down the step to the pavement. An almost equally elderly woman emerged from the Rover parked directly behind my van. Tonio handed him over, helped him into the car, came back to me.

"He likes to come at night," he explained. "Not so many fumes from the traffic, and easier parking."

"Lord Fore—Fore something," I said.

"Forlingham," Tonio nodded. "Do you know him?"

"Used to go racing. Poor old thing." I looked woozily up the street. "See that taxi?"

"Yes."

'Following us."

"Oh."

"So you take 'Lizabeth on to the nursing home. I'll top the taxi." A giggle got as far as the first ridiculous note. "What's worse than raining cats and dogs? I'll tell you—hailing taxis."

"You're drunk," Tonio said. "Wait while I change my coat." He was wearing formal consultant's dress and looked young and glamorous enough to be a pop singer. "Can we wait?"

I swung out a generous arm in a wide gesture. "The taxi," I said owlishly, "is waiting for *us.*"

He went to change his coat. I could hear Elizabeth's pump thudding safely away; wondered if I ought to go and reassure her; thought that in my state I probably couldn't. The Forlinghams started up and drove away. The taxi went on waiting.

At first I thought what I saw next was on the pink-elephant level. Not really there. Couldn't be there. But this time no hallucination. Edging smoothly around the corner, pulling gently into the curb, stopping behind the taxi, one Silver Wraith, property of Hire Cars Lucullus.

Raincoat emerged from the taxi and reported to the Rolls. Two minutes later he returned to the taxi, climbed in, and was driven away.

Tonio ran lightly down the stairs and came to a halt beside me in a black sweater instead of a coat.

"Let's get going," he said.

I put my hand clumsily on his arm.

"Shee—I mean, see that Rolls down there, where the taxi was."

"Yes."

"In that," I said carefully, "is the man who—oh God, why can't I think—who said he would . . . kill . . . 'Lizabeth if I didn't do what he wanted. . . . Well . . . he might . . . he might not . . . but can't rish—risk it. Take her. . . . Take her. I'll stop . . . him following you."

"How?" Tonio said unemotionally.

I looked at the Tower of Pisa holding the door open. "With that."

"It's heavy," he objected, assessing my physical state

"Oh for God's sake, stop arguing," I said weakly. "
want her to go where they can't find her. Please—pleas
get going. . . . Go on, Tonio. And drive away slowly."

He hesitated, but finally showed signs of moving
"Don't forget," he said seriously, "that you are no use t
Elizabeth dead."

"S'pose not."

"Give me your coat," he said suddenly. "Then they'l
think it's still you in the van."

Behind the van I took off my coat obediently, and h
put it on. He was shorter than me. It hung on him. Sam
dark head, though. They might mistake us from a dis
tance.

Tonio gave a rip-roaring impression of my drunke
walk, reeling right around the back of the van on hi
way to the driving seat. I laughed. I was that drunk.

He started the van and drove slowly away. I watche
him give one artistic weave across the road and back
Highly intelligent fellow, Tonio Perelli.

Down the road, the Silver Wraith began to move. Go
to stop him, I thought fuzzily. Got to stop him smashin
up our lives, smashing up other people's lives. Someone
somewhere, had to stop him. In Welbeck Street, with
doorstop. Couldn't think clearly beyond that one fact
Had to stop him.

I bent down and picked up the Leaning Tower by it
top two stories. As Tonio had said, it was heavy. Bruised
muscle tearingly heavy. Tomorrow its effect would b
awful. Fair enough. Tomorrow would be much mor
awful if I put it down again—or if I missed.

The Rolls came toward me as slowly as Tonio ha
driven away. If I'd been sober, I'd have had all the tim
in the world. As it was, I misjudged the pace and all bu
let him go cruising by.

Down one step. Don't trip. Across the pavement
Hurry. Swung the wrought-iron tower around with botl
hands as if I were throwing the hammer and forgot t
let go. Its weight and momentum pulled me after it; bu

although at the last moment Ross saw me and tried to
swerve away, the heavy metal base crashed exactly
where I wanted it. Drunks' luck. Dead center of the
windscreen.

Scrunch went the laminated glass in a radiating star.
Silver cracks streaked across Ross's vision. The huge
car swerved violently out into the center of the road and
then in toward the curb as Ross stamped on the brakes.
A screech of tires, a scraping jolt. The Rolls stopped
abruptly at a sharp angle to the pavement with its rear
end inviting attention from the police. No police appeared to pay attention. A great pity. I wouldn't have
minded being scooped in for being drunk and disorderly
and disturbing the peace.

I had rebounded off the smooth side of the big car
and fallen in a heap in the road. The Rolls had stopped,
and that was that. Job done. No clear thought of self-
preservation spearheaded its way through the mist in my
head. I didn't remember that Tonio's solid front door
stood open only a few yards away. Jelly had taken over
from bone in my legs. Welbeck Street had started revolv-
ing around me and was taking its time over straightening
out.

It was Ross who picked me up. Ross with his truncheon. I was past caring much what he did with it; and
what he intended I don't know, because this time I was
saved by the bell in the shape of a party of people in evening dress who came out into the street from a neighbor-
ing house. They had cheerful gay voices full of a happy
evening, and they exclaimed in instant sympathy over
the plight of the Rolls.

"I say, do you need any help. . . ?"

"Shall we call anyone—the police, or anything?"

"Can we give you a lift. . . ?"

"Or call a garage?"

"No, thank you," said Vjoersterod in his most charming voice. "So kind of you . . . but we can manage."

Ross picked me to my feet and held on grimly to my
arm. Vjoersterod was saying, "We've been having a little
trouble with my nephew. I'm afraid he's very drunk.

Still, once we get him home everything will be al
right."

They murmured sympathetically. Began to move
away.

"It's not true!" I shouted. "They'll prob'ly kill me."
My voice sounded slurred and much too melodramatic.
They paused, gave Vjoersterod a group of sympathetic
half-embarrassed smiles, and moved off up the street.

"Hey," I called. "Take me with you."

Useless. They didn't even look back.

"What now?" Ross said to Vjoersterod.

"We can't leave him here. Those people would remember."

"In the car?"

While Vjoersterod nodded, Ross shoved me toward
the Rolls, levering with his grasp on my right arm. I
swung at him with the left, and missed completely. I
could see two of him, which made it difficult. Between
them they more or less slung me into the back of the car
and I sprawled there face down, half on and half off the
seat, absolutely furious that I still could not climb out
of that crippling alcoholic stupor. There was a ringing
in my head like the noise of the livid green corridors of
gas at the dentist's. But no stepped-up awakening to
daylight and the taste of blood. Just a continuing extraordinary sensation of being conscious and unconscious,
not alternately but both at once.

Ross knocked out a few of the worst-cracked pieces
of the windscreen and started the car.

Vjoersterod, sitting beside him, leaned over the back
of his seat and said casually, "Where to, Mr. Tyrone?
Which way to your wife?"

"Round and round the mulberry bush," I mumbled
indistinctly. "And good night to you, too."

He let go with four-letter words which were much
more in keeping with his character than his usual elevated
chat.

"It's no good," Ross said disgustedly. "He won't tell
us unless we take him to pieces, and even then—if we

id get it out of him—what good would it do? He'll never
write for you. Never."

"Why not?" said Vjoersterod obstinately.

"Well, look at it this way. We threatened to kill his
wife. Does he knuckle under? Yes, as long as we're there.
The moment our backs are turned, first thing he does
is to move her out. We follow, find her, he shifts her off
again. That could go on and on. All we can do more is
actually kill her, and if we do that we've no hold on him
anyway. So he'll never write for you, whatever we do."

Full marks, I said to myself fatuously. Masterly summing up of the situation. Top of the class.

"You didn't hit him hard enough," Vjoersterod said
accusingly, sliding out of the argument.

"I did."

"You can't have."

"If you remember," Ross said patiently, "Charlie
Boston's boys made no impression either. They either
do or don't respond to the treatment. This one doesn't.
Same with the threats. Same with the drink. Usually one
method is enough. This time we use all three, just to make
sure. And where do we get? We get nowhere at all. Just
like Gunther Braunthal last year."

Vjoersterod grunted. I wondered remotely what had
become of Gunther Braunthal. Decided I didn't really
want to know.

"I can't afford for him to get away with it,"
Vjoersterod said.

"No," Ross said.

"I don't like disposals in England," Vjoersterod went
on in irritation. "Too much risk. Too many people
everywhere."

"Leave it to me," Ross said calmly.

I struggled up into a sitting position, propping myself
up on my hands. Looked out of the side window. Lights
flashing past, all one big whirl. We weren't going very
fast, on account of the broken windscreen, but the
December night air swept into the car in gusts, freezing
me in my cotton shirt. In a minute, when my head cleared
a fraction, I would open the door and roll out. We

weren't going very fast. If I waited for a bit of main street, with people. . . . Couldn't wait too long. Didn't want Ross attending to my disposal.

Vjoersterod's head turned my way. "You've only yourself to thank, Mr. Tyrone. You shouldn't have crossed me. You should have done what I said. I gave you your chance. You've been very stupid, Mr. Tyrone. Very stupid indeed. And now, of course, you'll be paying for it."

"Huh?" I said.

"He's still drunk," Ross said. "He doesn't understand."

"I'm not so sure. Look what he's done in the past hour. He's got ahead like a bullet."

My eyes suddenly focused on something outside. Something I knew, that everyone knew. The aviary in Regent's Park, pointed angular wire opposite the main entrance to the Zoo. Been there before with Vjoersterod. He must be staying somewhere near there, I thought. Must be taking me to where he lived. It didn't matter that it was near the Zoo. What did matter was that this was also the way to the nursing home where Tonio had taken Elizabeth. It was less than a mile ahead.

I thought for one wild horror-stricken moment that I must have told Vjoersterod where to go; then remembered and knew I hadn't. But he was much too close. Much too close. Supposing his way home took him actually past the nursing home, and he saw the van—saw them unloading Elizabeth, even. . . . He might change his mind and kill her and leave me alive . . . which would be unbearable, totally and literally unbearable.

Distract his attention.

I said with as much clarity as my tongue would allow. "Vjoersterod and Ross. Vjoersterod and Ross."

"*What?*" said Vjoersterod.

The shock to Ross resulted in a swerve across the road and a jolt on the brakes.

"Go back to South Africa before the bogies get you."

Vjoersterod had twisted round and was staring at me.

Ross had his eyes too much on the mirror and not enough
in the road. All the same, he started his indicator flashing
for the right turn which led over the bridge across
Regent's Canal and then out of the park. Which led
straight past the nursing home, half a mile ahead.

"I told the Stewards," I said desperately. "I told the
Stewards—all about you. Last Wednesday. I told my
paper. . . . It'll all be there on Sunday. So you'll remember me, too, you'll remember. . . ."

Ross turned the wheel erratically, sweeping wide to
the turn. I brought my hands around with a wholly un-
coordinated swing and clamped them hard over his eyes.
He took both of his own hands off the wheel to try and
detach mine, and the car rocked straight halfway through
the turn and headed across the road at a tangent, taking
the shortest distance to the bank of the canal.

Vjoersterod shouted frantically and pulled with all
his strength at my arm, but my desperation was at least
the equal of his. I hauled Ross's head back toward me
harder still, and it was their own doing that I was too
drunk to care where or how the car crashed.

"Brake!" Vjoersterod screamed. "Brake, you stupid
fool!"

Ross put his foot down. He couldn't see what he was
doing. He put his foot down hard. On the accelerator.

The Rolls leaped across the pavement and onto the
grass. The bank sloped gently and then steeply down
the canal, with saplings and young trees growing here
and there. The Rolls scrunched sideways into one trunk
and ricocheted into a sapling which it mowed down like
corn.

Vjoersterod grabbed the wheel, but the heavy car was
now pointed downhill and going too fast for any change
of steering. The wheel twisted and lurched out of his
hand under the jolt of the front wheel hitting another
tree and slewing to the side. Branches cracked around
the car and scraped and stabbed at the glossy coachwork.
Vjoersterod fumbled on the glove shelf and found the
truncheon, and twisted around in his seat and began hitting my arm in panic-stricken fury.

I let go of Ross. It was far too late for him both to size up the situation and to do anything useful about it. He was just beginning to reach for the hand brake when the Rolls crashed down over the last sapling and fell into the canal.

The car swung convulsively on impact, throwing me around like a rag doll in the back and tumbling Vjoersterod and Ross together in the front. Black water immediately poured through the broken windscreen and with lethal speed began filling the car.

How to get out. . . . I fumbled for a door handle in the sudden dark, couldn't find one, and didn't know what I had my feet on, didn't know which way up I was. Didn't know if the car was on its back or its nose. Didn't know anything except that it was sinking.

Vjoersterod began screaming as the water rose up his body. His arm was still flailing about and knocked into me. I felt the truncheon still in his hand. Snatched it from him and hit it hard against where I thought the rear window must be. Connected only with material. Felt around wildly with my hand, found glass above my head and hit at that.

It cracked. Laminated and tough. Cursed Rolls-Royce for their standards. Hit again. Couldn't get a decent swing. Tried again. Crunched a hole. Water came through it. Nor a torrent, but too much. The window was under the surface. Not far under. Tried again. Bash, bash. Made a bigger hole but still not enough . . . and water fell through it and over me, and from the front of the car the icy level was rising past my waist.

Great to die when you're dead drunk, I thought. And when I die don't bury me at all, just pickle my bones in alcohol. . . . Crashed the truncheon against the hole. Missed. My arm went right up through it. Felt it up there in the air, out of the water. Stupid. Silly. Drowning in less than an inch of Regent's Canal.

Pulled my arm back and tried again. Absolutely no good. Too much water, too much whiskey. One outside, one in. No push in my battered muscles and not much comprehension in my mind. Floating off on the river of death. . . . Sorry, Elizabeth. . . .

Suddenly there were lights shining down over me. Hallucinations, I thought. Hallelujah hallucinations. Death was a blinding white light and a crashing noise in the head and a shower of water and glass and voices calling and arms grasping and pulling and raising one up . . . up . . . into a free cold wind. . . .

"Is there anyone else in the car?" a voice said. A loud urgent voice, speaking to me. The voice of earth. Telling me I was alive. Telling me to wake up and do something. I couldn't adjust. Blinked at him stupidly.

"Tell us," he said. "Is there anyone else in the car?" He shook my shoulder. It hurt. Brought me back a little. He said again, "Is there anyone else?"

I nodded weakly. "Two."

"Christ," he muttered. "What a hope."

I was sitting on the grass on the canal bank, shivering. Someone put a coat around my shoulders. There were a lot of people and more coming, black figures against the reflection on the dark water, figures lit on one side only by the headlights of the car which had come down the path plowed by the Rolls. It was parked there on the edge, with its lights on the place where the Rolls had gone. You could see the silver rim of the rear window shimmering just below the surface, close to the bank. You could see the water sliding shallowly through the gaping hole my rescuers had pulled me through. You could see nothing inside the car except darkness and water.

A youngish man had stripped to his underpants and was proposing to go through the rear window to try to rescue the others. People tried to dissuade him, but he went. I watched in a daze, scarcely thinking, scarcely feeling. His head came back through the window into the air, and several hands bent over to help him.

They pulled Vjoersterod out and laid him on the bank.

"Artificial respiration," one said. "Kiss of life."

Kiss Vjoersterod. . . . If they wanted to, they were welcome.

The diver went back for Ross. He had to go down twice. A very brave man. The Rolls could have toppled over onto its side at any moment and trapped him inside. People, I thought groggily, were amazing.

They put Ross beside Vjoersterod, and kissed him, too. Neither of them responded.

Cold was seeping into every cell of my body. From the ground I sat on it rose, from the wind it pierced, from my wet clothes it clung clammily to my skin. Bruises stiffen fast in those conditions. Everything started hurting at once, climbing from piano to fortissimo. The noises in my head were deafening. A fine time for the drink to begin dying out on me, I thought. Just when I needed it most.

I lay back on the grass, and someone put something soft under my head. Their voices sprayed over me, questioning and solicitous.

"What did it happen?"

"We've sent for an ambulance. . . ."

"What he needs is some good hot tea. . . ."

"We're so sorry about your friends. . . ."

"Can you tell us your name?"

I didn't answer them. Didn't have enough strength. Could let it all go now. Didn't have to struggle any more. Old man alcohol could have what was left.

I shut my eyes. The world receded rapidly.

"He's out cold," a tiny faraway voice said.

It wasn't true at that moment. But a second later it was.

SIXTEEN

I was in a dim long room with a lot of bodies laid out in white. I, too, was in white, being painfully crushed in a cement sandwich. My head, sticking out of it, pulsed and thumped like a steam hammer.

The components of this nightmare gradually sorted themselves out into depressing reality. Respectively, a hospital ward, a savage load of bruises, and an emperor-sized hangover.

I dragged my arm up and squinted at my watch. Four-fifty. Even that small movement had out-of-proportion repercussions. I put my hand down gently on top of the sheets and tried to duck out by going to sleep again.

Didn't manage it. Too many problems. Too many people would want too many explanations. I'd have to edit the truth here and there, juggle the facts a little. Needed a clear head for it, not a throbbing dehydrated morass.

I tried to sort out into order exactly what had happened the evening before, and wondered profitlessly what I would have done if I hadn't been drunk. Thought numbly about Vjoersterod and Ross being pulled from the wreck. If they were dead, which I was sure they were, I had certainly killed them. The worst thing about that was that I didn't care.

If I shut my eyes, the world still revolved and the ringing noise in my head grew more persistent. I thought wearily that people who poisoned themselves with alcohol for pleasure had to to be crazy.

At six they woke up all the patients, who shook my tender brain with shattering decibels of coughing, spitting, and brushing of teeth. Breakfast was steamed haddock and weak tea. I asked for water and something for

195

a headache, and thought sympathetically about the man who said he didn't like Alka-Seltzers because they were so noisy.

The hospital was equipped with telephone trolleys, but for all my urging I couldn't get hold of one until nine-thirty. I fed it with coins salvaged from my now-drying trousers and rang Tonio. Caught him luckily in his consulting room after having insisted his receptionist tell him I was calling.

"Ty! *Deo gratias*. Where the hell have you been?"

"Swimming," I said. "I'll tell you later. Is Elizabeth O.K.?"

"She's fine. But she was extremely anxious when you didn't turn up again last night. Where are you now? Why haven't you been to find out for yourself how she is?"

"I'm in University College Hospital. At least, I'm here for another few hours. I got scooped in here last night, but there's not much damage."

"How's the head?"

"Lousy."

He laughed. Charming fellow.

I rang the nursing home and talked to Elizabeth. There was no doubt she was relieved to hear from me, though from the unusual languor in her voice it was clear they had given her some sort of tranquilizer. She was almost too calm. She didn't ask me what had happened when Tonio had driven her away; she didn't want to know where I was at that moment.

"Would you mind staying in the nursing home for a couple of days?" I asked. "Just till I get things straight."

"Sure," she said. "Couple of days. Fine."

"See you soon, honey."

"Sure," she said again vaguely. "Fine."

After a little while I disconnected and got through to Luke-John. His brisk voice vibrated loudly through the receiver and sent javelins through my head. I told him I hadn't written my Sunday column yet because I'd been involved in a car crash the night before, and held the receiver six inches away while he replied.

"The car crash was yesterday afternoon."

"This was another one."

"For God's sake, do you make a habit of it?"

"I'll write my piece this evening and come in with it in the morning before I go to Heathbury for the Lamplighter. Will that do?"

"It'll have to, I suppose," he grumbled. "You weren't hurt in the second crash, were you?" He sounded as if an affirmative answer would be highly unpopular.

"Only bruised," I said, and got a noncommittal unsympathetic grunt.

"Make that piece good," he said. "Blow the roof off."

I put down the receiver before he could blow the roof off my head. It went on thrumming mercilessly. Ross's target area also alternately burned and ached and made lying in bed draggingly uncomfortable. The grim morning continued. People came and asked me who I was. And who were the two men with me who had both drowned in the car? Did I know their address?

No, I didn't.

And how had the accident happened?

"The chauffeur had a blackout," I said.

A police sergeant came with a notebook and wrote down the uninformative truth I told him about the accident. I didn't know Mr. Vjoersterod well; he was just an acquaintance. He had insisted on taking me in his car to the nursing home where my wife was at present a patient. The chauffeur had had a blackout and the car had run off the road. It had all happened very quickly. I couldn't remember clearly, because I was afraid I had had a little too much to drink. Mr. Vjoersterod had handed me something to smash our way out of the car with, and I had done my best. It was very sad about Mr. Vjoersterod and the chauffeur. The man who had fetched them out ought to have a medal. The sergeant said I would be needed for the inquest, and went away.

The doctor who came to examine me at midday sympathized with my various discomforts and said it was extraordinary sometimes how much bruising one could sustain through being thrown about in a somersaulting car. I gravely agreed with him and suggested I go home as soon as possible.

"Why not?" he said. "If you feel like it."

I felt like oblivion. I creaked into my rough-dried crumpled shirt and trousers and left my face unshaven, my hair unbrushed, and my tie untied, because lifting my arms up for those jobs was too much trouble. Tottered downstairs and got the porter to ring for a taxi, which took me the short distance to Welbeck Street and decanted me on Tonio's doorstep. Someone had picked up the Leaning Tower and put it back in place. There wasn't a mark on it. More than could be said for the Rolls. More than could be said for me.

Tonio gave me one penetrating look, an armchair, and a medicine glass of disprin and nepenthe.

"What's this made of?" I asked when I'd drunk it.

"Nepenthe? A mixture of opium and sherry."

"You're joking."

He shook his head. "Opium and sherry wine. Very useful stuff. How often do you intend to turn up here in dire need of it?"

"No more," I said. "It's finished."

He wanted to know what had happened after he had driven Elizabeth away, and I told him, save for the one detail of my having blacked out the chauffeur myself. He was no fool, however. He gave me a twisted smile of comprehension and remarked that I had behaved like a drunken idiot.

After that he fetched my jacket from his bedroom and insisted on driving me and the van back to the flat, on the basis that Elizabeth needed me safe and sound, not wrapped around one of the lampposts I had miraculously missed the night before. I didn't argue. Hadn't the energy. He put the van in the garage for me and walked away up the mews to look for a taxi, and I slowly went up the stairs to the flat feeling like a wet dishcloth attempting the Matterhorn.

The flat was stifling hot. I had left all the heaters on the night before and Mrs. Woodward hadn't turned them off. There was a note from her on the table. "Is every-

hing all right? Have put milk in fridge. Am very anx-
ous. Mrs. W."

I looked at my bed. Nothing on it but sheets.
Remembered all the blankets and pillows were still
downstairs on the stretcher in the van. Going down for
them was impossible. Pinched Elizabeth's. Spread one
pink blanket roughly on the divan, lay down on it still
dressed, pulled another over me, put my head down gingerly on the soft cool pillow.

Bliss.

The world still spun. And otherwise far too little to
put out flags for. My head still manufactured its own
sound track. And in spite of the nepenthe the rest of
me still felt fresh from a cement mixer. But now there
was luxuriously nothing more to do except drift over
the edge of a precipice into a deep black heavenly
sleep. . . .

The telephone bell rang sharply, sawing the dream
in half. It was Mrs. Woodward, Lancashire accent very
strong under stress, sounding touchingly relieved that
no unbearable disaster had happened to Elizabeth.

"It's me that's not well," I said. "My wife's spending
a couple of days in the nursing home. If you'll ring again,
I'll let you know when she'll be back. . . ."

I put the receiver down in its cradle and started across
to my bed. Took two steps, yawned, and wondered if
I should tell Victor Roncey to go fetch Madge and the
boys. Wondered if I should tell Willy Ondroy to slacken
the ultra-tight security. Decided to leave things as they
were. Only twenty-four more hours to the race. Might
as well be safe. Even with Vjoersterod dead, there was
always Charlie Boston.

Not that Tiddely Pom would win. After all the trouble
to get him there his chances were slender, because the
bout of colic would have taken too much out of him.
Charlie Boston would make his profit, just as if they'd
nobbled him as planned.

I retraced the two steps back to the telephone and
after a chat with inquiries put through a personal call
to Birmingham.

"Mr. Boston?"

"Yes."

"This is James Tyrone."

There was a goggling silence at the other end punctuated only by some heavy breathing.

I asked, "What price are you offering on Tiddely Pom?"

No answer except a noise halfway between a grunt and a growl.

"The horse will run," I commented.

"That's all you know," he said. A rough bad-tempered voice. A rough bad-tempered man.

"Don't rely on Ross or Vjoersterod," I said patiently. "You won't be hearing from them again. The poor dear fellows are both dead."

I put down the receiver without waiting for the Boston reactions. Felt strong enough to take off my jacket. Made it back to bed and found the friendly precipice still waiting there. Didn't keep it waiting any longer.

A long while later I woke up thirsty and with a tongue which felt woolly and grass green. The nepenthe had worn off. My shoulders were heavy, stiffly sore, and insistent. A bore. All pain was a bore. It was dark. I consulted my luminous watch. Four o'clock, give or take a minute. I'd slept twelve hours.

I yawned. Found my brain no longer felt as if it were sitting on a bruise and remembered with a wide-awakening shock that I hadn't written my column for the *Blaze*. I switched on the light and took a swig of Tonio's mixture and, after it had worked, went to fetch a notebook and pencil and a cup of coffee. Propped up the pillows, climbed back between the blankets, and blew the roof off for Luke-John.

"The lawyers will have a fit," he said.

"As I've pointed out, the man who ran the racket died this week, and the libel laws only cover the living. The dead can't sue. And no one can sue them. Also you can't

ccuse or try the dead. Not in this world, anyway. So
othing they've done can be *sub judice*. Right?"

"Don't quote *Blaze* dictums to me, laddie. I was living
y them before you were weaned." He picked up my
ped sheets as if they would burn him.

"Petrified owners can come out of the caves," he read
oud. "The reign of intimidation is over and the scandal
the nonstarting favorites can be fully exposed."

Derry lifted his head to listen, gave me a grin, and
id, "Our trouble shooter loosing the big guns again?"

"Life gets tedious otherwise," I said.

"Only for some."

Luke-John eyed me appraisingly. "You look more
if you'd been the target. I suppose all this haggard-
ed stuff is the result of a day spent crashing about in
rs." He flicked his thumb against my article. "Did
u invent this unnamed villian, or did he really exist?
nd if so, who was he?"

If I didn't tell, Mike de Jong in his rival newspaper
ight put two and two together and come up with a
ling-in-the-gaps story that Luke-John would never
rgive me for. And there was no longer any urgent reason
r secrecy.

I said, "He was a South African called Vjoersterod,
d he died the night before last in the second of those
r crashes."

Their mouths literally fell open.

"Dyna . . . *mite*," Derry said.

I told them most of what had happened. I left Gail
d Ross's truncheon out altogether but put in the threat
Elizabeth. Left out the drunken driving and the hands
er Ross's eyes. Made it bald and factual. Left out the
eat.

Luke-John thought through the problem and then read
y article again.

"When you know what you've omitted, what you've
cluded seems pale. But I think this is enough. It'll do
e trick, tell everyone the pressure's off and that they
n safely bet antepost again, thanks entirely to the in-

vestigations conducted by the *Blaze*. That's, after al
what we wanted."

"Buy the avenging *Blaze*," said Derry only ha
sardonically. "Racket-smashing a specialty."

Luke-John gave him a sour look for a joke in bad tast
I asked him if he would ring up a powerful bookmakir
friend of his and ask him the present state of the Lamp
lighter market, and with raised eyebrows but no oth
comment he got through. He asked the question, listene
with sharpening attention to the answer, and scribble
down some figures. When he had finished, he gave
soundless whistle and massaged his larynx.

"He says Charlie Boston's main Birmingham offic
has been trying to lay off about fifty thousand on Tiddel
Pom since yesterday afternoon. Everyone smells a sewe
full of rats because of your articles and the *Blaze*'s u
dertaking to keep the horse safe, and they're in a tizz
whether to take the bets or not. Only one or two of th
biggest firms have done so."

I said, "If Boston can't lay off and Tiddely Pom win
he's sunk without trace, but if Tiddely Pom loses he'
pocket all Vjoersterod's share of the loot as well as h
own and be better off than if we'd done nothing at al
If he manages to lay off and Tiddely Pom wins, he'
be smiling, and if he lays off and Tiddely Pom lose
he'll have thrown away everything the crimes were con
mitted for."

"A delicate problem," said Derry judicially. "Or wh
you might call the antlers of a dilemma."

"Could he know about the colic?" Luke-John asked.

We decided after picking it over that as he was tryir
to lay off he probably couldn't know. Luke-John rar
back to his bookmaker friend and advised him to tak
as much of the Boston money as he could.

"And after that," he said gloomily as he put dow
the receiver, "every other bloody horse will fall, a
Tiddely Pom will win."

Derry and I went down to Heathbury Park togeth
on the race train. The racecourse and the sponsors

1e Lamplighter had been smiled on by the day. Clear,
nny, still, frosty: a perfect December morning. Derry
id that fine weather was sure to bring out a big crowd,
nd that he thought Zig Zag would win. He said he
1ought I looked ill. I said I felt better than yesterday.
Ve completed the journey in our usual relationship of
lerant acceptance and I wondered inconsequentially
hy it never solidified into friendship.

He was right on the first count. Heathbury Park was
ursting at the seams. I went first to Willy Ondroy's office
eside the weighing room and found a scattered queue
f people wanting a word with him, but he caught my
e across the throng and waved a beckoning hand.

"Hey," he said, swinging around in his chair to talk
me behind his shoulder. "Your wretched horse has
used me more bother. . . . That Victor Roncey, he's
bloody pain in the neck."

"What's he been doing?"

"He arrived at ten this morning all set to blow his
p if the horse arrived a minute after twelve, and when
found he was there already he blew his top anyway
d said he should have been told."

"Not the easiest of characters," I agreed.

"Anyway, that's only the half of it. The gateman rang
e at about eight this morning to say there was a man
ersistently trying to get in. He'd offered him a bribe
d then increased it and had tried to slip in unnoticed
hile he, the gateman, was having an argument with one
the stable lads. So I nipped over from my house for
recky, and there was this short stout individual walking
ong the back of the stable block looking for an
nguarded way in. I marched him round to the front
d the gateman said that was the same merchant, so
asked him who he was and what he wanted. He
ouldn't answer. Said he hadn't committed any crime.
othing else to do."

"Pity."

"Wait a minute. My racecourse manager came toward
as the man walked away, and the first thing he said to
e was "What's Charlie Boston doing here?""

"What?"

"Ah. I thought he might mean something to you. B
he was extraordinarily clumsy if he was after Tidde
Pom."

"No brains and no brawn," I agreed.

He looked at me accusingly. "If Charlie Boston w;
the sum total of threat to Tiddely Pom, haven't you bee
overdoing the melodrama a bit?"

I said dryly," "Read the next thrilling instalment
the *Blaze*."

He laughed and turned back decisively to his impatie
queue. I wandered out into the paddock thinking
Charlie Boston and his futile attempt to reach the hors
Charlie Boston who thought with his muscles. With oth
people's muscles, come to that. Having his boys on tl
sick list and Vjoersterod and Ross on the dead, he w;
as naked and vulnerable as an opened oyster.

He might also be desperate. If he was trying to l;
off fifty thousand pounds, he had stood to lose at lea
ten times that—upward to half a million—if Tiddely Po
won. A nose dive of epic proportions. A prospect to i;
duce panic and recklessness in ever-increasing intensi
as the time of the race drew near.

I decided that Roncey should share the care of h
horse's safety, and began looking out for him in tl
throng. I walked around the corner with my eyes scannir
sideways and nearly bumped into someone standing l
the Results at Other Meetings notice board. The apolo;
was halfway to my tongue before I realized who it wa
Gail.

I saw the pleasure which came first into her eyes, an
the uncertainty afterward. Very likely I was showing h
exactly the same feeling. Very likely she, like me, fe
a thudding shock at meeting. Yet if I'd considered
at all, it was perfectly reasonable that she should cor
to see her uncle's horse run in the Lamplighter.

"Ty?" she said tentatively, with a ton less than h
usual poise.

"Surprise, surprise." It sounded more flippant than
felt.

"I thought I might see you," she said. Her smooth black hair shone in the sun and the light lay along the bronze lines of her face, touching them with gold. The mouth I had kissed was a rosy pink. The body I had liked naked was covered with a turquoise coat. A week today, I thought numbly. A week today I left her in bed.

"Are Harry and Sarah here?" I said. Social chat. Hide the wound which hadn't even begun to form scar tissue. I'd no right to be wounded in the first place. My own fault. Couldn't complain.

"They're in the bar," she said. Where else?

"Would you like a drink?"

She shook her head. "I want to—to explain. I see that you know. . . . I have to explain."

"No need. A cup of coffee, perhaps?"

"Just listen."

I could feel the rigidity in all my muscles and realized it extended even into my mouth and jaw. With a conscious effort I loosened them and relaxed.

"All right."

"Did she, I mean, is she going to divorce you?"

"No."

"Ohhhh." It was a long sigh. "Then I'm sorry if I got you into trouble with her. But why did she have you followed if she didn't want to divorce you?"

I stared at her. The wound half healed in an instant.

"What's the matter?" she said.

I took a deep breath. "Tell me what happened after I left you. Tell me about the man who followed me."

"He came up and spoke to me in the street just outside the hotel."

"What did he look like?"

"He puzzled me a bit. I mean, he seemed too—I don't know—civilized, I suppose is the word, to be a private detective. His clothes were made for him, for instance. He had an accent of some sort and a yellowish skin. Tall. About forty, I should think."

"What did he say?"

"He said your wife wanted a divorce and he was working on it. He asked me for—concrete evidence."

"A bill from the hotel?"

She nodded, not meeting my eyes. "I agreed to go in again and ask for one."

"Why, Gail?"

She didn't answer.

"Did he pay you for it?"

"God, Ty," she said explosively. "Why not? I needed the money. I'd only met you three times and you were just as bad as me, living with your wife just because she was rich."

"Yes," I said. "Well, how much?"

"He offered me fifty pounds, and when I'd got used to the idea that he was ready to pay I told him to think again; with all your wife's money she could afford more than that for her freedom."

"And then what?"

"He said . . . if I could give him full and substantial facts, he could raise the payment considerably." After a pause, in a mixture of defiance and shame, she added "He agreed to a thousand pounds, in the end."

I gave a gasp which was half a laugh.

"Didn't your wife tell you?" she asked.

I shook my head. "He surely didn't have that much money on him? Did he give you a check?"

"No. He met me later, outside the art school, and gave me a brown carrier bag. Beautiful new notes, in bundles. I gave him the bill I got, and told him—everything I could."

"I know," I said.

"Why did she pay so much, if she doesn't want divorce?" When I didn't answer at once, she went on. "It wasn't really only the money. I thought if she wanted to divorce you, why the hell should I stop her? You said you wouldn't leave her, but if she sort of left you, then you would be free, and maybe we could have more than a few Sundays. . . ."

I thought that one day I might appreciate the irony of it.

I said, "It wasn't my wife who paid you that money.

was the man himself. He wasn't collecting evidence
or a divorce, but evidence to blackmail me with."

"Ohh." It was a moan. "Oh, no, Ty. Oh God, I'm so
sorry." Her eyes widened suddenly. "You must have
thought—I suppose you thought—that I sold you out for
that."

"I'm afraid so," I apologized. "I should have known
better."

"That makes us about quits, then." All her poise came
back at one bound. She said, with some concern but less
emotional disturbance, "How much did he take you
for?"

"He didn't want money. He wanted me to write my
column in the *Blaze* every week according to his instructions."

"How extraordinary. Well, that's easy enough."

"Would you design dresses to dictation by threat?"

"Oh."

"Exactly. Oh. So I told my wife about you myself. I
had to."

"What—what did she say?"

"She was upset," I said briefly. "I said I wouldn't be
seeing you again. There'll be no divorce."

She slowly shrugged her shoulders. "So that's that."

I looked away from her, trying not to mind so ap-
pallingly much that that was that. Tomorrow was Sunday. Tomorrow was Sunday and I could be on my
own, and there was nothing on earth that I wanted so
much as to see her again in her smooth warm skin and
hold her close and tight in the half dark. . . .

She said thoughtfully, "I suppose if that man was a
blackmailer it explains why I thought he was so nasty."

"Nasty? He was usually fantastically polite."

"He spoke to me as if I'd crawled out of the cracks. I
wouldn't have put up with it—except for the money."

"Poor Gail," I said sympathetically. "He was South
African."

She took in the implication and her eyes were furious. "That explains it. A beastly Afrikaner. I wish I'd
never agreed—"

"Don't be silly," I interrupted. "Be glad you cost hi▮
so much."

She calmed down and laughed. "I've never even bee▮
to Africa. I didn't recognize his accent or give it ▮
thought. Stupid, isn't it?"

A man in a check tweed suit came and asked us ▮
move, as he wanted to read the notices on the board b▮
hind us. We walked three or four steps away, an▮
paused again.

"I suppose I'll see you sometimes at the races," sh▮
said.

"I suppose so."

She looked closely at my face and said, "If yo▮
really feel like that, why—*why* don't you leave her?"

"I can't."

"But we could. . . . You want to be with me. I kno▮
you do. Money isn't everything."

I smiled twistedly. I did after all mean something t▮
her, if she could ever say that.

"I'll see you sometimes," I repeated emptily. "At th▮
races."

SEVENTEEN

I caught Victor Roncey coming out of the luncheo▮
room and told him that the danger to Tiddely Pom wa▮
by no means over.

"He's here, isn't he?" he said squashingly.

"He's here thanks to us," I reminded him. "And ther▮
are still two hours to the race."

"What do you expect me to do? Hold his hand?"

"It wouldn't hurt," I said flatly.

There was the usual struggle between aggressive in▮
dependence and reasonable agreement. He said grudg▮
ingly, "Peter can sit outside his box over in the stables.▮

"Where is Peter now?"

He waved a hand behind him. "Finishing lunch."

"You'll have to take him in yourself, if he hasn't got a stable lad's pass."

He grumbled and agreed, and went back to fetch his son. I walked over to the stables with them and checked with the man on the gate, who said he'd had the usual number of people trying to get in, but not the man he'd turned away in the morning. Wing Commander Ondroy had told him to sling that man in the storeroom and lock him in if he came sniffing around again.

I smiled appreciatively and went in with Roncey to look at the horse. He stood patiently in his box, propped on one hip, resting a rear leg. When we opened the door, he turned his head lazily and directed at us an unexcited eye. A picture of a racehorse not on his toes, not strung up by the occasion, not looking ready to win Lamplighter Gold Cups.

"Is he always like this before a race?" I said. "He looks doped."

Roncey gave me a horrified glance and hurried to his horse's head. He looked in his mouth and eyes, felt his neck and legs, and kicked open and studied a small pile of droppings. Finally he shook his head.

"No dope that I can see. No signs of it."

"He never has nerves," Peter observed. "He isn't bred for it."

He looked bred for a milk cart. I refrained from saying so. I walked back into the paddock with Roncey and got him to agree to saddle up his horse in the stables, not in the saddling boxes, if the Stewards would allow it.

The Stewards, including Eric Youll, didn't hesitate. They said only that Tiddely Pom would have to walk the three stipulated times around the parade ring for the public to see him before the jockey mounted, but were willing for him to walk six feet in from the rails and be led and guarded by Peter and myself.

"All a waste of time," Roncey muttered. "No one will try anything here."

"Don't you believe it," I said. "You'd try anything if you stood to lose half a million you hadn't got."

I watched the first two races from the press box and spent the time in between aimlessly wandering about in the crowd trying to convince myself that I wasn't really looking out for another glimpse of Gail.

I didn't see her. I did see Dermot Finnegan. The little Irish jockey walked in front of me and gave me a huge gap-toothed grin. I took in, as I was supposed to, that he was dressed in colors, ready to ride in a race. The front of his jacket was carefully unbuttoned. I added up the purple star on the pink and white horizontal stripes and he laughed when he saw my astonishment.

"Bejasus, and I'm almost as staggered as yourself," he said. "But there it is, I've got my big chance on the Governor's first string, and if I make a mess of it it may God have mercy on my soul, because I won't."

"You won't make a mess of it."

"We'll see," he said cheerfully. "That was a grand job you made of me in *Tally,* now. Thank you for that. I took that when it came and showed it to the Governor, but he'd already seen it, he told me. And you know I wouldn't be certain that it wasn't the magazine that put him in mind of putting me up on Rockville, when the other two fellows got hurt on Thursday. So thank you for that, too."

When I told Derry about it in the press box during the second race, he merely shrugged. "Of course he's riding Rockville. Don't you read the papers?"

"Not yesterday."

"Oh. Well, yes, he's got as much as he can chew this time. Rockville's a difficult customer, even with the best of jockeys, and our Dermot isn't that." He was busy polishing the lenses of his race glasses. "Luke-John's bookmaker friend must have accepted a good deal of Boston's fifty thousand, because the price on Tiddely Pom has come crashing down like an express lift from a hundred to eight to only four to one. That's a stupid price for a horse like Tiddely Pom, but there you are."

I did a small sum. If Boston had taken bets at 10

or 12 to 1 and had only been able to lay them off at 4 to 1, that left him a large gap of 6 or 8 to 1. If Tiddely Pom won, that would be the rate at which he would have to pay, which added up still to more than a quarter of a million pounds and meant that he would have to sell off the string of betting shops to pay his debts. Dumb Charlie Boston, trying to play with the big boys and getting squeezed like a toothpaste tube.

There was no sign of him in the paddock. Roncey saddled his horse in the stables and brought him straight into the parade ring very shortly before the time for the jockeys to mount. Peter led him around and I walked along by his quarters; but no one leaned over the rails to squirt him with acid. No one tried anything at all.

"Told you so," Roncey muttered. "All this fuss." He put up his jockey, slapped Tiddely Pom's rump, and hurried off to get a good position on the trainers' stand. Peter led the horse out onto the course and let him go, and Tiddely Pom cantered off unconcernedly with the long lolloping stride so unlike his appearance. I sighed with relief and went up to join Derry in the press box to watch the race.

"Tiddely Pom's favorite," he said. "Then Zig Zag, then Rockville. Zig Zag should have it in his pocket." He put his race glasses to his eyes and studied the horses milling around at the start. I hadn't taken my own glasses, as I'd found the carry strap pressed too heavily on tender spots. I felt lost without them, like a snail without antennae. The start for the Lamplighter was a quarter of a mile down the course from the stands. I concentrated on sorting out the colors with only force-four success.

Derry exclaimed suddenly, "What the devil!"

"Tiddely Pom," I said fearfully. Not now. Not at the very post. I should have foreseen . . . should have stationed someone down there. . . . But it was so public. So many people walked down to watch the start. Anyone who tried to harm a horse there would have a hundred witnesses.

"There's someone hanging on to his reins. No, he's been pulled off. Great God!" Derry started laughing incredulously. "I can't believe it, I simply can't believe it."

"What's happening?" I said urgently. All I could see was a row of peacefully lining-up horses, which miraculously included Tiddely Pom, and some sort of commotion going on in the crowd on the far side of the rails.

"It's Madge. . . . Madge Roncey. It must be. No one else looks like that. . . . She's rolling about on the grass with a fat little man . . . struggling. She pulled him away from Tiddely Pom. . . . Arms and legs are flying all over the place. . . ." He stopped, laughing too much. "The boys are with her. . . . They're all piling onto the poor little man in a sort of Rugger scrum. . . ."

"It's a pound to a penny the poor little man is Charlie Boston," I said grimly. "And if it's Madge and not the *Blaze* who's saved the day, we'll never hear the end of it from Victor Roncey."

"Damned Victor Roncey," Derry said. "They're off."

The line of horses bounded forward, heading for the first jump. Seventeen runners, three and a half miles, and a gold trophy and a fat check to the winner.

One of them crumpled up over the first. Not Tiddely Pom, whose scarlet and white chevrons bobbed in a bunch at the rear. Not Zig Zag, already positioned in the fourth place, from where he usually won. Not Egocentric, leading the field up past the stands to give the Huntersons their moment of glory. Not Rockville, with Dermont Finnegan fighting for his career in a battle not to let the horse run away with him.

They jumped the water jump in front of the stands. A gasp from the crowd as one of them splashed his hind legs right into it. The jockey in orange and green was dislodged and rolled.

"That horse always makes a balls of the water," Derry said dispassionately. "They should keep it for hurdles." No tremor of excitement in his voice or hands. It had cost him nothing to get Tiddely Pom onto the track. It had cost me too much.

They swept around the top bend and started out around the circuit. Twice around the course to go. I watched Tiddely Pom all the way, expecting him to fall, expecting him to drop out at the back and be pulled up, expecting him to be too weak from colic to finish the trip.

They came around the bottom bend and up over the three fences in the straight toward the stands. Egocentric was still in front. Zig Zag still fourth. Dermot Finnegan had Rockville in decent control somewhere in the middle, and Tiddely Pom was still there and not quite last.

Over the water. Zig Zag stumbled, recovered, raced on. Not fourth any more, though. Sixth or seventh. Tiddely Pom scampered over it with none of the grace of Egocentric but twice the speed. Moved up two places.

Out they went again into the country. Derry remarked calmly, "Tiddely Pom has dropped his bit."

"Damn," I said. The jockey was working with his arms, urging the horse on. Hopeless. And half the race still to run.

I shut my eyes. Felt the fatigue and illness come swamping back. Wanted to lie down somewhere soft and sleep for a week and escape from all the problems and torments and disillusionments of weary life. A week alone, to heal in. A week to give a chance for some energy for living to come creeping back. I needed a week at least. If I were lucky, I'd have a day.

"There's a faller at that fence." The race commentator's amplified voice jerked my eyes open. "A faller among the leaders. I think it was Egocentric. . . . Yes, Egocentric is down. . . ."

Poor Huntersons. Poor Harry, poor Sarah.

Gail.

I didn't want to think about her. Couldn't bear to, and couldn't help it.

"He's still going," Derry said. "Tiddely Pom."

The red and white chevrons were too far away to be clear. "He's made up a bit," Derry said. "He's taken a hold again."

They jumped the last fence on the far side and began the sweeping bend around into the straight, very strung out now, with great gaps between little bunches. One or two staggered fifty yards in the rear. There was a roar from the crowd and the commentator's voice rose above it: "And here is Zig Zag coming in the front, opening up a commanding lead. . . ."

"Zig Zag's slipped them," Derry said calmly. "Caught all the others napping."

"Tiddely Pom?" I asked.

"He's well back. Still plodding on, though. Most we could expect."

Zig Zag jumped the first fence in the straight five seconds clear of the rest of the field.

"Nothing will catch him," Derry said. I forgave him the satisfaction in his voice. He had tipped Zig Zag in his column. It was nice to be right. "Tiddely Pom's in the second bunch. Can you see him? Even if he hasn't won, he's not disgraced."

Zig Zag jumped the second-last fence well ahead, chased after an interval by four horses more or less abreast. After these came Tiddely Pom, and behind him the other half dozen still standing. If we had to settle for that, at least the antepost punters had had some sort of run for their money.

It was clear twenty yards from the last fence that Zig Zag was meeting it wrong. The jockey hesitated fatally between pushing him on to lengthen his stride and take off sooner or shortening the reins to get him to put in an extra one before he jumped. In the end he did neither. Simply left it to the horse to sort himself out. Some horses like to do that. Some horses like to be told what to do. Zig Zag went into the fence like a rudderless ship, took off too late and too close, hit the fence hard with his forelegs, slewed around in midair, crashed down in a tangle of hoofs, and treated his rider to a well-deserved thump on the turf.

"Stupid *bastard*," Derry said, furiously lowering his glasses. "An apprentice could have done better."

I was watching Tiddely Pom. The four horses ahead of him jumped the last fence. One of them swerved to avoid Zig Zag and his supine jockey and bumped heavily into the horse next to him. Both of them were thoroughly unbalanced and the jockey of one fell off. When Tiddely

Pom came away from the fence to tackle the straight, he was lying third.

The crowd roared. "He's got a chance!" Derry yelled. "Even now."

He couldn't quicken. The low lolloping stride went on at the same steady pace and all the jockey's urging was having no constructive effect. But one of the two in front of him was tiring and rolling about under pressure. Tiddely Pom crept up on him yard by yard, but the winning post was coming nearer and there was still one more in front. . . .

I looked at the leader, taking him in for the first time. A jockey in pink and white stripes, riding like a demon on a streak of brown straining hard-trained muscle. Dermot Finnegan on Rockville, with all his future in his hands.

While I watched he swept conclusively past the post, and even from the stands one could see that Irish grin bursting out like the sun.

Three lengths behind, Tiddely Pom's racing heart defeated the colic and put him second. A genuine horse, I thought thankfully. Worth all the trouble. Or, at least, worth some of it.

"All we need now," said Derry, "is an objection."

He wrapped the strap around his race glasses, put them in their case, and hurriedly made for the stairs. I followed him more slowly down and edged gingerly through the crowd milling around the unsaddling enclosure until I reached the clump of other press men waiting to pick up something to print. There was a cheer as Rockville was led through into the winner's place. Another cheer for Tiddely Pom. I didn't join in. Had nothing to contribute but a dead feeling of anticlimax.

All over. Tiddely Pom hadn't won. What did I expect?

The crowd parted suddenly like the Red Sea and through the gap struggled a large untidy earth mother surrounded by planets. Madge Roncey and her sons.

She walked purposefully across the comparatively empty unsaddling enclosure and greeted her husband with a gentle pat on the arm. He was astounded to see her and stood stock-still with his mouth open and Tiddely Pom's girth buckles half undone. I went across to join them.

"Hullo," Madge said. "Wasn't that splendid?" The faraway look in her eyes had come a few kilometers nearer since fact had begun to catch up on fantasy. She wore a scarlet coat a shade too small. Her hair floated in its usual amorphous mass. She had stockings on. Laddered.

"Splendid," I agreed.

Roncey gave me a sharp look. "Still fussing?"

I said to Madge, "What happened down at the start?"

She laughed. "There was a fat little man there going absolutely berserk and screaming that he would stop Tiddely Pom if it was the last thing he did."

Roncey swung around and stared at her. "He started hanging on to Tiddely Pom's reins," she went on, "and he wouldn't let go when the starter told him to. It was absolutely crazy. He was trying to kick Tiddely Pom's legs. So I just ducked under the rails and walked across and told him it was our horse and would he please stop it, and he was frightfully rude." A speculative look came into her eye. "He used some words I didn't know."

"For God's sake," said Roncey irritably. "Get on with it."

She went on without resentment: "He still wouldn't let go so I put my arms round him and lifted him up and carried him off and he was so surprised he dropped the reins, and then he struggled to get free and I let him fall down on the ground and rolled him under the rails, and then the boys and I sat on him."

I said, trying to keep a straight face, "Did he say anything after that?"

"Well, he hadn't much breath," she admitted judiciously. "But he did say something about killing you, as a matter of fact. He didn't seem to like you very much. He said you'd smashed everything and stopped him getting to Tiddely Pom, and as a matter of fact he was so hysterical he was jolly nearly in tears."

"Where is he now?" I asked.

"I don't know exactly. When I let him get up, he ran away."

Roncey gave me a mean look. "So it took my wife to save my horse, not the *Blaze.*"

"Oh, no, dear," she said placidly. "If Mr. Tyrone hadn't been looking after him, the little man would have been able to reach him sooner, and if I hadn't come back from the Isle of Wight because I thought it would be quite safe if no one knew, and we all wanted to see the race, if I hadn't been there at the starting gate, someone else would have taken the little man away. Lots of people were going to. It was just that I got to him first." She gave me a sweet smile. "I haven't had so much fun for years."

The day fragmented after that into a lot of people saying things to me that I didn't really hear. Pieces still stick out. Dermot Finnegan being presented with a small replica of the Lamplighter Gold Cup and looking as if he'd been handed the Holy Grail. Willy Ondroy telling me that Charlie Boston had been slung off the racecourse, and Eric Youll outlining the Stewards' plan for warning him off permanently, which would mean the withdrawal of his betting license and the closing of all his shops.

Derry telling me he had been through to Luke-John, whose bookmaker friend had taken all of Charlie Boston's fifty thousand and was profoundly thankful Tiddely Pom hadn't won.

Colly Gibbons asking me to go for a drink. I declined. I was off drink. He had his wife with him, and not an American colonel in sight.

Pat Roncey staring at me sullenly, hands in pockets. I asked if he'd passed on my telephone number along with the whereabouts of Tiddely Pom. Belligerently he tried to justify himself: the man had been even more keen to know where I lived than where the horse was. What man? The tall yellowish man with some sort of accent. From the *Guardian,* he'd said. Didn't Pat know that

the *Guardian* was the one paper with no racing page?
Pat did not.

Sandy Willis walking past leading Zig Zag, giving
me a worried smile. Was the horse all right, I asked. She
thought so, poor old boy. She muttered a few unfeminine
comments on the jockey who had thrown the race away.
She said she'd grown quite fond of Tiddely Pom; she
was glad he'd done well. She'd won a bit on him, as he'd
come in second. Got to get on, she said; Zig Zag needed
sponging down.

The Huntersons standing glumly beside Egocentric
while their trainer told them their raffle horse had broken
down badly and wouldn't run again for a year, if ever.

That message got through to me razor sharp and clear.
No Egocentric racing, no Huntersons at the races. No
Gail at the races. Not even that.

I'd had enough. My body hurt. I understood the full
meaning of the phrase "sick at heart." I'd been through
too many mangles, and I wasn't sure it was worth it.
Vjoersterod was dead, Bert Checkov was dead, the nonstarter racket was dead . . . until someone else tried it,
until the next wide boy came along with his threats and
his heavies. Someone else could bust it next time. Not
me. I'd had far far more than enough.

I wandered slowly out onto the course and stood beside
the water jump, looking down into the water. Couldn't
go home until the race train went, after the last race.
Couldn't go home until I'd phoned in to Luke-John for
a final check on what my column would look like the
next day. Nothing to go home to anyway, except an
empty flat and the prospect of an empty future.

Footsteps swished toward me through the grass. I
didn't look up. Didn't want to talk.

"Ty," she said.

I did look then. There was a difference in her face.
She was softer; less cool, less poised. Still extraordinarily
beautiful. I badly wanted what I couldn't have.

"Ty, why didn't you tell me about your wife?"

I shook my head. Didn't answer.

She said, "I was in the bar with Harry and Sarah, and someone introduced us to a Major Gibbons and his wife, because he had been in your *Tally* article, too, like Harry and Sarah. They were talking about you. . . . Major Gibbons said it was such a tragedy about your wife. I said, what tragedy, and he told us. . . ."

She paused. I took a deep difficult breath: said nothing.

"I said it must be some help that she was rich, and he said what do you mean rich; as far as I know she hasn't a bean, because Ty is always hard up with looking after her, and he'd be reasonably well off if he put her in a hospital and let the country pay for her keep instead of struggling to do it himself. . . ."

She turned half away from me and looked out across the course. "Why didn't you tell me?"

I swallowed and loosened my mouth. "I don't like—I didn't want—consolation prizes."

After a while she said, "I see." It sounded as if she actually did.

There was a crack in her cool voice. She said, "If it was me you'd married, and I'd got polio. . . . I can see that you must stay with her. I see how much she needs you. If it had been me—and you left me. . . ." She gave a small laugh which was half a sob. "Life sure kicks you in the teeth. I find a man I don't want to part with—a man I'd live on crumbs with—and I can't have him—even a little while, now and then."

EIGHTEEN

spent Sunday alone in the flat, mostly asleep. Part of the time I pottered around tidying up, trying to put my mind and life into order along with my house. Didn't have much success.

On Monday morning I went to fetch Elizabeth. Sh
came home in an ambulance, with two fit uniformed me
to carry her and the pump upstairs. They laid her o
the bed I had made up freshly for her, checked that th
pump was working properly, helped replace the Spiroshe
on her chest, accepted cups of coffee, agreed that th
weather was raw and cold but what could you expec
in December, and eventually went away.

I unpacked Elizabeth's case and made some scramble
eggs for lunch, and fed her when her wrist packed up
and fixed another mug of coffee into the holder.

She smiled and thanked me. She looked tired, but ver
calm. There was a deep difference in her, but for som
time I couldn't work out what it was. When I finall
identified it, I was surprised. She wasn't anxious an
more. The long-established deep-rooted insecurity n
longer looked out of her eyes.

"Leave the dishes, Ty," she said. "I want to talk t
you."

I sat in the armchair. She watched me. "It still hur
. . . what that man did."

"A bit," I agreed.

"Tonio told me they were both killed that night . .
trying to find me again."

"He did, did he?"

She nodded. "He came to see me yesterday. We ha
a long talk. A long, long talk. He told me a lot c
things."

"Honey," I said, "I—"

"Shut up, Ty. I want to tell you . . . what he said."

"Don't tire yourself."

"I won't. I am tired, but it feels different from usua
I feel just ordinarily tired, not . . . not *worried* tire
Tonio did that. And you. I mean, he made me unde
stand what I saw on Thursday, that you would let you
self be smashed up . . . that you would drive when yo
were drunk and risk going to prison . . . that you woul
do anything, however dangerous . . . to keep me safe. .
He said, if I'd seen that with my own eyes, why did

oubt . . . why did I ever doubt that you would stay
vith me? . . . It was such a relief. . . . I felt as if the
vhole world were lighter. . . . I know you've always told
ne . . . but now I do believe it, through and through."

"I'm glad," I said truthfully. "I'm very glad."

She said, "I talked to Tonio about . . . that girl."

"Honey—"

"Hush," she said. "I told him about the blackmail.
Ve talked for ages. . . . He was so understanding. He
aid of course I would be upset, anyone would, but that
 shouldn't worry too much. . . . He said you were a
ormal healthy man and if I had any sense I would see
hat the time to start worrying would be if you *didn't*
vant to sleep with someone." She smiled. "He said if
 could face it, we would both be happier if I didn't
iind if sometimes . . . He said you would always come
ome."

"Tonio said a great deal."

She nodded. "It made such sense. I haven't been fair
 you."

"Elizabeth," I protested.

"No. I really haven't. I was so afraid of losing you
 couldn't see how much I was asking of you. But I un-
erstand now that the more I can let you go, the easier
ou will find it to live with me . . . and the more you
ill want to."

"Tonio said that?"

"Yes, he did."

"He's very fond of you," I said.

She grinned. "He said so. He also said some pretty
ar-burning things about you, if you want to know." She
old me some of them, her mouth curving up at the
orners and the new security gleaming in her eyes.

"Exaggeration," I said modestly.

She laughed. A breathy giggle. Happy.

I got up and kissed her on the forehead and on the
heek. She was the girl I'd married. I loved her very
uch.

On Tuesday morning, when Mrs. Woodward came
back, I went out along the mews, around the corner and
into the telephone box, and dialed the number of the
Western School of Art.

Become more noticeably beautiful two weeks from now with GLAMOUR'S BEAUTY & HEALTH BOOK

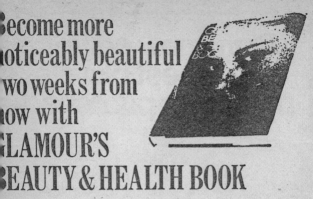

In just two weeks, you can be visibly more attractive, healthier-looking and more self-confident than you would have believed possible. Your appearance and manner will have improved so much women will notice and men will actually react to your presence.

EASY-TO-FOLLOW INSTRUCTIONS, PHOTOGRAPHS & DIAGRAMS OFFER YOU A COMPLETE COURSE IN MAKING THE MOST OF YOUR MAKE-UP, BODY, HEALTH AND PERSONALITY!

5-step makeovers for you • special ways to make up eyes and mouth • tips to improve hair, complexion, figure • exercises for problem spots • changing your self-image • your health & your sex and *much more!*

FOR TWO-WEEK FREE EXAMINATION MAIL COUPON TODAY!

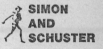